"WHAT IF....?"

Penelope sipped happily at her coffee while big Mike tucked into his bowl of lima beans. All was well with the world.

Almost. There was still a murder to be solved.

Penelope tried to put herself in the mind of the murderer. Reduced to the simplest common denominators, she believed there were only two motives for felonious murder—love and money. All others—passion, greed, power, jealousy, blackmail, hatred, revenge, et al.—were variations of one or the other. And although she was not yet ready to eliminate love as the motive, she decided to focus on money.

"So, Mikey, who would be interested in money and benefit from Peter Adcock's death?"

Mikey barely looked up from his lima beans. He heard her— he rarely missed anything of importance—but he thought the answer was too obvious for a reply.

Penelope answered her own question. "Just about anyone connected with the team," she said. What if Blake knew that she was about to be fired? Ditto for Rats. That might make either Rats or Feathers commit murder? What if Adcock was cheating on his partners? What if a player was about to be cut from the team, losing his last chance for renown? What if . . . oh, bother, the possibilities are endless. Let's go to work."

Mycroft yawned, stretched, yawned again. 'Meow," he said.

In exchange for that interesting theory, Penelope offered one of her own. "What if. . . .." she began.

BOOK YOUR PLACE ON OUR WEBSITE AND MAKE THE READING CONNECTION!

We've created a customized website just for our very special readers, where you can get the inside scoop on everything that's going on with Zebra, Pinnacle and Kensington books.

When you come online, you'll have the exciting opportunity to:

- View covers of upcoming books
- Read sample chapters
- Learn about our future publishing schedule (listed by publication month *and author*)
- Find out when your favorite authors will be visiting a city near you
- Search for and order backlist books from our online catalog
- Check out author bios and background information
- Send e-mail to your favorite authors
- Meet the Kensington staff online
- Join us in weekly chats with authors, readers and other guests
- Get writing guidelines
- AND MUCH MORE!

**Visit our website at
http://www.kensingtonbooks.com**

BASEBALL CAT

GARRISON ALLEN

KENSINGTON BOOKS

http://www.kensingtonbooks.com

For Robert Youdelman
A True Friend
And a True Fan of the Game

THE CAST
More or Less
In Their Batting Order

Big Mike aka Mycroft, Mikey. A twenty-five pound Abyssinian alley cat originally from Abyssinia, where he learned the rudiments of baseball as a kitten, as well as perfecting his bear imitation (useful for intimidating an assortment of wild dogs, jackals, and hyenas).

Penelope Warren. Once a pretty fair country shortstop before she threw her arm out and took up literature, the United States Marine Corps, and the Peace Corps (not necessarily in that order). Now, she is the sole proprietress of Mycroft & Company, a mystery bookstore in Empty Creek, Arizona, and a pretty fair country detective.

The Empty Creek Coyotes Professional Baseball Club. Empty Creek's latest entry in the civic pride parade and a member of the fledgling Arizona-New Mexico League. The players are enthusiastic, if somewhat inept, with a talent for making the National Pastime look like Roller Derby.

Peter Adcock. Erstwhile graduate of the George Steinbrenner school of baseball ownership and *the* managing general partner of the Empty Creek Coyotes.

Blake Robinson. The young, MBA-wielding General Manager of the Coyotes who received her given name because of her mother's fondness for William Blake, a sentiment not shared by the players who embark on a nickname contest for their GM. Blake also doubles as a groundskeeper, Coyote Dog saleswoman, ticket taker, and equipment manager.

Jimmy "Rats" McCoy. The crusty, tobacco-chewing and spitting, ex-major league legend who manages the Coyotes. Rats once hit .387 for the Detroit Tigers, asked for a contract renegotiation, and was told, "Jimmy, we could have finished last without you." He came by his nickname when his second wife forced him to alter his formerly most colorful vocabulary.

Martha "Feathers" McCoy. The aforementioned second wife and a former Las Vegas showgirl who retired two days after winning Jimmy's heart, mind, and money during a marathon session of five card stud. "Jimmy, darling," she said, raking in the last pot, "all those feathers are heavy, and unless you've got something else to bet, I'm going to bed and taking you with me."

Elaine Henders. Laney is Penelope's best friend and a prolific author of a number of rather explicit romance novels set in the Old West.

Wally, Alexander, and Kelsey. An unemployed cowboy and

two diminutive Yorkshire Terriers, respectively, who share Laney's bed and breakfast. Alexander is Big Mike's buddy.

Harris Anderson III. The editor of the *Empty Creek News Journal* who, more often than not, is invited by Penelope for slumber parties enlivened by Laney's fertile suggestions for games of midnight madness.

Nora Pryor. The preeminent historian of Empty Creek, a petite single mother with beautiful strawberry-blonde hair and a deep sultry voice that would make her a superstar answering any 900 number in the land.

Anthony Lyme-Regis. A tweedy English gentleman and former rugby player who has taken up directing television commercials for Super Bra (among other products). He flies into Empty Creek on weekends to see the woman with the 900 number voice.

Storm Williams aka Cassandra Warren. Penelope's little sister and star actress of such memorable films as the remakes of *Nyoka of the Jungle* and *Wrestling Women Meet the Aztec Mummy.* Until she wins an Academy Award, the place of honor on Stormy's mantel holds the championship trophy of a wet tee shirt contest which she won fair and square over . . .

Debbie Locke aka Debbie D and Dee Dee. A cocktail waitress at the Double B Western Saloon and Steakhouse, unofficial watering hole of the Coyotes—and everyone else in town. Possessed of twin national treasures, Debbie is convinced the contest was rigged. She is the official poster girl of the Coyotes.

Sam Connors. One of Empty Creek's finest and a former suitor to Penelope (things didn't work out with Big Mike), he is now greatly enamored of Debbie.

John "Dutch" Fowler. Police Chief and Penelope's future brother-in-law, because the first time he saw Stormy, that little love cherub beaned him with a high hard one (and he wasn't wearing a batting helmet at the time).

The Robbery-Homicide Bureau. Lawrence Burke and Willie Stoner, aka Tweedledee and Tweedledum, share a cubicle, a daily bag of jelly doughnuts, and a healthy respect for Big Mike's claws.

Lora Lou Longstreet. When she is not posing in the nude for her significant other, Lora Lou presides over The Tack Shack and, political correctness be damned, is the prettiest president of any Chamber of Commerce between Piscataway, New Jersey and El Cajon, California.

David Macklin. Lora Lou's artist, a talented painter who sketches Snow Birds during Empty Creek's various town fests, paints magnificent oils of desert scenes, and is largely responsible for Lora Lou's lofty position in the Chamber hierarchy.

Kathy Allan. Part-time assistant at Mycroft & Company, part-time college student, and full-time inspiration for her boyfriend's rewrite of Homer's epic poem, *The Iliad.*

Timothy Scott. Said author of *The Kathiad.*

Harvey McAllister. A displaced surfer and owner of the Desert Surf and Flower Shop.

Teresa Sandia. Harvey's helpmate and publicist. She is also a pretty mean massage therapist.

L. Malcolm Osterburg. Empty Creek's Director of Planning and Development. Left to his druthers, he would pave over Empty Creek because that's what a Director of Planning and Development should do.

Erika von Sturm. A Teutonic Valkyrie in charge of physical fitness training for the Empty Creek Coyotes. Her chant of "*Eins, zwei, drei, vier,*" inexhaustibly repeated drives her charges into exhaustion.

Kendall McCoffey, Senior. A not-so-silent partner in Empty Creek's professional baseball club.

Kendall McCoffey, Junior. A traveler on the Information Superhighway and a reluctant recruit to baseball.

Rose McCoffey. McCoffey, Senior's trophy wife.

Angelique Lamont. A semi-retired exotic dancer and the new owner of The Dynamite Lounge.

Belinda Baxter. A single mother of two rambunctious boys, aged nine and eleven.

Discreet Investigations. A firm founded by Justin Beamish. He is an old friend of Penelope's as are his principal assistants, Ralph and Russell, twin brothers who also operate a business for discriminating adults.

"AND NOW, THE STARTING LINE UP FOR *YOUR* EMPTY CREEK COYOTES!"

Jesus "The Snake" Gomez. 2b.

Luke "Shrimp" Federov. 3b.

Earl "Big Rap" Rapp. 1b.

Eddie "The Man" Stiles. cf.

Abraham "Prez" Jefferson Washington. lf.

Quincy "Little Rap" Smith. ss.

Emilio "Scooter" Hernandez. rf.

Hank "The Tank" Easter. c.

Ralph "Buddy" Peterson. lhp.

Jackson "The Peeper" Elliott. rhp.

The Rest of the Lineup. Assorted players, managers, coaches, scouts, mascots, fans, parents, girlfriends and boyfriends, the odd astrologer or two, a displaced surfer, Jimmy Buffet and the Coral Reefers, a Town Crier, the mayor and city council members, planning commissioners, a public address announcer, senior citizens, Stanley and Livingstone, a whole bunch of assorted pigs, various other four-legged critters, one no-legged critter, a 36 ounce Cecil Fielder model Louisville Slugger, and a buzzard on a saguaro cactus.

PLAY BALL!

BASEBALL CAT

PROLOGUE

It was a spiritual moment always.

Jimmy "Rats" McCoy had opened baseball seasons everywhere from Binghamton, New York and Durham, North Carolina to Tiger Stadium, Yankee Stadium, and Fenway Park, but there was nothing that compared with emerging from the dugout after the long wait between seasons and seeing the pristine grass, the crisp chalk lines of the batter's boxes, the foul lines, the smooth dirt of the infield. This was not something that Rats ever told either his first or second wife. Both had been stunning beauties when he married them. Both still were, as a matter of fact, and neither would appreciate an unfavorable comparison between them and a baseball diamond.

But it had always been that way, even when Rats was a kid sneaking into Lane Field, the home of the old San Diego Padres of the old Pacific Coast League, dreaming of his own baseball glories. Back then—ushers permitting—Rats always paused for a moment, closed his eyes, and walked down the tunnel, feeling his way until the moment was right. And when he suddenly opened his eyes, there it was.

A baseball field.

Truly, it was a field of dreams, awaiting new triumphs, new heartbreaks, the crack of the bat on the ball, the effortless beauty of the double play, the thrill of the ball and the base runner arriving at third simultaneously.

The fact that he was now the manager of the Empty Creek Coyotes in the new Arizona-New Mexico League didn't bother Rats McCoy one little bit. It was still opening day of the baseball season and it was still, as always and forever, a spiritual moment.

At least, it should have been.

But this time when Rats opened his eyes and took it all in, from the left field foul pole to center to right—the mound, the coaching box at first, the batter's box—there was something amiss.

Big-time amiss.

Major league amiss.

"Rats," said Rats, although he thought of several other phrases more appropriate to the situation. "Double rats."

"Can I please come out now?" a feminine voice implored from the dugout. "Is it my turn?"

"Yeah, I think you'd better," Rats said.

Following his instructions and seeking her own spiritual revelation on this, her first opening day as general manager of a professional baseball club, Blake Robinson nervously tripped over the dugout steps and opened her eyes too soon to get the full impact of the moment.

Instead of the auspicious moment Rats had promised— the grace and splendor of the diamond and all its many promises—Blake's untidy entry into pro ball was marred by an unwelcome sight. Instead of visions of fleet-footed outfielders chasing down a long drive in the gap, a perfect drag bunt, a close play at the plate, or even a strikeout or infield fly, Blake saw what appeared to be a body sprawled in the visiting team's dugout.

"Urgle," said Blake Robinson, turning the same delicate shade of green that Rats did whenever he swallowed his chew of tobacco—which had happened several times during the course of spring training.

Now, when Blake Robinson wasn't turning green, she was a vision of her own, a tawny-haired belle with exquisite features, long coltish legs—which contributed to her untimely tumble—and a figure which encouraged her apparently liberated young baseball players to issue frequent invitations to join them in the showers.

"Aw, come on, Blake," one or another of the players would whine. "Look at the money you'd be saving the club. Look at all that extra soap and water you're using taking showers all alone."

Blake always smiled and tossed her thick mane and threatened to buy a supply of saltpeter to sprinkle on their food. She wasn't exactly sure what saltpeter was, except that her father had always complained about the army putting that particular substance in the food to discourage young libidos from raging amuck. Since her players didn't know what saltpeter was either, they were hardly discouraged by her threat. "Aw, come on, Blake, I'll wash your back."

"You okay?" Rats asked as he helped Blake to her feet. "You look a little queasy."

"I am a *lot* queasy. Do you see what I see?"

"Yep. Better take a look. Come on."

With his protegée in hesitant tow, Rats led the way to the visitor's dugout. Since it was early—not yet seven a.m.—they were the only people in the newly-renovated Coyote Stadium. Rats preferred to take his spiritual moments alone, or nearly alone, in this case. It was the same way he went to church—when he went—before the preachers and parishioners arrived, preferring the solitude to greater appreciate the splendor of God.

Blake followed Rats somewhat reluctantly, managing not to trip over the chalked foul lines. She would have elected to sit down and put her head between her legs until the nausea passed, the body disappeared, and she awakened from what she hoped was a nightmare. But she *was* the General Manager and she supposed an important, although undefined, part of her duties was to investigate bodies in the visiting team's dugout, especially when the body appeared from a distance to be that of the club's majority owner and managing general partner.

"It's Peter Adcock," Rats confirmed. "Dead. Someone used his head for a baseball."

"Urgle," Blake repeated.

Rats leaned over for a closer look. "Cecil Fielder model," he said. "I would have used a lighter bat myself. You can get around on the fast ball better."

During his long and mostly-distinguished baseball career, Rats had never seen a game called because of murder. Rain, snow, sleet, tornados, an earthquake, a collapsed dome, an occasional hurricane, and even amoebic dysentery on one memorable barnstorming tour had caused postponements, but never a murder.

"At least," Rats observed, "it was in the visiting dugout."

"My God," Blake cried, "what are we going to do? It's opening day."

"You're the general manager. General away." Hmm, Rats mused, wondering if he should enter *General* in the club's Blake Robinson Nickname Contest. Nah, not colorful enough. *Urgle* might do, but it was too hard to pronounce. A nickname had to be clean and quickly characterize some trait of the bearer.

Now that the gurgling in her stomach had subsided somewhat, Blake was feeling a little indignant. "They didn't have a course in business school that covered this exact situation," Blake said. She reached into the visiting dugout, averting her eyes from the late Peter Adcock, and gingerly picked up the telephone hanging on the wall.

"What are you doing?" Rats asked mildly.

"Calling the police, of course."

"That's the bullpen phone," Rats pointed out. "It ain't hooked up to the outside world."

"Oh, right."

CHAPTER
ONE

The jangling telephone persisted, finally penetrating
Penelope Warren's somnolent state.

Her partner in life's adventures, one rather gargantuan cat
aptly nicknamed Big Mike, irritated at the unwelcome distur-
bance, curled into a tight ball in a futile effort to slumber on.
But it was not to be.

Had Penelope believed in such twentieth century devices
as an answering machine, she—and Mycroft—might have
continued sleeping, blissfully unaware of the outside world's
attempted intrusion into a very agreeable dream. But Penelope rejected most of the twentieth century's conveniences,
believing the telephone to be an instrument of the devil, the
answering machine a product of his evil imagination, and
call waiting—well, that was *rudus interruptus* and not to be
tolerated.

"Whazzit," Penelope said by way of greeting when she
finally untangled the cord and managed to put the correct
end of the receiver to her ear.

"Twenty-six," was the reply from an oddly familiar voice. The voice's owner had only an hour or so ago whispered several provocative and risqué ideas into the ear of the hibernating Penelope, believing that the power of suggestion would penetrate her subconscious and resurface later during an amorous moment.

Even in a state of semiconsciousness, Penelope hated repeating herself. As an alternative, she said, "Twisixwhat?"

"The telephone rang twenty-six times before you answered," Harris Anderson III said. "I counted."

Penelope slowly pulled herself to an upright position, dragging the bed covers along to cover a very pretty chest although she was alone in the bedroom except for Mikey. He continued to express his displeasure at the unwarranted interruption of sleep by digging his claws into the blanket and, as a result, Penelope dragged a twenty-five pound Abyssinian alley cat from Abyssinia into her lap, which didn't help either of their moods at the moment.

"Are you awake now?" Andy asked, raising his voice.

Penelope, who had been on the verge of nodding off again, said, "There's no need to shout."

"Yes, there is," Andy replied. "You were falling asleep again."

"And why shouldn't I?"

"There's been a murder. Nora Pryor just called."

That got Penelope's attention as though he had splashed a glass of icy water into her face. She forced her brain into alert, grinding a gear or two along the way, and asked, "Who? Where? When?"

Andy replied crisply and concisely, as the editor of the

Empty Creek News Journal should. "Peter Adcock. Coyote Stadium. Sometime last night or early this morning."

"Where are you?"

"The stadium."

"I'm on my way."

"That's my girl."

Penelope hung up and headed off for the kitchen without bothering to pause for a robe. This was not the time for frills and, as isolated in the desert as her home was, there would be no one around to see her in the altogether, not at the ungodly hour of—she glanced at the clock on the kitchen wall—eight-fifteen in the morning. But coffee was not a frill; indeed, it was a necessity of life, and Penelope had just set it to bubbling nicely when the twenty-five pound Abyssinian alley cat from Abyssinia grumped into the kitchen, complaining loudly about all the disruption in his life. The sound of the electric can opener at work on a can of lima beans, however, alleviated Big Mike's discontent somewhat. Having spent his formative years in Africa, Big Mike believed he was a full-blooded, card-carrying lion. He tucked into the lima beans, growling softly as though he had just been presented with a nice juicy zebra or wildebeest steak.

The front door banged open.

"Penelope," another familiar voice cried, "get up!"

Penelope peeked around the corner of the kitchen door. "I am up," she told Elaine Henders, her best friend, confidante, and sometime co-adventurer. "Hi, Wally," she added.

"Hi," Wally said. He was an unemployed cowboy who lived with Laney, assisting her in the research for the highly erotic romance novels she wrote.

"So you are," Laney said, sounding rather disappointed,

"but why are you hiding?" She tossed her red hair indignantly. "We have news."

"Because I'm starkers and because I already know."

"You know?" Laney operated a desert telegraph that would make the CIA envious, providing the latest news updates and gossip of Empty Creek. She had a dedicated network of informants who could be counted on to provide the most lurid details of the latest happenings. "About the murder? But I just found out. Nora was out for her morning jog when every police car in town descended upon the baseball stadium."

"Why didn't she call me?"

"She did. You didn't answer. That's why we just came in. I thought we'd have to throw you in a cold shower to get your attention."

"And that's why you brought Wally? To throw me in the shower?"

"Yes, isn't he sweet? Always willing to pitch in and help."

"I'll bet. Well, tell him not to peek. I'm going to take my shower. Alone."

"Don't peek, Wally."

"I won't."

Penelope ran for the bedroom.

When she returned, showered and fully-clothed, Penelope punched Wally in the arm. Hard.

"Ow, what was that for?"

"You peeked. I know you did."

"Nice butt," Wally said, grinning sheepishly.

"Yes, it is," Penelope agreed as she filled her San Diego State Aztecs football coffee cup. She knew it was the wrong season but didn't believe anyone would notice or care, especially Peter Adcock. "Now, can we get on with it?"

After four years in the United States Marine Corps—where she rose to the exalted rank of Sergeant—obtaining three degrees in English literature, and serving as a Peace Corps Volunteer in Ethiopia—where a tiny Mycroft had belly-flopped into her life from out of the bougainvillea, barely missing her gin and tonic in the process—Penelope had sought a new home. Having developed a fondness for the desert during her graduate studies at Arizona State University, Penelope consulted Mycroft and assured him that lizards were plentiful in the Grand Canyon State. Lizard chasing was, along with intimidating wild dogs, jackals, and even the occasional hyena, a favorite sport of the fledgling lion in training.

Now, driving through their adopted home town followed by Laney and Wally, neither Penelope nor Mycroft regretted the choice. Empty Creek, Arizona suited both temperaments perfectly. They fit right in with the other free-spirited, always colorful, and frequently loony individuals who inhabited the little town bordering the usually dry creek bed that provided the community its name. After all, where else in the nation— or the world for that matter—were you likely to find Red the Rat, an old desert prospector whose mule was best man at his wedding even though the animal's name was Daisy? Fortunately, it had been an outdoor wedding. And there was Timothy Scott, a demented young poet rewriting the *Iliad* in his beloved's honor. Cackling Ed was an equally deranged senior citizen of indeterminate years who used his post as a Geezer World security guard to peer down the blouse of any woman younger than himself, which included most of womankind.

Penelope didn't even count such luminaries as her own younger sister, Cassandra, the heroine of nearly a dozen B movies under her screen and stage name of Storm Williams, or Samantha Dale, a conservative bank president with a fondness for strip poker. Nor did Penelope wonder what a detached observer might think of her own role in the community as the sole proprietress of Mycroft & Company, a successful mystery bookshop, and as an amateur detective of some note who was always assisted in her inquiries by a big and fearless cat with a passion for lima beans.

Yes, indeed, Penelope thought, Empty Creek is just the place. Then, unfortunately, her thoughts turned to darker deeds—violence and murder.

As Laney and Wally took seats in the stands of Coyote Stadium, Penelope and Big Mike joined the local constabulary who were gathered around the on deck circle near the visitor's dugout.

"Well," Larry Burke demanded, "what took you so long?"

"Yeah," Willie Stoner said, echoing his partner, "what kept you?"

Both members of the Robbery-Homicide Bureau kept wary eyes on Big Mike. They had experienced his wrath—and claws—in the past, but Big Mike ambled right on by and began his own investigation as a no-nonsense cat should.

Penelope glanced at her watch. "An elapsed time of some thirty-six minutes between notification and arrival."

"We were here in four minutes," Burke said.

"Don't start," Dutch Fowler warned.

"Yes," Penelope said, ignoring the chief of police, her right as his future sister-in-law, "but you were only six blocks away and you weren't sound asleep."

"I said, don't start."

"Too slow," Burke said.

Stoner got in right on cue. "Yeah, too slow."

Dutch groaned.

"And I'll bet you stopped for jelly doughnuts, too," Penelope said. The evidence was apparent on the shirts of both detectives.

"Did not. Sent out after we secured the crime scene."

"Well, send out for some more, please. I'm hungry. And get some coffee." As honorary members of the Empty Creek Police Department, Penelope felt that she and Mycroft should be accorded certain prerogatives.

"Aw, boss, do we have to?"

"Do it," Dutch said. "Otherwise, we'll be here all day."

The two detectives wandered off to find a handy patrol officer to send on the errand.

"Tweedledee and Tweedledum are at the top of their game," Penelope said. She looked around and took in the scene, waving at Andy who was apparently interviewing Nora Pryor, the preeminent local historian as well as the informant who had called the news to him and Laney. She recognized the ex-Major League legend. Rats was standing behind the pitcher's mound with a young woman Penelope did not know. But Penelope averted her eyes from the crime lab technicians, medical examiners, and the police photographer clustered around the visitor's dugout.

"I don't know why you can't get along with them," Dutch complained.

"We get along fine. I can't help that they got their detective licenses from a cereal box." Penelope was actually quite fond of Tweedledee and Tweedledum, although she wasn't about to admit it. Their relationship over the years had often been adversarial, but in weak moments the two detectives sometimes demonstrated a grudging affection for their nemesis, which in equally weak moments, Penelope reciprocated.

"Hey, boss, we're about done," a technician called. "Can we take him away?"

"Just a minute," Dutch answered. "You want to take a look, Penelope?"

"I hate this part," Penelope said. Despite having solved several murders, Penelope could not accept violent death and always thought of John Donne's memorable words: " . . . any man's death diminishes me, because I am involved in mankind; and therefore never send to know for whom the bell tolls; it tolls for thee."

"Me, too," Dutch said.

"Even after all these years?"

"It's why I left Los Angeles. I thought I'd have a nice quiet retirement job in Empty Creek."

"Well, at least, you met Stormy," Penelope pointed out, still postponing the confrontation with death.

"Thank God. She's the only normal person around here."

Penelope thought this an odd observation from the fiancé of the woman whose film roles consisted mainly of cavorting around in various states of dishabille, laying waste to hordes of villains with sword and sorcery, and the occasional well-placed kick to an unsuspecting wizard's groin. Instead of pointing out that her sister was as wacky as anyone else, Penelope took a deep breath and said, "Let's do it."

The body was covered and when the M.E. asked if she wanted to see it, Penelope shook her head.

"What we think happened," Dutch said, "was Adcock and the killer were at the dugout steps. Must have been an argument and the killer used a bat to cave in the skull. Adcock fell back and the killer took off."

"Right-handed or left-handed?"

Dutch snorted. "Right, of course. Why make it easier for us by eliminating righties."

"Could have been a switch-hitter."

"You just had to think of *that*, too."

"Do you have the murder weapon?"

"Over here."

The baseball bat was brand new—relatively speaking— with a gleaming enamel surface, its handle not yet marred by the application of pine tar by hopeful young sluggers seeking a better grip. There was a slight nick on the knob. The barrel of the bat was tinged with blood, already darkening to a rusty color.

"You might be able to get some prints," Penelope said, already knowing the likelihood of *that*.

Dutch snorted. "Mycroft might fly too."

"Just a thought."

"We'll try," Dutch said, "but. . . ."

"What were they doing out here in the middle of the night?"

Dutch shrugged. "What do you know of Adcock?"

"Not much. I watched some of the city council meetings when they were negotiating to bring the Coyotes to town. He drove a hard bargain, getting the city to finance stadium renovations. I thought he was rather arrogant."

Dutch, who attended all city council meetings—from boring beginning to tedious conclusion—as part of the normal course of his duties, said, "Peter Adcock was a jerk. Nobody on the council liked him. The city staff hated him. He was always interfering in the stadium renovations. That's why it went so far over budget."

"This isn't narrowing the list of suspects any."

"No," Dutch said grimly, "but this might." He pulled a small baggie from his shirt pocket. "We found it clutched in Adcock's hand."

Penelope took the baggie and read the crumpled business card inside.

Lora Lou Longstreet
President
Empty Creek Chamber of Commerce

"I don't believe it," Penelope said. "Surely you don't suspect Lora Lou?"

"Did I hear my name mentioned?"

Lora Lou Longstreet, in addition to her duties as the reigning queen of the Empty Creek Chamber of Commerce, owned and operated The Tack Shack, the principal dispenser of all things horsey for Empty Creek and its environs. Her beauty belied the fact that she was a most astute and accomplished businesswoman, as many a macho male had discovered to their chagrin. Tall with short blonde hair, Lora Lou was a "fine figger of a woman" as Red the Rat always declared, at least until his marriage to Mattie Bates had somewhat curtailed his public observations on the distaff portion of the local population. A larger than life nude portrait of Lora Lou hung behind the bar of the Double B Western Saloon and Steakhouse offering visible proof of old Red's observation. Her full bosom and long, shapely legs were there for all God's critters to see. Always quick to smile, a radiant sunbeam that brightened any room she happened to be in, Lora Lou was one of Penelope's best friends, and not only because they happened to serve on the Chamber's board of directors together.

But Lora Lou's smile quickly vanished when she discovered that Peter Adcock—as she had heard rumored only a few minutes earlier—was, indeed, dead, and further learned that one of her business cards had been found in his hand.

"Where were you last night?" Dutch asked.

"But . . . but . . . you don't suspect me?"

"Of course, he doesn't," Penelope said. "And neither do I."

"I do, too," Dutch said, "and so do you."

"I do not!"

"Well, I do. Where were you last night?" he repeated.

Now, in the normal course of events, Penelope knew that Lora Lou would have spent the previous evening in the company of her very close friend, David Macklin, happily posing for yet another portrait, until the painting reached the point where young Dave (he was nearly fifteen years her junior) would feel impelled to do something to ward off the chill—real or imaginary—that Lora Lou inevitably felt. Or they could have been experimenting with whatever products they might have ordered with the gift certificate Laney had thoughtfully given to all of her lady friends for Valentine's Day. The certificate was accompanied by a mail order catalog filled with a variety of the most interesting and highly erotic items available from a combination adult bookstore, mail drop, and private detective agency, fronted by Ralph and Russell, twin behemoths in the employ of one Justin Beamish, the principal in Discreet Investigations. Penelope's own certificate and catalog were carefully hidden away from lascivious eyes on the very top shelf of her closet beneath a pile of carefully folded San Diego State University sweatshirts. But Penelope also knew that young Dave was out of town. He had complained often enough about having to miss the opening game of the season.

Lora Lou frowned as she looked back and forth between Penelope and Dutch. "I was home—taking care of the horses."

This pronouncement satisfied Penelope immediately because she knew that Lora Lou also boarded a number of horses that kept her busy during her hours away from The Tack Shack. Dutch, however, looked as if he was about to bring out an inquisitorial rubber hose, but further grilling of the suspect was momentarily postponed by the arrival of coffee and jelly doughnuts. Penelope quickly took charge and organized a picnic in the home team dugout.

Big Mike, having completed his investigation, ambled across the diamond to join them, stepping daintily over the chalked lines around the batter's box. When he found nothing but jelly doughnuts, Big Mike looked as though he was ready to run away from home. Lora Lou soothed his feelings by going into her purse and emerging with a chicken-flavored cat treat. If he couldn't have lima beans, a liver-flavored anything was Mycroft's next favorite repast, but given a choice between jelly doughnuts and a chicken-flavored treat, he

would take chicken every time. Big Mike chewed carefully—
Penelope thought it was done rather contemptuously to make
his point—and when he was finished, looked up at Lora Lou
as if to say, 'Now, here's a woman who knows how to treat
a cat,' and turned his purring motor on as he settled down in
her lap, thus eliminating her as a suspect once and for all.
To Penelope's knowledge—which was extensive—Big Mike
had never sat in a killer's lap and had certainly never purred
within a hundred yards of a murderer.

Dutch, who had considerably less confidence in Mycroft's
judgment of human beings, said, "I suppose you were alone
last night."

"No, Andy stayed over," Penelope offered, before taking
a delicate bite of a doughnut. Apparently the contents were
under some considerable degree of pressure because a fat
dollop of red jelly squirted out and landed on Dutch's hereto-
fore clean shirt.

"Damn it, Penelope!" Dutch exclaimed.

"When you get back to the office," Penelope said calmly,
"you should soak that in cold water before it stains." She
turned to Lora Lou. "Or is it warm water? I can never
remember."

Dutch scooped the blob of jelly off with his forefinger and
flipped it at Penelope, missing her by a good three feet but
managing to hit Tweedledee squarely in the nose as he lumbered down the dugout steps.

Big Mike watched these proceedings with some degree of
amusement. There were hard feelings between the burly
detective and the equally-burly cat, stemming back to an
unfortunate disagreement over who got to drive a certain
police car. Tweedledee still carried the scars, evidence of Big

Mike's displeasure, on his cheek. As a result, Mycroft had been briefly detained, along with Penelope who had come to his immediate defense, in the Empty Creek hoosegow, but this was no hardship as he was fawned over, and rightly so, by two female cops.

"Jeez, boss, what'cha do that for?" Feeling Big Mike's steely gaze, Tweedledee grabbed two jelly doughnuts and hastily retreated to safety.

"Were *you* alone?" Dutch repeated.

"Yes," Lora Lou replied. "I got home about six, made a salad, ate, and went directly to the stables to feed the horses. Afterward, I poured a glass of wine, and read for a while. I was asleep by midnight. The alarm went off at six, as usual, and I was at a breakfast meeting at seven-thirty. That's where I heard about . . . about this."

"Did anyone call?" Dutch asked.

"Mrs. Burnham, but I was screening calls and so I didn't pick up. You know what Mrs. Burnham is like."

Penelope and Dutch did, indeed, know what Eleanor Burnham was like. Empty Creek's very own Town Crier could rattle on forever, usually somewhat incomprehensibly about inconsequential topics.

"Dave didn't call?" Penelope asked hopefully.

Lora Lou shook her head. "I talked to him the night before."

"Why did you come out here when you heard about the murder?"

"To see if it was true, I suppose. The Chamber of Commerce was planning several promotions in conjunction with the team, including our Fourth of July picnic. I met with

Peter Adcock any number of times to talk about the various events."

"Did you like him?"

Lora Lou hesitated. "Not very much," she said finally. "He was rather overbearing. I called him the Octopus."

"Why?"

"He was all hands, always touching and pushing me to have dinner with him." Again, Lora Lou hesitated. "I suppose you'll hear this sooner or later so I might as well tell you. I threatened to break his fingers with one of his own baseball bats if he touched my knee one more time. Mona heard me." Mona, another of Laney's prized informants, worked in The Tack Shack, dispensing gossip as she womaned the cash register.

"Good for you," Penelope said.

"But I didn't kill him." Lora Lou looked up at Dutch. "Are you going to drag me off in handcuffs?"

"Of course not," Dutch said. "There are a million reasons why Adcock could have had your card in his hand."

"Oh."

Penelope thought Lora Lou sounded a little disappointed. Perhaps she and Dave *had* been playing with Laney's exotic gift. "Well," she humphed, "I thought Lora Lou was a suspect."

"Lora Lou Longstreet? Really, Penelope, where is your mind today? How could you suspect Lora Lou?"

CHAPTER
TWO

L ora Lou, having been dismissed as a suspect, called The Tack Shack on her cell phone (it was a perk of Chamber office; like Penelope, she was not enamored of twentieth century inventions and, left to her own devices, would never have one), told Mona she would be late, and joined the spectators in the stands.

Penelope and Mycroft emerged from the dugout to question Jimmy McCoy and Blake Robinson. Having already told their stories on separate occasions to Dutch, Tweedledee and Tweedledum, and the dean of the Empty Creek press corps, Rats was a little testy until Penelope said, "You should have been the Most Valuable Player the year you hit .387 for the Tigers. You were robbed." Penelope was a lifelong fan of Detroit's professional baseball and football teams. How could you not root for Tigers and Lions?

"That's what happens when your team finishes last," Rats said modestly.

"I don't care. I still think you were robbed."

Having accepted her baseball credentials, Rats looked around surreptitiously before pulling a package of chewing tobacco from a pocket. He bit off an unhealthy mouthful and began munching contentedly. Big Mike watched the procedure with some interest, probably wondering if the product came in a liver flavor. Looking like a big old cow chewing its cud, Rats said, "I might as well tell you what I told them other fellas. I didn't like Adcock. I kicked his butt out of my dugout more than once."

"Rats is in very good shape," Blake offered.

"What about you?" Penelope asked. "Did you like your boss?"

Blake looked uncomfortable. "He was a genius," she said hesitantly.

"He was a jerk," Rats said.

"The two are not incompatible," Penelope said. "In fact, they often go together, but did you like him?"

"Not very much."

"Why not?"

"He only hired me because he wanted to sleep with me."

"Did you?"

"Good Lord, no!" Blake exclaimed.

"Why did you put up with it?" Penelope asked, suspecting she already knew the answer. "You could have filed a sexual harassment suit."

"Do you know how many jobs there are in baseball for women? I love baseball. I was a softball player in college, not great, but I didn't want to just give up the game. So I got my MBA and applied for jobs everywhere. Mostly, I got form letters saying they would keep my résumé on file. Adcock hired me, even if it was for the wrong reasons. I'm good and

I'm going to get better. This is my career and I wasn't going to let him drive me out just because he had eight hands."

Penelope nodded and wondered if the young woman had ever exchanged notes with Lora Lou.

Rats spit.

Big Mike jumped at the sudden expectoration.

"What were you two doing out here so early?"

Rats looked uncomfortable now. He spit again. "Opening day," he mumbled. "Kinda Zen."

"Zen?"

"You know, at one with the diamond. It's hard to explain."

"Rats wanted me to feel the spirituality of the moment at the first sight of the ball park on opening day when everything is pristine and pure. All the teams are in first place and all the hitters are going to hit a ton and the pitchers will win twenty games. It's like the opening lines of a poem about baseball."

"Yeah," Rats said. "Like that. A poem."

"And then you found the body."

"Sorta spoiled the moment."

"I'll bet. What did the players think of Adcock?"

"Not much."

"How about the other people in the organization?"

"About the same."

"The other owners in the league?"

"Hated him."

"Did anyone like him?"

"Not that I know of. Even his mother probably couldn't stand him."

"What about his family? Where are they?"

"He didn't have any," Rats said. "He was pretty much of a loner."

"Except for women," Penelope said, looking at Blake.

"I guess he was a lonely loner," Blake said. "I feel sorry for him now."

Penelope nodded. "Who takes over for him?"

"I don't know," Blake said. "I'll have to call the board of directors."

"Do you have a roster of the team and the other club personnel?"

"The police asked for that. I sent for a box of the opening day souvenir programs. They should be here soon. It has everyone and everything about the Coyotes in it."

Again, Penelope nodded before turning to Rats. "I'd like to meet the team."

"You think one of us did it." Rats didn't bother making it a question.

"I don't know," Penelope replied, "but the possibility has to be considered."

Rats spit. "Team meeting in the clubhouse before batting practice."

"I'll see you then."

"You shy?"

"Not particularly."

"That's good."

"Rats means they'll probably try to get you in the showers with them, but they're good guys."

And so, the investigation into the death of Peter Adcock at the hands of a person or persons as yet unknown began as most murder investigations began in Empty Creek. The principal unofficial sleuth of Empty Creek and her stalwart feline assistant repaired to the Double B Western Saloon and Steakhouse with such other members of her retinue as cared to accompany her. Since the police officers all scattered to work on the case, Laney and Wally went off to research an important point for her current romance novel in progress, and Andy went back to the newspaper office to begin work on his story, Penelope and Big Mike were dutifully followed only by the former suspect Lora Lou Longstreet and the early morning informant Nora Pryor.

At the Double B, as the trio of women headed for their usual corner table, Big Mike left the parade and leaped gracefully to his customary stool at the bar to await his ration of nonalcoholic beer, cheerfully dispensed by Pete the Bartender, and whatever wisdom might be forthcoming from Red the Rat.

"Morning, Red."

"Morning, ladies. Big Mike." Red the Rat gave his feline drinking buddy a scratch behind the ears.

"How's Mattie?" Penelope asked.

"She's a pistol, that one," Red said of the rifle-wielding woman who had recently entered his life in holy matrimony. The rifle hadn't really been necessary to get the old desert rat to the altar, but it helped.

"Give her our best."

"Will do."

The Double B was the heart and core for Empty Creek's somewhat dubious aristocracy, although its functions never appeared in the society pages of Andy's *News Journal.* Still, almost anything worth reporting passed through the Double B in one fashion or another. It was a combination of restaurant—the best cheeseburgers and steak fries in Western civilization—and bar, where Pete, in addition to serving the odd cat or two, dispensed the hottest damned Bloody Marys going, with gargantuan jalapeño peppers in place of the traditional celery stalks, which were considered too wimpy by the regular clientele.

It had recently become an art gallery as well, with its larger than life-size portrait of Lora Lou Longstreet reclining in her zaftig altogether. If the Bloody Marys didn't set the hormones to raging, Lora Lou certainly would. In fact, it was the fabled and much anticipated unveiling of her portrait that inspired an impromptu quorum of the Chamber board of directors to nominate Lora Lou for the presidency (Penelope provided the second), thereby setting what was believed to be a record for political incorrectness.

The Double B was also pool hall, sports center, dance floor, unofficial city hall, and home base to Debbie Locke, also known as Debbie D and Dee Dee, an always cheerful cocktail waitress, whose nicknames did not come from her grades in college (she graduated magna cum laude from the University of Pennsylvania), but rather from what was popularly believed to be the cup size of her bra.

"Good morning, all," Debbie said, pouring coffee without being asked, knowing their habits well. "You're early today, especially Penelope. It's barely eleven o'clock."

"'Glamis hath murder'd sleep, and therefore Cawdor/Shall sleep no more, Macbeth shall sleep no more!'" Penelope quoted. "Except, Macbeth is in the clear this time."

"I was a psych major," Debbie said. "Would you translate that please?"

"Someone killed Peter Adcock."

"Oh, no!" Debbie cried, splashing coffee over the rim of Lora Lou's cup, staining the table cloth. "Oh, God, I'm sorry."

"Accidents happen," Nora said, grabbing some paper napkins to soak up the mess.

"*Et tu*, Debbie?" Penelope asked, completing her store of Shakespearean quotations for the nonce.

"What do you mean?"

"Did Peter Adcock hit on you?"

"How did you know?"

"I've been on the case less than four hours, and the one thing I've learned is that Peter Adcock had an eye for the ladies and wasn't shy about making his intentions known."

Coffee pot in one hand, wet napkins in the other, Debbie glanced around the table. "All of you, too?"

Penelope shook her head. "Just Lora Lou."

"Well," Nora said, "that's not quite true. He. . . ."

"Good God," Penelope interrupted. "Am I the only woman in Empty Creek he didn't find attractive and worthy of attention?"

"He probably would have gotten around to you," Lora Lou said. "You're not bad for an old lady. David wants to paint you."

Penelope ignored the Chamber president. It was not a news flash. David wanted to paint all of Lora Lou's friends. As for that old lady crack. . . . "Why don't you get rid of that stuff, Debbie, and come back? You can tell us about Mr. Adcock then." She turned to Nora. "Well. . . ."

Nora blushed. In addition to being Empty Creek's foremost local historian, a devoted single mother, and enamored of a certain Englishman who directed television commercials, the slightest reference to anything of a personal sexual nature set

Nora Pryor to blushing. Possessed of long strawberry-blonde hair, her cheeks soon surpassed the pale red of the fine strands until she glowed like an out-of-work traffic signal stuck on red.

"I outran him," Nora said.

"Of course you did. But why?"

"I was running past the stadium as I usually do, minding my own business, thinking of something Anthony said . . ."

Nora's blush grew deeper—if such a thing were possible—immediately making Penelope wonder what the usually proper Anthony Lyme-Regis might have suggested. When he got into the cooking sherry. . . .

". . . when Peter Adcock thundered up beside me and asked if I had ever made love in a dugout."

"And . . . ?"

"And what? I left him in the dust."

"No, *have* you ever made love in a dugout?"

"Penelope!"

"I was just curious."

Debbie's return diverted attention from Nora, and the crimson glow of her cheeks soon receded. Nora had no inhibitions when it came to the sexual mores of others.

"It was that damned poster," Debbie said without preamble, pulling out the fourth chair at the table. "I thought it would be fun, but he wouldn't leave me alone until I told him my boyfriend was a cop. That shut him up quick."

"By he, I take it you mean Peter Adcock?"

"*And* the photographer," Debbie said. "He was just as bad."

"That figures."

"Why does that figure?" Lora Lou asked.

"It just does."

"You always say that when you're stuck."

"I am *not* stuck," Penelope protested. "Peter Adcock was a man. All men are womanizers. Therefore, Peter Adcock was a womanizer. And . . ." Penelope paused dramatically. "And, a further therefore and a whereas or two, indicate that Peter Adcock might have met his fate at the hands of a woman wronged, a jealous husband or boyfriend, or . . ."

"Or?"

"Or just about anyone else in or out of town." Penelope shook her head with some considerable degree of disgust. "Just once I'd like to see someone caught with the smoking gun."

"Or bat."

"Why a bat, and what was it doing in the dugout in the middle of the night?" Penelope asked. "And what was Peter Adcock doing meeting a murderer there?"

"An assignation?" Lora Lou suggested.

"You've been reading Laney's latest novel."

"Rereading all of them, actually. Where does she come up with all those ideas? Her novels are veritable sex manuals."

"Which reminds me, Lora Lou, have you and David used Laney's Valentine's Day present?"

For such a freespirited individual, Lora Lou produced a most credible blush of her own.

"Gotcha," Penelope said. "That was for the old lady remark." She glanced around the table and saw Nora's cheeks rushing past the one hundred mark on the blush-o-meter and heading for the stratosphere. Debbie's cheeks, too, were suddenly a bright red. "Got all of you, it would seem. It's too bad that killers aren't so easily trapped."

———

After lunch, Debbie remained at the epicenter of Empty Creek's social hub, while Lora Lou headed for The Tack Shack and Nora went off to the library to do some of her own research on a hitherto obscure facet of Empty Creek's history, having to do with an early bawdy house, the town's founder, and a shoe box full of letters recently found in an attic in Ohio and donated to the local library. Penelope gathered up Big Mike who was sleeping on his bar stool and made an appearance at Mycroft & Company, where she was greeted by complaints from Kathy Allan, her devoted, if somewhat disgruntled, assistant.

"I suppose I won't see you again until this is all over," Kathy said frowning. The frown was out of place on her pretty face, but she had seen Penelope consumed by tracking down a killer before. It wasn't that Kathy disapproved. Not at all. Each of Penelope's forays into the mean streets of Empty Creek only added to Kathy's admiration of her boss, friend, and mentor. Indeed, she thought Penelope was the greatest thing since the invention of the fat free blueberry muffin.

"Don't be silly. Have I ever left you in the lurch?"

"Yes."

"Oh. Well, give yourself a raise then."

This pronouncement altered Kathy's outlook on life. "How much?"

"A dollar an hour if you promise not to whine. Fifty cents if you do."

"I'd rather have you around," Kathy said, "but. . . . All right, no whining."

"Good. I knew I could count on you. How's Timmy?"

"Stuck on Book II of *The Kathiad*. This may be the shortest epic poem in history."

"I wondered how he was going to sustain it. I mean, really, twelve books devoted to one woman?"

"I'll renew his inspiration. David Macklin is going to paint me."

"In the nude?"

"Of course, in the nude. This is the nineties."

"Well, I suppose it would look nice over the mantel." Mycroft & Company had a very serviceable fireplace with Victorian armchairs before it where customers could sit and browse through novels at their leisure *if* the bookstore's name-sake happened to like them and allowed them to enter his space.

"Good God, Penelope! You wouldn't. Not in public. It's Timmy's birthday present."

"I was just thinking it might be nice for sales."

"Penelopeeeeee."

"You're whining."

"Sorry. But . . . you wouldn't . . . would you?"

Penelope smiled. "Just kidding, but it's nice to see you still have some sense of propriety."

"Whew."

"Well, I'm off. Come on, Mikey."

"Where are you going to start?"

"At the beginning."

"I knew that."

"By the way, did Peter Adcock ever proposition you?"

"No. Why?"

"Just curious."

After an unproductive afternoon, Penelope drove home and went into the kitchen. She took a bag of lettuce and carrots from the refrigerator and headed out to feed Chardonnay and the rabbits who congregated each evening for their handout. Big Mike liked both Chardonnay and the rabbits, so he followed Penelope down the path to the stables on the banks of Empty Creek. It was dry now, but it could become a raging torrent during rains.

Chardonnay was a golden Arabian filly with a sweet and even temper who happened to like peppermint candies as much as Big Mike went for lima beans. Penelope had long ago decided that she didn't know any normal animals either. But, of course, just like the people, they drank from the Empty Creek water supply, which Penelope blamed for the zany behavior of the local populace. The big horse whinnied an affectionate greeting from her pen, shaded now from the heat by a green mesh canopy. She took the peppermints delicately from Penelope's hands and munched her hors d'oeuvres happily, while Penelope distributed largess to the waiting rabbits and then prepared a healthy concoction for the filly's dinner.

Chores completed, Penelope went to the little patch of grass beneath the scrub oak. It was the only cultivated piece of ground on Penelope's twelve acres. All the rest was natural desert, as beautiful as anything she might have grown. She sat in the lawn chair—checking first to make sure that Clyde the Rattlesnake hadn't taken up occupancy beneath it—and watched the rabbits munch politely. Big Mike stretched out on the grass, content to watch as well. Often, he played with the rabbits, stalking them until they leaped in the air and hopped off. It was a game that the cat and rabbits all enjoyed, but it had been a long day.

Penelope sighed, waiting for a second wind, and tried to decide on suitable opening game attire. It was a way to let her subconscious work on the events of the day.

Then, she turned to the souvenir program of the Empty Creek Coyotes.

The opening day program was like a high school yearbook: a book of dreams, hopes, and lofty aspirations. Most of the younger players grinned foolishly for the camera, while the older players, perhaps realizing this was their last chance to succeed in baseball, were solemn. As Penelope leafed through it, she thought all it needed were appellations added to each of the write-ups—Most Likely to Succeed, Class Clown, Party Animal, and, of course, Class Murderer.

Like a yearbook, too, several pages were devoted to the faculty. The late Peter Adcock's photograph was casual. He wore an open-necked shirt and a baseball cap, cocked jauntily over one eye. Blake Robinson smiled shyly. Rats McCoy glowered, befitting the heavy responsibilities of his managerial role. His two coaches were no less forbidding. Erika von Sturm, a native of Germany and the team trainer, looked suitably Teutonic. The Head Groundskeeper squinted.

Penelope felt like she could close her eyes, meditate, and open the program at random, allowing her finger to act as a divining rod and point to a killer. However, when she put this curious theory into practice, Penelope found herself pointing to a quarter-page ad for Empty Creek Diablo, a beer from a local micro-brewery. Deciding to try for two out of three, Penelope first accused Adcock of his own murder and then another advertisement, this one for The Dynamite Lounge, which proclaimed itself under new management, offering exotic dancing for the discriminating taste. "Meditation is vastly overrated in police work," Penelope announced to Mycroft as she turned back to the write-up beneath Adcock's mug shot.

An hour later, having read through the entire program, including the advertisements, Penelope had learned that Adcock was an entrepreneur in real estate investments and later, having made a killing in the stock market, had devoted himself to his boyhood love—baseball. She had also learned that Rats McCoy had finished his major league career needing just one hit for a lifetime batting average of .300, that James "Gnarly" Bridges, the third base coach, had hit into an unassisted triple play in his only major league at bat, and the amount of water needed to keep the outfield grass green in the desert environment (reclaimed water at the insistence of a vehement organization of environmentalists called Save Our Desert, SOD, for short).

Of the players, most were high school or college players who hadn't been drafted by any of the big league teams. A few, however, were professionals who had been cut from their previous minor league teams and were looking to rejuvenate their faltering careers with a good season for the Coyotes, hoping that their efforts would not go unnoticed.

One outfielder stood out from among the rest, besides his being the oldest player on the roster at twenty-nine and besides his photograph revealing a gaunt face and worried eyes. At the age of twenty, Eddie Stiles had been named American League Rookie of the Year, hitting .319 with twenty-seven home runs and ninety-two runs batted in. Great things had been predicted for him—batting championships, home run crowns, leading the league in RBI's, perhaps all three in a single season for the coveted triple crown, and quite likely a Hall of Fame career. He had been compared with the greatest of all time—Willie Mays, Mickey Mantle, Hank Aaron, Al Kaline. Cooperstown waited.

All that was before he ran his career into the cesspool of fast living, women, and drugs. Dubbed Cocaine Eddie Stiles by the media, he had been in and out of rehab programs, suspended three times, sent to the minors, brought up again, and finally released, his career and life a tortured shambles. None of that was included in the program—only the high-lights of Eddie's career were described—but everyone knew.

Penelope turned back to his picture. With a few numbers beneath his face, it would look like every other police mug shot Penelope had ever seen.

Penelope turned back to the center of the program, glancing down the roster quickly. There were twenty-five players on the roster. Of the ten pitchers, six were right-handers. One of the four left-handed pitchers, Jonathan Luke, was also listed as a switch-hitter. Among the outfielders and infielders, there were two switch-hitters and six who hit from the left side of the plate. If the true southpaws were eliminated as potential suspects, there were sixteen possibilities on the team who could have taken a pretty good swing at Peter Adcock, assuming, of course, that one of them had a motive to kill the team's owner.

CHAPTER
THREE

Rats McCoy was standing outside the clubhouse door when Penelope and Big Mike arrived. "I don't know if you're shy or not, but I thought you might like an escort the first time."

"That's very considerate of you, Mr. McCoy."

"Call me Rats. Everyone does."

"How did you come by the nickname?"

"Feathers, she's my second wife, took exception to some of my language. I told her it was colorful and all baseball players talked like that, but she said it was filthy and disgusting. So now I substitute 'rats' for certain other words. Like, 'Rats, Ump, he was safe.' I ain't colorful no more."

"I think you're very colorful, indeed. Even more so."

"Yeah?" Rats grinned and opened the door.

The clubhouse was subdued. The players were sitting around on stools in front of their lockers. Most of them were too young to have encountered death in its many guises, particularly a violent murder of someone they knew. But

youth was resilient and they all watched Penelope and Big
Mike enter with wary curiosity.

Mikey hopped on a vacant stool and looked around with
interest. It appeared there were any number of fascinating
areas to explore and exotic objects to examine.

"This is Penelope Warren," Rats announced, "and Big
Mike. And she's not taking showers with you, so get that out
of your minds right now."

A collective groan rose from the team, but the attempt at
levity brought a few smiles.

"Now, she's helping the cops out on this case and she's
gonna want to talk with you guys. So help her out. The sooner
we find out who . . . what happened, the better off this team
will be. So cooperate with her. From what I hear around town,
she's one of the good guys."

"Can I say something, Rats?" Eddie Stiles asked.

He should get a new picture taken, Penelope thought. He
doesn't look like a three-time loser at all.

"Sure, Eddie."

"I just wanna clear the air. The cops already talked with
me. I know I've screwed up pretty bad and done some really
stupid things, but they're looking at me like I killed Adcock.
I don't drink anything stronger than Diet Coke anymore. As
for the drugs, I won't even take aspirin now. I just want a
chance to prove myself again. You and Adcock gave me that
chance. I wouldn't kill him. Man, I just want to play baseball
and it doesn't look like they're gonna let me. And now, *she*
comes in here. What do I have to do? I just wanna be left
alone."

Twenty-four players looked at Penelope. The suspicious

expressions on their faces formed a symbolic shield around their teammate.

Rats started to speak but Penelope motioned him to silence. "Eddie, I'm not a cop and you don't have to talk with me if you don't want to, but I seem to have a talent for police work. I walked through that door with an open mind and I'll keep it open. That's all I can say. I hope you make it. People are going to look at you with suspicion. That would have been true even if Adcock hadn't been murdered. I can't do anything about that and you have to learn to deal with it. But I'd love to see you back in the big leagues. I'd love to see you make another catch like the one in dead center that day in Yankee Stadium. Prettiest catch I ever saw."

"You remember that?"

"I remember, Eddie."

"Well, thanks."

"One other thing, Eddie."

"Yeah?"

Penelope grinned. "If I didn't have a boyfriend, I'd take a shower with you anytime."

Penelope was batting a thousand in the Making People Blush department

When Penelope and Big Mike left the clubhouse, they headed for the concession stand to find Blake Robinson behind the counter. "What are you doing here? I thought you were the General Manager."

"I am. I'm also the equipment manager, part-time trainer, promotions manager, groundskeeper, Coyote Dog saleswoman, and big sister to whichever player happens to be homesick. How did the meeting go?"

"You're right. They're good guys."

"What can I get you?"

"A beer and two Coyote Dogs, one with everything and one with just the Dog, and could you chop it up? He'll eat it here."

Blake Robinson was obviously a prime candidate for permanent citizenship in Empty Creek because she didn't bat an eyelash at serving a cat. "How about a side of lima beans?" Blake asked, immediately transporting herself to a place of honor in Big Mike's Culinary Hall of Fame, right beside Penelope and her magic electric can opener.

"Now, how did you know that?"

Blake smiled. "We asked around after you left this morning."

"And what did you find out? I mean, besides Mikey's passion for lima beans."

"Don't mess with the Cat Lady."

A mariachi band roamed the stands serenading the fans.

The faithful turned out for any number of reasons, slowly filling the stands during batting practice and infield. There were true baseball fans among them, parents and their children, single women acting as both mom and dad to their sons, aging jocks already enhancing their memories of old feats on the diamond, and a contingent of Senior Citizens from Geezer World, otherwise known as the Burning Cactus Condominium and Golf Club. They were led by Cackling Ed, who appeared to have been born sometime during the late Cenozoic Era. Others came out of civic pride and to cheer on the boys of Empty Creek against the Sedona Red Rocks, the team from that pretentious little New Age community to the north. The society crowd showed up because without a cotillion or some other charitable event, Coyote Stadium was *the* place to be that particular evening.

And, of course, there were relatives and friends of the young men who made up the roster of the Empty Creek Coyotes, present to witness their debut in professional baseball and the beginning of their long and hopefully successful quest to reach the major leagues. It was a journey fraught with disappointment at each way station and few—if any—would survive. Injury, a suddenly dead arm, that old hitter's lament—they're throwing the curve ball now—and a dozen other reasons were all cause to be left behind. But not on this special occasion. This was the opening game of the season and hopes soared to the heavens.

Hardly anyone came to mourn Peter Adcock.

Big Mike promptly staked out his territory on the roof of the dugout. Penelope sipped her beer and watched as Rats McCoy stepped into the batting cage to demonstrate one of the finer points of hitting to a player. Rats looked like he could still win the American League batting championship as he hit three screaming line drives to left, center, and right. For good measure, he went deep with a towering fly ball over the center field fence. He returned the bat to his young charge who stepped back into the cage and promptly popped it up.

Rats spit tobacco juice.

A player popped his head up over the dugout and smiled shyly at Penelope after a hasty glance down the aisle.

"That's the biggest cat I've ever seen. What'd Rats say his name was?"

"Mycroft."

"That's a strange name."

"He's a strange cat." Penelope said. "Why aren't you out there?" she asked, pointing vaguely at the field. "Are you hurt?"

"I'm the starting pitcher tomorrow, so tonight I'm the lookout."

"Lookout for what?"

"Mrs. McCoy. She'll kill Rats if she catches him chewing tobacco."

"How does he hide it?"

"He brushes his teeth about a hundred times a day. The good thing is it gets me out of running with the rest of the pitchers."

Penelope looked out to left field where the pitching staff was running under the tutelage of a woman with short blonde hair. "Is that Erika von Sturm?"

"Erika the Hun. Everybody's got to have a nickname."

"What's yours?"

His face turned red. "Peeper," he said. "I got caught looking at Blake when she was in the shower. I got fined, but it was worth it. I'm going to win the Blake Robinson Nickname Contest."

Penelope laughed. "How's that, Peeper?"

"She's got a butterfly tattoo on her butt. I'm going to enter either Butterfly or Tattoo in the contest, but I can't decide. Which do you think is best?"

"Why not enter both of them?"

"That's a good idea. Oops. Here she comes. Gotta go."

Penelope turned to find a statuesque woman gliding down the aisle. By the time Penelope turned back, Peeper was at the batting cage and Rats was sprinting down the foul line toward the cramped little clubhouse, presumably to eliminate the evidence.

"Hi, I'm Martha McCoy, but you can call me Feathers. Everyone does. And that's my beloved on his way to brush his teeth." Feathers looked after her fleeing husband fondly. "He thinks I don't know he still chews. And you must be the Cat Lady."

"Penelope Warren."

"Rats told me about you."

"Why do they call you Feathers?" Penelope asked.

"Because that's all I wore during my career in Vegas," she answered with an impish smile and a devilish twinkle in her eyes. "All on my head."

Feathers McCoy was tall, at least six feet, and took forever to sit down, as though she were a beautiful temptress retreating gracefully into a charmer's basket, arranging her body seductively for her next appearance. Although Feathers was on the wrong side of fifty—barely—she looked like she could resume her career and send younger show girls scurrying to the cosmetic surgeon.

Mycroft, having lost interest in batting practice, marched over Penelope and into Feathers' lap, thereby taking another potential suspect out of consideration.

"Do you mind? Mikey's very friendly."

"Not at all. I love cats. If we ever settle down, I'm going to adopt about a hundred of them." She scratched Mycroft under the chin as he gazed into her eyes. "Do you have any suspects?"

"Not yet," Penelope said, wondering if Adcock's taste extended to an older woman who just happened to be a beautiful ex-Las Vegas show girl. She decided it wouldn't hurt to toss a metaphoric hook in the sand and see if she caught anything other than a lizard. "Did he ever come on to you?"

"Peter? Of course, but nothing ever happened. *I* would have brained him with a baseball bat."

"Or Rats?"

Feathers was quiet for a long time, staring wistfully out at the field. "Rats has been out of baseball a long time," she said finally, turning to Penelope, stroking Mycroft softly. "That happens sometimes. Even big stars get lost, drift away from the game. We live in Las Vegas. Rats could have worked at one of the casinos. They'd love to have a star like him on the payroll, but he thought that would hurt his chances of getting back in the game. So he sold insurance, and it was killing him. He was good at it—everyone wanted to buy a policy from Jimmy McCoy. But this is his big chance, and he wouldn't do anything to hurt his chances of a comeback. I wouldn't either."

Good answer. Mycroft showed his approval with a steady purr, but Penelope wondered if the Big Mike lap test was infallible.

"Hi, Sis, when did you get back?"

"This afternoon. I called but you weren't home."

"Where's Dutch?"

"Working. Why aren't you?"

"I am," Penelope said. "Feathers, this is my sister Cassandra, but call her Stormy. Everyone does."

"Nice to meet you."

"Welcome to Empty Creek."

"How was Glamour City?" Penelope asked.

"We wrapped a couple of days ago, but I stayed over—power lunches with my agent. I want to do a play, but Myron wants me to do a film called *The Last Best Burlesque Show.*"

"That's our Myron." While a pretty good agent—if your specialty happened to be Grade Double B Straight to Video films—Myron Schwartzman tended to retrogress more and more toward his younger days. He had been in the Navy, stationed in San Diego, where he moonlighted as a bouncer at the old Hollywood Burlesque house, falling in unrequited love with a succession of strippers. It was Myron who gave Cassandra Warren her stage name of Storm Williams, a tribute to one or another of his lost loves.

"I think he wrote the script, but he won't admit it."

"I think he writes all your scripts, but won't admit it. I wouldn't."

As the stadium filled, Penelope spent a considerable amount of time making introductions.

"Laney and Wally, this is Feathers McCoy. . . ."

"Andy's editor of the *News Journal.*"

"I'd like to do a feature on you. What it's like to be the wife of a minor league manager. . . ."

"This is Samantha and Big Jake. . . ."

"Lora Lou is president of the Chamber of Commerce. Her boyfriend is quite a talented painter. You'll see some of his work later at the Double B. . . ."

"Meet Ed, he was old when the Titanic sailed."

The high school band played the Marine's Hymn as the flags were carried onto the field by a color guard from the Marine Corps Reserve. The Marine Corps flag was carried by a woman Marine. Penelope stood at attention for *the* Hymn.

The rest of the crowd joined her for the National Anthem and remained standing for the obligatory minute of silence for the late Peter Adcock. A multidenominational contingent from Empty Creek's clergy pronounced a blessing on the field, the teams, and the fans.

Before throwing out the first ball, Mayor Tiggy "Anything-for-a-Vote" Bourke led the crowd in a discordant rendition of "Take Me Out to the Ball Game." They were joined by the enthusiastic musicians of the mariachi band.

Hoopla finished, the boys of Empty Creek's summer ran onto the field, chattering nervously as they tossed the ball around the infield. The first Red Rock stepped into the batter's box. Buddy Peterson, the Coyote pitcher, went into his windup.

"Steerike!" the umpire shouted.

And that was the highlight of the Coyotes first game.

Penelope started yawning in the bottom of the fifth inning. By the seventh inning stretch, she was nearly comatose as were the Empty Creek Coyotes who were behind by twelve runs at the time. Even a brief rally in the home half of the stretch inning, as the Coyotes loaded the bases with no outs, failed to completely revive her. It was hard for even the truest fan to get excited about the strikeout and double play that ended the inning.

But she lasted longer than Big Mike who had taken refuge in the Coyote Dog stand with Blake Robinson after the third inning (the Coyotes were already losing by six).

"We'll get 'em tomorrow," Feathers said after the last out. Her voice was hoarse from cheering her husband's managerial debut.

Penelope, Feathers, and Stormy decided to wait for their men at the Double B. Rats was talking to his team. Andy was helping out his one-man sports staff and waited for post-game interviews. And Stormy knew that Dutch would catch up to her eventually.

A goodly number of fans also stopped by the Double B to go over the game and to belly up to the bar, clamoring for service as a harassed Pete and a substitute waitress attempted to keep up with the demand for service.

"Where's Debbie?" Penelope asked.

"Arrested." Pete shouted. "Took her away just before the dinner hour started."

"What?" Penelope shouted. "Why? Who?"

"Don't know. Wouldn't talk to me. Damned cops. I said, wait until the rush's over, but no. Had to be right then. Been scrambling ever since."

Penelope retreated with three glasses of wine to the table where Stormy and Feathers waited. "Debbie's been arrested."

"No, she hasn't," Stormy said. "She's just being questioned."

"You knew?"

"Didn't you?"

"No. Why are they questioning Debbie? What good is your engagement to the chief of police," Penelope demanded of her sister, "if you don't tell me anything?"

Stormy dug into her purse and pulled out a cell phone, quickly punched in Dutch's beeper number, and pressed 9-1-1 after the signal. Handing the phone to Penelope, she said, "You ask him. No one ever tells me anything."

Penelope took the phone and prepared for a good sulk while waiting for Dutch to call.

"Is that the Chamber of Commerce president in the painting behind the bar?" Feathers asked.

"Yes," Stormy said.

"Oh, my."

"He's quite good," Stormy continued. "I'm thinking of having one done."

"Oh, God," Penelope groaned. She would have tossed a peanut at Stormy, but the telephone rang.

"Hi, honey," Dutch said.

"Don't honey me," Penelope said. "What have you done with Debbie?"

"Nothing. Where's Stormy?"

"She ran off with Brad Pitt."

"I did not. I wouldn't leave my sweetie for anyone less than Robert Redford."

"Good choice," Feathers said, "as aging hunks go."

"Will you please tell me what's going on?"

"Baseball poster. Did you take a close look at it?"

"No," Penelope said. Since the walls were plastered with Debbie's poster, Penelope got up and peered at the nearest one. "So, I'm looking at one now."

"She's holding the murder weapon."

"How do you know it's the same bat?" Penelope demanded.

"Oh, darling, I can hardly wait for you to get home and tickle my feet. . . ."

"Who is this?" Penelope demanded. "Get off my line."

"And nibble my toes. . . ."

"And what are you going to do for me?"

"Oh, darling, I'll. . . ."

Penelope waited. Might as well pick up a few tips. . . .

The phone went dead. A red light glowed telling Penelope that the batteries were low. Penelope looked at it in disgust and handed it back to Stormy. "What good is it if you don't keep your batteries charged?"

"My batteries *are* charged. When is Dutch coming?"

"I don't know. We were interrupted by a pervert."

"Were they talking about toes?"

Penelope nodded wearily.

"Our wires have crossed before," Stormy said. "They say the most interesting things."

"There are no wires in those portable contraptions." Penelope pointed out. She knew *that* much about the twentieth century.

"Whatever."

"Did you ever stop to think that if you can hear them, they can probably hear you."

"Oh, my God. . . ."

Stormy's review of recent telephone conversations with her chief of police was interrupted by the arrival of Debbie and *her* policeman, Sam Connors, and then the chief himself. During the confused babble that passed for civilized conversation in Empty Creek, further interrupted by the appearance of a newspaper editor and a baseball manager, Penelope managed to piece the story together.

Detective Willie Stoner, at the end of an exhausting day, had apparently been mooning over the poster of Debbie tacked to a prominent spot on the cubicle of the Robbery-Homicide Division, when he noticed a nick on the bat she held. As a trained observer, he remembered seeing a similar nick on the bat that had apparently inflicted the fatal injury to Peter Adcock.

"Tweedledum discovered it?" Penelope exclaimed. "I'll be damned."

"After the photo shoot," Debbie offered, "they gave me the bat as a souvenir. Good thing, too, because the check bounced the first time."

"Well, why didn't you just produce the bat in question?"

"I couldn't. It's missing."

"It's not missing," Dutch said. "We have it."

"I meant it's missing from my house."

Like many residents of the usually placid community, Debbie rarely locked her door. Penelope had been cured of the delusion that Empty Creek, while one of the safest communities in the nation according to the FBI's *Uniform Crime Reports*, was totally secure when a body had been discovered on her doorstep. The ensuing warnings from the killer—in the form of pennies glued to her door—had caused a brief flurry in the deadbolt business, to say nothing of bringing out the Colt Sporter, the civilian version of the military's M-16 rifle that Penelope now kept handy.

"Who knew you had the bat?"

"Just about everybody."

"This doesn't make any sense. Why go to all that trouble to get Debbie's souvenir bat? A baseball team must have plenty of bats."

"But not with Debbie's prints on them."

"Oh, come on, Dutch, *I* could get that thrown out of court."

Penelope went to the wall and ripped one of the posters down. At the table, she pointed to Debbie's grip high up on the bat. "She's choking up," Penelope said. "You can see that she's holding the bat lightly. That's where you found the prints, right?"

Dutch nodded.

"And lower down, where a killer would probably hold the bat, you found nothing but smudges, right? From the pressure of swinging the bat hard enough to deliver a killing blow?"

Again, Dutch nodded.

"You see?" Penelope said triumphantly. "Reasonable doubt. Debbie had a reason for leaving her prints on the bat. Circumstantial evidence."

"Unless . . ." Dutch shrugged, "Debbie is the person who smudged the prints."

"Motive?"

"The check bounced."

"How much did you get for the poster, Debbie?"

Debbie looked back and forth between Penelope and Dutch, a look of disbelief on her face. "A hundred dollars," she said finally. "I make more than that in tips each night."

"People have been killed for ten cents," Dutch said.

"Opportunity?" Penelope looked at Sam Connors.

"I've been working graveyard," he said sadly. "Debbie was alone last night. This morning. Whenever."

"You don't believe Debbie did it," Penelope said to Dutch, "anymore than you believe Lora Lou Longstreet did."

Everyone looked at Dutch, even Andy who had been scribbling furiously in his reporter's notebook. Debbie bit her lip nervously. Sam took her hand and squeezed reassuringly. Rats looked like he could use a big chaw right about now. Feathers held her breath. Big Mike made his way across the room and jumped into Stormy's lap. After all, she was his favorite aunt.

Dutch smiled and shook his head. "No, I don't believe Debbie did it." He looked fondly at Debbie. "She's an Ivy League graduate. She's not that stupid, although I don't know what she sees in Sam."

"Thanks for the vote of confidence, boss."

"But somebody is sure as hell that stupid and we better find him or her."

"Or that smart," Penelope said.

CHAPTER
FOUR

Penelope and Big Mike resumed their normal schedule on the morning after the double play perpetrated on the local baseball club—the demise of their managing general partner and the collapse of glory at the hands of the Sedona Red Rocks—which is to say they slumbered on, insensible to the world long after the departure of Andy. Penelope was the first to grudgingly register her surroundings, which included a rumpled king-sized bed, an all-too-cheerful bird singing happily outside, and a very large cat ensconced on her legs, matching her wink for wink and then some. As Penelope stirred, Big Mike's ears twitched a warning: Don't do it.

Penelope did it anyway. Rudely tossed from his snug little nest, Mycroft landed, paws akimbo, ears alert and swiveling, and eyes darting about, searching for any laggards from the elephant stampede that had awakened him without so much as a 'by your leave, sir.'

"Morning, Mikey, time to get up," Penelope mumbled.

Oh, that.

His eyes glazed over again as Penelope stumbled down the hall toward the kitchen and the still relatively new coffee maker. This latest acquisition had an automatic timer that could be preset, ensuring that coffee was brewed and waiting at any designated hour. But, it also had a pause feature which delighted Penelope so much that she continued to ignore the timer. Sleepwalking on automatic pilot, Penelope poured the water, measured coffee into the filter, and waited. The pot slowly filled with the dark brown liquid and when it reached the three cup level, Penelope confidently pulled the pot out.

And the damned thing immediately stopped brewing, waiting patiently for its mistress to fill her coffee cup and replace the pot before resuming its duties, all without spilling a drop.

Now, *that* was one worthwhile twentieth century invention.

Penelope sipped happily at her coffee. It was almost worth getting up.

Big Mike, jolted from his second-most favorite activity, grumped into the kitchen ready for his favorite. Penelope obligingly filled his bowl with lima beans and Big Mike tucked in for *his* eye opener.

Soon, all was well with the world.

Almost.

Stupid?

Or smart?

After a time, the reasoning became too convoluted. Knowing Peter Adcock's attraction to the distaff portion of the world's population, his killer apparently tried to focus attention on Lora Lou Longstreet and Debbie Locke. But why, and why not one or the other? Why both? It made no sense.

Of course, Lora Lou's business card was all over the place. There was even a card holder on the counter at The Tack Shack. Anyone who passed through for a bridle, a bag of feed, or one of the horsey knickknacks the shop carried could easily take a card.

Penelope tried to put herself in the mind of the murderer. Taking the bat from Debbie's house had been an act of premeditation. Even knowing that her fingerprints were probably on the bat, he—or she—couldn't possibly know that the connection would be made. And who would believe Debbie to be a killer for very long anyway?

As for Lora Lou. . . .

Here, hold my business card while I turn your brain into an omelette.

Too stupid to consider.

Reduced to the simplest common denominators, Penelope believed there were only two motives for felonious murder—love and money. All others—passion, greed, power, jealousy, blackmail, hatred, revenge, et al.—were variations of one or the other. While Penelope was not yet ready to eliminate love as a motive, she decided to focus on money.

"So, Mikey, who would be interested in money and benefit from Peter Adcock's death?"

If Mycroft, who was dozing on the windowsill, heard her— and he rarely missed anything of importance—he thought the answer was too obvious for a reply, so Penelope answered her own question.

"Just about anyone connected with the team," she said. "What if. . . . What if Blake knew that she was about to be fired? Ditto for Rats. That might make either Rats or Feathers commit murder. What if Adcock was cheating on his partners?

What if a player was about to be cut from the team, losing his last chance for renown? What if. . . . Oh, bother, the possibilities are endless. Let's go to work."

Mycroft yawned, stretched, yawned again, stretched some more. "Meow," he said finally, jumping gracefully from the sill to the floor. Penelope took that to mean either "Okey-dokey" or "About time."

Lola LaPola and her crew were at Mycroft & Company when Penelope and Big Mike pulled up to their parking space behind the store. Lola alternated between reporting hard news and roaming the Valley of the Sun—the greater Phoenix metropolitan area which included Empty Creek—seeking out interesting features for an independent television station.

"Hi, Penelope, we would have been here yesterday, but we were stuck on an assignment."

Penelope took pride in that Lola no longer used the personal pronoun several times within each utterance, but now included her crew in a gesture of teamwork. Her reporting had also improved to a calm and matter-of-fact recitation of the facts. Penelope claimed some little credit in Lola's transformation, going back to a time when tragic circumstances had forced Penelope to play the role of Queen Elizabeth I at the Empty Creek Authentic Elizabethan Spring Faire. Lola had provoked the Queen's ire on that occasion, and was sentenced to an uncomfortable hour in the pillory for her transgression, to the delight of her much-abused television crew. Since then, with the help of the arresting bailiff whom she later married, Lola had mellowed considerably.

"Lola, it's good to see you, but you're not here to interview me, I hope."

"Absolutely. And Big Mike, of course. Anytime the Cat Lady and Big Mike go on a case . . . well, it's news and an interesting feature."

Penelope sighed. "Just don't call me the Cat Lady on television." She was going to have to do something about that nickname. . . .

Lola beamed. "I promise, although it's really too good to pass up."

They did the interview in front of Mycroft & Company, which meant that hordes of people would drive by tomorrow to satisfy their morbid curiosity. Some might even buy a book or two.

Big Mike, an old hand at television interviews, settled comfortably in Penelope's arms and peered at the camera.

Lola did the setup and then turned to Penelope. "What leads do you and Big Mike have on your latest investigation?"

Now, Penelope could have been honest and forthright, as her character demanded, truthfully replying, "We haven't the foggiest." But that would accomplish nothing and would be no fun at all. So she decided to hold a metaphorical shotgun to the sky, blast away, and see what might plummet to earth. Penelope didn't feel a few little lies in the interests of justice would be held against her on Judgment Day. "Of course, it's too early to be certain, but we have reason to suspect either financial misdealings or a possible love tryst. Those are the usual motives for murder."

"Unless it was a psychopath."

"Someone truly evil, someone who kills for the joy of it? It's possible, of course, but remote."

Lola probed, but Penelope danced around the questions like an astute politician.

Big Mike's only comment was, "Meow."

During the obligatory cutaways—shots of Lola nodding sagely, reacting to answers to questions already asked— Penelope inquired, "How's Mark?"

Lola nodded.

Penelope took that to mean Lola's husband was fine.

"Do you still have the pillory in your bedroom?"

Lola sputtered and broke character. "Penelope!"

Penelope took Lola's outraged wail as affirmation. It was known among a select few that the young couple had purchased the object which had brought them together and Penelope approved. After all, she and Andy had experimented with the aphrodisiacal properties of the pillory once in their roles as Queen and courtier.

"I was just curious."

"Next time, I'm calling you the Cat Lady."

Penelope sighed, stood, stretched, and wandered out of the back room—a combination office and storage area—into the store proper. Kathy was rearranging the window display with the assistance of Mycroft, which meant that he was generally making a nuisance of himself, purring and rubbing against her legs. Inexplicably struck by an affection attack, Mikey had decided that he wanted a lap to sit in, one that was stationary, not hopping about putting books into the window, and one that belonged to Kathy. Mikey had his mind set on that particular lap and no other would do.

As a result, Penelope found Kathy sitting in the window, Big Mike on her lap, reading. Fortunately, there were no customers clamoring for attention at the moment. Mycroft might have inflicted grievous bodily harm on anyone who caused his dislodgement.

"I don't think Peter Adcock's womanizing had anything to do with his death," Penelope said. "At the moment," she added hastily.

Kathy looked up from her book. "What then?"

"The answers are conspicuous by their absence," Penelope announced.

"Aren't they always?"

"For a time, Kathy, for a time."

The offices of the Empty Creek Coyotes Professional Baseball Club occupied a double wide mobile home that had been set up in the parking lot behind the left field fence. Converted to commercial office space now, the former living room served both as a reception area and a conference room.

Waiting for Blake to get off the telephone, Penelope examined the three framed photographs hanging on the wall. Blake Robinson beamed happily for the camera. Rats McCoy scowled, looking as though he had just struck out in the game of life. Adcock, however, his photograph draped in black crepe, looked serious. He had been a handsome man of perhaps forty with brown hair, receding slightly, a straight nose, slightly too thin for Penelope's taste, and deep brown eyes. With a more subtle approach, many a woman would have found those eyes seductive and compelling. Penelope turned away, wondering why he acted like such a jerk with women. With those looks, he wouldn't have to.

The bedrooms were now offices for the Managing General Partner—empty—the General Manager, and Telephone Ticket Reservations, Group Sales, and Promotions. The kitchen served in its original function as did the two bathrooms.

Penelope and Big Mike had no sooner settled into their respective chairs than the roof was struck by a projectile of some sort.

Ka-blam!

Penelope and Mikey jumped. Blake Robinson merely flinched.

"My God!" Penelope exclaimed. "What was that?"

"Home run," Blake said. "Early batting practice. Rats doesn't like losing."

Ka-blam!

Jump. Flinch.

"You get used to it after a while. That was probably Big Rap. He's got good power to left."

Penelope remembered Earl "Big Rap" Rapp's photograph from the program. He was a heavy-set young black man with a goatee that made him look sinister until he smiled and his easy, good humor showed. He was also the player who used the Cecil Fielder model bat, but he had an excellent alibi—he had been with his wife. "Or Rats," Penelope said.

"Yep. He's still got good power to everywhere. I love to watch him hit."

Ka-blam!

Penelope managed to reduce her jump to a mere start. Big Mike, having decided the roof wasn't caving in, decided to take a bath.

"Why don't you put up a net?" Penelope asked. "It would cut down on the noise and you could gather the baseballs afterwards."

"Good idea." Blake made a note on a yellow legal pad.

"Of course, you'd have to go back to the city for permits."

Blake hastily scratched the note out. "My new boss thinks all politicians are crooks."

"And who is that?"

"Kendall McCoffey, Senior," Blake answered. "He's exercising an option to buy Peter's share of the team. He's supposed to be a silent partner, but he thinks Peter was snookered by the city."

"Snookered?"

"That's what he said."

Since Penelope's Jeep carried a fading bumper sticker that proclaimed JIMMY BUFFET FOR PRESIDENT, the silent partner's sentiment on elected officials was one she could sympathize with. Still, much to Big Mike's disgust—he was a devoted fan of Jimmy's—Penelope had not cast her ballot for the balladeer, wanting to make her vote count just in case the presidential sweepstakes ended in a tie. But snookered? Apparently, Kendall McCoffey didn't know Empty Creek's true capacity for the Big Rip Off.

"And when do we meet Kendall McCoffey, Senior? I'd like to talk to him about a number of matters."

"I don't know. He's sending his son down to take over as the managing general partner."

"What's he like?"

"Which one?"

"Start with Senior. I assume the son is Kendall McCoffey, Junior."

"I've never met him. Just talked to him on the phone. He seems nice enough, if you don't get him started on politicians."

Penelope smiled. "I'll try to avoid that," she said, but in

fact, that was another bit of a little white lie in the pursuit of justice. Penelope intended to get him started on that topic as soon as possible after his arrival. Kendall McCoffey, Senior's view of the deal between the city and the club didn't match very well with the record. Penelope also wanted to know more about the club's financing. "What's he do besides own part of a baseball club?"

"He's an attorney."

"And Junior?"

"He writes computer games."

"You mean, like Pac Man?"

Blake nodded. "I think so. He's supposed to be some kind of genius."

"He should be tried for crimes against the youth of this nation and the English language!" Penelope declared. As a book lover of long standing—she could read before she started school—Penelope believed that computer games would be the demise of civilization with entire generations trained to do nothing but stand in darkened arcades feeding coins into machines in order to blast various alien invaders from artificial heavens. Penelope supposed it to be suitable training for fighter pilots or vaguely useful in the case of an actual hostile alien invasion, but how many fighter pilots did one nation need, the cost of airplanes being what it was, and as for invasion from space . . . well, Penelope wasn't missing any meals over that one.

"Let me show you around," Blake said hastily.

Penelope was not to be mollified. "Computer games! Did you hear that, Mikey?"

Big Mike couldn't miss it since Penelope had raised her voice considerably, but he shared her view of computer games. The one arcade he had visited was unbearably noisy and not at all refined and sophisticated, like the library or a certain bookstore where cultivated conversations were the norm, or should have been in a more perfect world conducive to sleep and other genteel pursuits like dining by candlelight, stalking mice and lizards, or paying a visit to Murphy Brown, the mother of his kittens.

"Readers of the world!" Penelope shouted. "Unite!"

Blake was beginning to realize there were certain subjects that shouldn't be brought up in the presence of the Cat Lady.

Despite Peter Adcock's apparent propensity to make unwanted advances to nearly every woman in town, Penelope's thoughts turned back to money and decided the true beginning was to be found with the first proposal for bringing the Coyotes to Empty Creek. A baseball team didn't just plop down, choose up sides, and start banging the old horsehide around. There were applications to be made to the city, environmental impact studies to be conducted, traffic reports, noise impacts, public hearings. While Penelope, the city fathers and mothers, the business community, and many of the residents could see little harm in having their own professional baseball team, there were citizens who attended planning commission hearings and city council meetings, complaining bitterly about the environment, traffic, noise, glaring lights, and even one sustained diatribe about the alleged unhealthy properties that would be contained in the Coyote Dogs to be sold at the stadium.

But for a little desert backwater like Empty Creek, a professional baseball team—even one without a major league affiliation—meant additional revenues without the inconveniences of big shopping centers, resort hotels and championship golf courses, invasive housing developments, or more of the ugly little strip malls that multiplied like rabbits. The denizens of Empty Creek, Arizona, were content to leave such desert-destroying advancements to Western Civilization for Phoenix and Scottsdale.

After the planning commission had imposed their conditions of approval, a ten percent surtax on all tickets sold, as well as a share of the beer and food concessions, and the city council had exacted their pound or two of revenues—contributions to the city's art program, the library, and the pothole abatement campaign—the city was in a firm profit-sharing mode with the Empty Creek Coyotes Professional Baseball Club, and not one lizard, rattlesnake, or cactus would be dislodged in the process.

The arrangement should have made everyone happy but, quite possibly, someone had expressed his or her displeasure at the intrusion of professional sports in Empty Creek.

Penelope explained all this to Big Mike while they drove to City Hall. The top was off the Jeep now and would remain in the garage until the first rains, many months away. But Mycroft was distracted and paid little attention. The month of May in Empty Creek meant the temperatures were soaring. By Memorial Day, they would be well over the century mark and the hot summer would be upon them. Although everyone else in town said "But it's a dry heat," Mikey didn't care. Dry or not, it was hot and he was shedding.

The cold blast from the city's air conditioners revived the big cat and he jumped to the counter of the Planning Department, gave a cursory glance to some blueprints, and turned his attention to Jennie Davenport, the Senior Planner, who just happened to be at the counter and who just happened to be the individual who had shepherded the baseball team through the maze of city regulations.

"Hi, Penelope," she said. "We've been expecting you." If Jennie was disconcerted at a twenty-five pound cat suddenly appearing on her counter, she didn't show it as she reached to a lower shelf and pulled out a carton of liver treats. Obviously, Mycroft's reputation as a lady's cat had preceded him.

"Then you know why I'm here."

"He said 'no.'"

He was L. Malcolm Osterburg, the city's director of planning and development. *He* stated his name before the planning commission or city council as though announcing that *he* was King of all the Russias.

"Did you remind him of the First Amendment, the Freedom of Information Act, and that it is a matter of public record?" Penelope had once threatened to subpoena the city manager's desk calendar under the Freedom of Information Act, endearing her once and for all to the hard-working city employees.

"No," Jennie laughed, "but I'd be happy to." Jennie was a pretty young woman, a few years younger than Penelope, with long and lustrous black hair that was the envy of many a female around town. Before Osterburg had been hired, there were those—Penelope among them—who urged Jennie to apply for the position. But she had insisted that she needed a few more years' experience and declined to submit her application, a decision she and her supporters now regretted.

L. Malcolm Osterburg was determined to live up to his title whether the citizens he served wanted development or not. He was in a perpetual orgasm over one grandiose scheme or another and would go to his grave happy only after high rise office buildings, industrial complexes, resort hotels, and housing tracts replaced the quaint desert ambiance of Empty Creek. If he had a family crest, it would consist of crossed bulldozers.

"No!" Osterburg thundered from his office.

"Yes!" Penelope shouted, throwing open the leaf in the counter, letting it bang loudly as she headed for Osterburg's office. Big Mike, startled by the shouting and banging, was right behind her, his recently groomed fur bristling. He was followed by the office staff who were all grinning and whispering, "This oughta be good."

It wasn't bad by normal standards, but for Empty Creek it ranked only about a seven on a scale of one to ten for puncturing bureaucratic pomposity.

L. Malcolm Osterburg stood behind his desk, drawing himself up to his full height of five feet nine and three-quarter inches. If this was meant to intimidate either Penelope or Big Mike, Osterburg failed miserably.

Penelope was just as tall as Osterburg, for one thing. And after the Marine Corps, she wasn't impressed by some Lieutenant Junior Grade in the Navy Reserve which she knew Osterburg to have been.

Nor was Big Mike overwhelmed. Anything less than a charging elephant or rhino failed to get *his* attention, although he was a little afraid of those sticks that occasionally slithered through the yard accompanied by their own sound effects. So unless Osterburg had a rattlesnake handy in one of his desk drawers, Mikey wasn't about to be swayed by some idiot jumping to his feet.

When Mycroft leaped to his desk top, Osterburg, horrified,

backed away a step and cried, "Animals are not allowed on city premises."

Mycroft promptly coughed up a hair ball. Score one for the visiting team.

"Where's the luau, Malcolm?" Penelope asked, a reference to the gaudy Hawaiian shirt he wore.

"The authorities have already requested the files. You can't have them."

Penelope reached into her purse and brought out the leather case with the badge and identification that proclaimed her to be an honorary member of the Empty Creek Police Department. Big Mike had a similar case and badge, but he didn't carry it. "I'm one of them and I want the files," Penelope said.

"No."

"Yes." Without asking his permission, Penelope took the phone and quickly punched in the number of Mycroft & Company. When Kathy answered, Penelope said, "Start the paperwork to get all files pertaining to the city and the baseball club under the Freedom of Information Act. Name L. Malcolm Osterburg, the mayor, and the city manager specifically and throw in a few John and Jane Does just in case. I want it filed in court immediately and the papers by close of business today."

"Wait," Osterburg said, depressing the button on the phone, leaving Kathy listening to a dial tone. Having known Penelope for a long time, Kathy was only slightly bewildered.

Score two for the visitors.

"Yes, Malcolm?" Still holding the telephone, she smiled her very sweetest smile.

"Upon reflection, you can have the files. But it's twenty cents a copy."

"Fifteen cents and you know it."

"All right, fifteen, but you have to do it yourself."

"That's not what the mayor's memo says and you know that too." The city was on one of its periodic campaigns to be nice to the public. It wouldn't last long, but Penelope intended to take advantage of it.

"Jennie."

"Yes, Malcolm."

"Would you see that Ms. Warren gets everything she needs?"

"Certainly, Malcolm."

Penelope and Big Mike left the field of battle—and a hair ball—to Osterburg.

They almost wore out the copy machine, but Penelope soon had a huge cardboard box crammed with papers. It cost her $137.15, but that didn't matter, since she intended to submit the receipt to Dutch for reimbursement.

"Thanks, Jennie, guys," Penelope said to the people who had helped.

"Anytime."

Despite their success at irritating the pompous L. Malcolm Osterburg, her blood was still dangerously near Fahrenheit 451, the temperature at which books burned, according to Ray Bradbury's classic novel. Penelope went back to Mycroft & Company fuming and raging, seriously considering dropping a note to Mr. Bradbury suggesting he write a sequel concerned with the temperature at which computer games would be consumed by flames.

She might have done it, too, had she not been distracted by a telephone call from Dutch.

"Guess what?"

"Tell me, please, that you've arrested a psychopathic author of computer games, although the term 'author' is much too good for someone of his ilk."

"What are you talking about?"

"High crimes and misdemeanors, of course. Really, Dutch, if you're going to marry my sister you have to learn to keep up with conversations."

"This is babble, not a conversation."

"Oh, never mind, I'll explain later. What do you have?"

"Guess."

"You're running off to join the circus. My mother will be so relieved. She's never approved of police officers, not since that time she got a ticket for going one mile over the speed limit."

"Your mother likes me."

"Another unfathomable mystery of the universe. Are you going to tell me or not?"

"No."

"I'll eat worms."

"Go ahead."

Penelope laughed. "That never worked with Mom either. I almost did it once."

"Did what?" Dutch asked warily.

"Ate a worm, of course, but I set it free. Like Elsa in *Born Free.* I think that's why I wanted to go to Africa. It's all my mother's fault for taking us to see *Born Free.* That doesn't explain Stormy, though. I don't remember any nudity in that particular motion picture."

"She doesn't do that anymore."

"Has she told you about *The Last Best Burlesque Show?*"

"What?"

"I didn't think so. Now, what have you discovered?"

Dutch surrendered, as he usually did when dealing with either Stormy or Penelope. "We sent the bat to Phoenix for some further testing. They did some of that scientific stuff lab guys are so fond of and guess what?"

"Let's not go back to that."

"More fingerprints turned up. Small ones, like from a kid, a woman, or a relatively small man."

"Now what in the hell does that mean?" Penelope asked.

Good question.

Very good question.

CHAPTER
FIVE

The Coyotes had lost their second game in another blow-out. Jackson "The Peeper" Elliott started, walked the bases loaded, and told Rats he wasn't warmed up yet. The disgusted manager waved in a relief pitcher who grooved a fast ball for the Red Rock clean-up hitter, who promptly cleaned up with a shot to right field that was probably passing Santa Fe, New Mexico, by now. Things looked up after that, however, as the Red Rocks were held scoreless in two of the subsequent eight innings.

Nothing much plummeted to earth—or anywhere else, for that matter—as a result of Penelope's televised comments. After watching the piece on the late news with Andy, she had to change into something a lot more comfortable to convince him that she had not betrayed him by speaking to the electronic media, promising to make some suitable comment for the next edition of the *News Journal*. That took time but turned out to be a lot of fun as well.

As Penelope, accompanied by the ever faithful Mycroft, drove to work the next day, snatches of environmental impact reports, staff reports, additions and deletions to conditions of approval, written comments submitted to both the planning commission and city council by the citizenry, and a miscellany of other documentation buzzed through her brain. It was enough to make her glad she had not gone into city planning as a profession, and she was grateful for her own eclectic career to date. Running a mystery bookstore promised something new with every publisher's catalog that arrived by mail and the hopeful postcards sent by authors urging her to order their latest mystery. Each carton of books from the distributors meant another Christmas, weekly bonuses throughout the year, looking forward to the latest from Elmore Leonard, or Rochelle Krich, or Sara Paretsky, or James Lee Burke. Penelope doubted that she would anticipate the latest in environmental impact reports.

But the pleasure of opening the current delivery of new mystery novels was greatly diminished by the many questions raised by the voluminous city records. Going through the files, even hurriedly, Penelope found a love-in between the city officials, certain key players, and Peter Adcock who represented the baseball club throughout the prolonged negotiations. That, in itself, was curious. Where were the battalions of lawyers who usually hovered close at hand, whispering in one ear or another at each step of the process? In addition, all payments to the city had been delayed—the library, the art fund, the beautification fund, and the pothole abatement program would not see civic contributions from Empty Creek's latest business enterprise for months.

And why would Kendall McCoffey, Senior say that Peter Adcock had been snookered by the city?

But in the greater scheme of the master plan for the western hemisphere, Penelope and Big Mike did not find anything else amiss in Empty Creek as they drove to work. There were all the usual comings and goings, befitting a bustling little community waiting patiently for the Big One in California to provide ocean front property for Arizonians. Indeed, Harvey McAllister and Teresa Sandia were taking their morning break, catching a few rays in front of the Desert Surf and Flower Shop while they waited. Their bodies glistened with oil.

Harvey, an enterprising young man, was a quintessential surfer with long bleached-blond hair and a deep tan, but a refugee from his beloved California waves. He had opened the Desert Surf and Flower Shop on the advice of both his psychiatrist and astrologer in anticipation of the inevitable earthquake, the ultimate in urban renewal. It was considered by some to be one of the more eccentric enterprises to barrel down Empty Creek's pike in recent years, but Harvey—known professionally as Surf Dude—did quite well, shaping very fine surf boards and selling them to satisfied customers around the world. Penelope and Big Mike didn't know anything about the niceties of surfing, of course, both having an aversion to immersing themselves in large bodies of water—"Fish pee in it," Penelope always pointed out—but they did admire ingenuity.

Surf Dude had once confided to Penelope that he couldn't take the anxiety of sitting on his board waiting for the Big One—wave, not earthquake—only to see California sink beneath the surface of the Pacific Ocean. "Made my skin break out something awful. I looked like the before picture in an acne commercial."

"I would have thought riding a tidal wave from Malibu to Empty Creek to be the ultimate surfing experience."

"Yeah, cool," Surf Dude said dreamily, "but girls took one look at me and ran."

That particular problem had been alleviated after only a few months in Empty Creek when he met Teresa—his skin had cleared up in the dry desert air—a dark and sultry Latina with a remarkable resemblance to the young Rita Moreno and a flair for marketing surf boards from a desert location where summer temperatures frequently closed in on 120 degrees (Teresa also was a skilled massage therapist with fingers like iron that could work magic). The cover of the promotional brochure Teresa put together showed her dude surfing down a sand dune. Inside, he posed with his board propped against a towering saguaro cactus. These photographic images appealed to the eccentricities of the surf board-buying public, who didn't really care where a good board came from anyway. With his reputation as a board shaper, Harvey could have been a Tibetan monk living in a cave on Mt. Everest, but Teresa didn't know that. The result was a six month waiting list for delivery of a Harvey McAllister desert special.

Across the street, Alyce Smith, Empty Creek's own astrologer and psychic—and Harvey's spiritual advisor—was in a trance meditating, oblivious for the moment to the passage of the stars. At least Alyce was in the shade. Down at Mom's Doughnut Shop, the safest place in town, a black and white was parked while two police officers took *their* morning pause in crime fighting. Samantha Dale emerged from the Empty Creek National Bank, crossed the street, and entered Mom's.

Since everyone seemed to be on morning recess, Penelope decided it was time for her own intermission, although she had yet to accomplish anything of note. Big Mike agreed with the decision. He'd had a most strenuous morning—eating, bathing, falling from the windowsill twice. Thus it was that Penelope and Big Mike entered Mom's just as Rats McCoy threw a pretty good right cross at the owner of the Sedona Red Rocks, knocking him to his ample backside.

Apparently, the situation had been building. Sam Connors and Peggy Norton were prepared for swift action and quickly hustled the two men outside before any damage could be done to the furnishings.

"What was that all about?" Penelope asked.

A rather astonished Samantha Dale said, "It was something about how his granddaughter's Little League team could beat the Coyotes. Rats popped him a good one. Quite justified, I would say. I would have popped him myself." For a usually most proper businesswoman—Samantha was president of Empty Creek National Bank, president-elect of Rotary, and the immediate past president of the Chamber of Commerce— she occasionally astounded Penelope. Like the time she revealed her passion for playing strip poker on her home computer with Big Jake Peterson, the man in her life. Unfortunately, Big Jake couldn't play poker worth a damn and Samantha had to draw to inside straights, against the advice of her father, in order to move the proceedings along to the more interesting parts of the evening. "There I was, fully clothed, and Jake was down to his boxer shorts. . . . My God, I had to do something."

"Of course, you did," Penelope commiserated at the time. It had taken her forever to get the painfully shy Andy around to seducing her. Of course, she hadn't installed the strip poker game on the computer yet. And to Andy's credit, after he got around to kissing her on about the thirtyumpteenth date, he had been an apt learner.

Outside, the altercation seemed over. Edwin Heath walked off down the street holding a hand to his eye. As soon as his back was turned, Sam and Peggy shook Rats's hand and escorted him back into Mom's where he received a standing ovation from the other customers and Pop promptly gave him another cup of coffee on the house. "Way to go, Rats," Pop said.

Rats would have autographed several napkins thrust at him, but he kept shaking his hand and saying, "Damn, that hurt."

Big Mike sympathized. He had once sprained his right front paw rather badly belting the nose of a rambunctious Rhodesian Ridgeback.

It seemed the community had taken the Empty Creek Coyotes and their manager to its collective bosom. Coyote fever was thriving.

With the excitement over, Rats headed off to the stadium to figure out a starting lineup that would give the Red Rocks what for, Sam and Peggy went back on patrol, Pop started another pot of coffee, and Samantha asked, "What's new on the case?"

"You know about Lora Lou's business card and Debbie's missing bat and all the other women Adcock propositioned?"

Samantha nodded. "I threatened to call my security guard."

I really must be the only woman in Maricopa County he

didn't approach, Penelope thought, nodding as she added another woman to Adcock's list of attempted conquests. "That all seems too obvious," she said, "so I threw a few other concepts out there to see what happened."

"Yes, we saw you on the news last night."

Penelope had expected any number of outraged calls from the mayor, the Developer Kid, assorted attorneys threatening legal action, but . . . nothing. There should have been something from someone. What self-respecting guilty party would not call and feign indignation? Even Dutch had failed to call with a lecture about the folly of conducting investigations through the media.

"Apparently, you were the only one," Penelope replied.

"Jake and I watched it together. It got us to talking. Do you really think Peter Adcock was killed because of some wheeling and dealing gone wrong?"

"I really don't know. I took a look at city records."

"And?"

"So far, nothing. There's nothing that really stands out, something that says, 'I am a crook,' but I have a feeling about it. Peter Adcock and the Coyotes got an uncharacteristically good deal from the city." Penelope smiled at her friend. "I don't know how Perry Mason and Matlock and Jessica Fletcher did it. They were always getting someone to confess."

"Have you talked to Marty Gault?"

"Not yet, but the distinguished president of Save Our Desert is on my list."

Save Our Desert was a powerful lobby at City Hall and any local politician who wanted to be elected or reelected better be a member or solicit their support. It wasn't like

SOD to roll over and play dead lizard. They usually exacted *their* pound of flesh in the form of land deeded over to open space in perpetuity—no matter what the issue. Buy a new toilet seat for your home and SOD wanted your backyard in exchange.

"If there was some sort of a deal, Marty probably would have gotten a hint of it."

"Unless he was in on it. I've heard he has some financial problems."

"It was a pretty nasty divorce."

"I know you can't tell me much, but is the baseball club solvent? Debbie's check for the poster bounced."

"Quite solvent. The check must have bounced when funds were being transferred."

Penelope had avoided thinking about fingerprints—small fingerprints—for just about as long as she could, hoping that some reasonable explanation would suddenly occur to her if she didn't think about it. But revelations, divine or otherwise, were in short supply around Empty Creek today. Well, more than one writer in town for a book signing had told her if they waited for inspiration, nothing would ever get written. Penelope had adopted the same credo as Rule Number One for Detecting: When on a case, detect every day, whether inspired or not.

Penelope took a look at the fingertips of her right hand. There they were, those distinctive little ridge line patterns formed on the fetus before birth and carried through a lifetime without changing—except in size. Penelope pulled out the magnifying glass that came with her compact edition of the *Oxford English Dictionary* and took another look. There was definitely a ridge line pattern, but she didn't know which were arches, loops, or whorls. No matter. Penelope's First Rule of Life was: Don't fill your head with unnecessary information. That's what reference librarians and experts were for. A corollary was: Keep your memory banks open for the important stuff—like the generally acknowledged date of Shakespeare's birth (April 23, 1564), Malawi Independence Day (July 6, 1964), or the time to feed the cat (although that was a no-brainer; Mycroft was always ready to eat).

Magnifying glass held high, Penelope marched to the counter of Mycroft & Company, and said, "Let me see your hand."

"Which one?" Kathy asked.

"I don't care. The right will do."

Kathy offered her hand.

Penelope examined her fingertips through the glass. "Very delicate," Penelope said. "I don't know why Timmy doesn't write odes to your fingers."

"Do you want to tell me what you're doing?"

"Ruminating on the mysteries of life in general and fingerprints in particular. Small fingerprints."

"Fingerprints are overrated in the solution of crimes," Kathy said. She hadn't worked at Mycroft & Company for nothing. "All the best mystery novelists know that."

"Police officers, as well, but fingerprints, when found, must be considered, even small ones."

"Well, here come the smallest fingerprints I know."

Penelope looked up to see the petite Nora Pryor crossing the street and heading for Mycroft & Company. "Ah, just in time for a little experiment. Hand me a tissue, please."

Penelope fogged the magnifying glass with her breath,

wiped it clean, held it to the light, and pronounced it smudge-free just as Nora entered the store.

"Good morning," Penelope said. "Give me your hand, please."

"What for?"

"I want to take your fingerprints for comparison purposes."

"Oh."

"You look befuddled," Penelope said.

"Naturally. I enter a bookshop in order to replenish my reading supply and the next thing I know I'm being finger-printed, apparently on a magnifying glass. Why wouldn't I be befuddled? And where did you come up with that word, anyway? No one says befuddled."

"It comes from the verb to fuddle which is to say to confuse or render tipsy with strong drink," Penelope replied.

Big Mike, observing the exchange from his accustomed warm weather hideaway in the fireplace, did what any self-respecting cat would do while a state of befuddlement reigned about him—he assumed that wise and all-knowing expression, an aloof serenity and confidence that announced, 'Call me when you have something important to say.'

Penelope managed to make quite serviceable impressions of Nora's fingerprints on the magnifying glass. Of course, the glass had to be held to the light in a certain way in order to be taken as anything but smeared or just plain dirty. By catching the light, however, Penelope had a set of small fingerprints similar to those that had apparently been found on the murder weapon.

"You don't think. . . ."

"Of course not, Nora. I know you didn't kill Peter Adcock.

You'd just tell him to fuddle off. But I wanted something to provoke thought and possible avenues of investigation."

"And has it?"

"Not much," Penelope admitted glumly.

A later prolonged examination of Nora Pryor's fingerprints in solitude provoked nothing more thoughtful and revealing than the fact that they were, indeed, small. And since it seemed impractical—and probably unconstitutional as well—to take the fingerprints of everyone, young and old, male and female, who happened to have smallish hands, Penelope replaced the magnifying glass and suggested a little trip to Mycroft, who quickly agreed.

Marty Gault was a self-made businessman and financier who had made pots of money and felt guilty about it. His personal redemption came through preservation of the desert surrounding Empty Creek, even after some disastrous investments and an expensive divorce. He spoke long and passionately about the necessity for saving local habitat in its natural state, sans cracker box housing developments, strip malls, hotels, golf courses, mini-mart gas stations, and theme parks. Just to ensure that the list was all-inclusive, anything that involved cement, asphalt, or the mass destruction of forests was included. His own credo was; If it doesn't grow or reproduce the way God intended, we don't want it. There were a great many like-minded individuals in Empty Creek, which is why Save Our Desert was such a powerful influence.

"Come to join SOD, Penelope?"

While Penelope sympathized with many of SOD's goals, she also believed that sensible growth, carefully measured and monitored, was not always a bad thing. After all, following Marty Gault's philosophy to its logical—albeit extreme—conclusion, meant that Mycroft & Company would be selling its novels from the limited shade provided by a saguaro cactus.

"Nope," Penelope said cheerfully, noting the presence of a baseball on Gault's desk. Interesting. "We're here to find out why SOD didn't extort more concessions from the Coyotes."

During his many years of dealing with City Hall, Gault had developed the politician's skill of ignoring a disliked and pointed question and answering another one entirely, even if it hadn't been asked.

"Don't you want Big Mike to enjoy the natural environment he's entitled to as one of God's chosen creatures?" Gault asked.

Now, Mycroft enjoyed a good romp through nature as much as the next cat. In point of fact, he dominated his turf—which was wherever he happened to be at any given moment—ruling firmly but benevolently. He was also fearless, and unwanted intruders up to and including mountain lions, better mind their manners. He also enjoyed his comforts, a good hidey hole for protection from the elements, seasonal flings with Murphy Brown, the electric can opener that provided access to lima beans, and a nice feminine lap for sleeping, bathing, and purring. He was a devotee of William Shakespeare (he had shredded the *Complete Works* instead of his scratching post), enjoyed soft music as well as Jimmy Buffet's more bawdy ballads, and was a pretty good movie critic, giving two paws down to most of Stormy's epics. In short, he was the epitome of the Renaissance Cat, skilled in the arts of war *and* all of the more refined pursuits life offered.

"As you know," Penelope responded, "baseball is the

national pastime, but that still doesn't explain why Save Our Desert rolled over and let Peter Adcock have everything he wanted."

"He was born free. He should live free."

That reminded Penelope of her own reference to *Born Free* in conversation with Dutch. It also reminded her that it was just about time for another African weekend from the video store. Andy hated it, of course, although he enjoyed watching *Born Free*, *Out of Africa*, *Zulu*, and *Naked Prey*. But the movies always set Penelope to blubbering nostalgically for Africa and she was inconsolably homesick for days, threatening to head for the airport, until Andy would finally offer to drop her off. That usually snapped her out of it, but one of these days. . . .

Penelope was ready for that one. "Quit stalling or I'll sic Big Mike on you."

Tales of Mycroft's exploits and derring-do had spread throughout the community. Just ask Tweedledee, or Doctor Bob, Big Mike's vet, or any number of large dogs. . . . What Marty Gault didn't know was that Mycroft only sicked when he good and damned well felt like it.

"All right," Gault said, "all right."

Penelope waited while Gault appeared to order his thoughts. Big Mike, bored with the discussion of how he should live his life, batted halfheartedly at the baseball on Gault's desk.

"Civic pride," he said finally.

"That's it?"

"You said it yourself. It's the national pastime. We felt we'd alienate people if Sedona had a baseball team and we didn't. When Adcock threatened to take his team someplace else. . . ." Gault shrugged. "I convinced the board of directors to bless the project. After all, the stadium was already there. It just needed renovations. It wasn't like the desert would get plowed up. It just seemed better to save our resources for a bigger battle."

Mycroft lost control of the baseball and it rolled off the desk top. Penelope caught it deftly.

"Good hands," Gault said.

The baseball was autographed. Penelope looked at it, expecting to find the signature of one or another of the Coyotes, or perhaps even Rats McCoy. Instead, it was signed Peter Gault. Penelope tossed the ball to Gault. "Who's Peter Gault?" she asked.

Gault hesitated, looking at the baseball. "My son from my first marriage. He lives in Tucson with his mother. She's remarried."

"He's a ball player?"

"Just finishing his junior year in high school." Again, Gault hesitated. "Adcock promised him a tryout if he doesn't get drafted or get a baseball scholarship. But there's nothing wrong with that. It had nothing to do with the board's decision."

Well, well, well. Marty Gault might be one of those Little League parents who became obsessed about their offspring's playing time and athletic career. "Did you tell the board?"

Gault had the good grace to look a little sheepish. "No. I probably should have, but it hardly matters now."

"Did you hear anything else during the negotiations, anything at all, that might have a bearing on Adcock's death?"

"Well . . . the Mayor threatened to turn the Developer Kid loose if Save Our Desert screwed it up for the city and the team. It seemed excessive since we had already given our blessing."

The Empty Creek Coyotes were rapidly writing the new league's record books for futility. After losing again, they had established the marks for most runs given up in a three game series, a game, and an inning. If there was any consolation to be found in another loss to the Red Rocks, it was in the gloriously colorful shiner worn by the Sedona owner, although Rats spent the game with his right hand stuffed in an ice bucket.

The faithful filed out, muttering among themselves.

"Make your plans now," the public address system boomed, "to attend Designer Key Chain Night. The first one hundred fans through the gates will. . . ."

"Am I ugly?" Penelope asked.

"You are the most beautiful woman I have ever seen," Andy replied, "in this or any other life."

"Yes, I know," Penelope said, "but am I ugly?"

Andy hesitated, searching desperately for the right answer. He had once made the mistake of telling Penelope he occasionally found Daryl Hannah cavorting through his dreams. His ribs had been sore for several days, the result of a well-placed elbow. The Land of Ugly seemed filled with treacherous quicksands. A verbal misstep now. . . . In dealing with Penelope in one of her moods, Andy firmly held to the principle of, when in doubt, equivocate like crazy. "I would trudge a thousand miles to gaze upon your serene beauty."

"Not bad, but why serene?"

"Well, I didn't have time to think it completely through,

but I shall immortalize your magnificent beauty in prose. I promise."

"You better not."

"I must, darling. I am consumed by your stunning and exquisite ... exquisite...."

"Quit stalling. Am ... I ... ugly?"

"No, no, no! You are *not* ugly. What brought this up anyway?"

"I seem to be the only woman in Empty Creek that Peter Adcock did not find attractive enough to proposition."

"Oh, that's easy."

"It is?"

"Sure. If Peter Adcock was mixed up in something shady, and his murder seems to indicate that, the last person he would want to attract the attention of would be the woman known as a skilled detective. Ergo, he steered clear of you."

"You're not just trying to save my face, so to speak?"

Andy shook his head. "He considered you a dangerous adversary, if only by reputation."

In exchange for that interesting theory, Penelope offered one of her own. "What if...."

CHAPTER
SIX

When Penelope and Big Mike arrived at the police station, they found the two members of the Robbery-Homicide Bureau going through Peter Adcock's extensive collection of glossy magazines displaying numerous color and black and white photographs of women in various stages of undress. There were several stacks of magazines distributed on the two desks pushed together in their cubicle.

"What *are* you doing?"

"Searching for clues," Tweedledee said indignantly. "Whadda ya think?"

"I think you're growing up to be disgusting old men," Penelope said, although she couldn't find fault with their diligence. They were not simply leafing through the magazines. Each and every page was individually turned and carefully scrutinized. Their concentration reminded Penelope of Big Mike when he got his mind set on something—like stalking a bird or lizard, just keeping his paw in should the lima bean crop fail.

"We are disgusting old men."

"There's yet time to repent," Penelope said, "and atone for your multitude of sins."

"Look on this as a reward for good behavior," Tweedledee said.

"Yeah," Tweedledum said, adding his magazine to a small stack and taking another. "Besides, we're doing a public service."

"Spending the taxpayer's money by looking at naked women is a public service?"

"Sure, we're on a meticulous search for information."

"What are all the different stacks for?"

"Gotta have a system. These haven't been gone through yet. We've looked at the ones in these two stacks, but they're the ones we figure are worth another look. Just in case we missed something."

"And where is your Completed-and-Not-Worth-Another-Look-Pile?"

"Don't have one yet."

"I see."

"Hey," Tweedledee said, "it's hard to concentrate with all this talking. I'm gonna have to start all over with this one."

To Penelope's astonishment, they actually found something.

Rather, Penelope found it when what appeared to be one of those ubiquitous subscription forms inserted into all magazines fell to the floor as Tweedledee took a new magazine. When she picked it up, however, she found a postcard advertising The Dynamite Lounge.

That was not unique. The Dynamite, located on the edge of town on the road to Scottsdale and Tempe, periodically went on an advertising campaign, hiring a horde of minimum wage messengers to place their postcards beneath windshield wipers on cars all over town. Penelope had a small collection of them in the glove compartment of the Jeep. They would eventually be recycled when she got around to cleaning out the glove compartment again. The Dynamite's new management team was simply carrying on the tradition, as evidenced by their ad in the Coyote program.

"Well, well, well," Penelope said.

"What'cha got?"

Never one to claim credit for another's labor, Penelope said, "I think you found something."

"I did?"

Penelope handed the postcard to Tweedledee who whistled before passing it over the desk to his partner, who said, "Wow."

"Angelique must be new," Tweedledee said. "I haven't seen her before."

"Well, she's been there long enough to get to know Peter Adcock."

"We better check this out," Penelope said.

"You can't go to a place like that."

"Why not? Sleaze is my life."

Which is how two sworn police officers, a gifted, although nonprofessional detective, and a cat happened to visit The Dynamite Lounge, hoping to chat with an exotic dancer who had inscribed her postcard with the sentiment:

For Peter, With Love Always, Angelique.

The two detectives accepted Penelope's offer to drive since the air conditioning on their official car had an aversion to the hot summer months and only worked during the cold winter nights when the heater went on the fritz.

"God damn car hates us," Tweedledee said.

Big Mike rode shotgun, as was his custom, while Tweedledee and Tweedledum, fearful of having Big Mike's claws anywhere near their laps, clambered into the back seat.

To the detectives' annoyance, Penelope, who was determined to learn what else they had discovered in their search of Adcock's Empty Creek apartment and belongings, drove slowly, questioning them all the way.

"Aw, come on, Penelope, the place'll be closed by the time we get there."

"Give. Was Angelique in his address book?"

"Didn't have one. Everything was on one of those notepad things."

"Was she in there?" Penelope asked, restraining her urge to scream.

"Nah. Nothing but business acquaintances."

"And most of the people around town. Mayor, city council, planning department. Lora Lou. Samantha. People like that."

"Was I listed?"

"No."

Damn the man. "How about his other stuff?"

"What other stuff?"

Penelope gritted her teeth. "Clothes, books, kitchen utensils. You know, stuff, like all those magazines."

"That was about it. There wasn't anything else. Clothes, sure. Nothing much there. He had instant coffee and half a bottle of wine in the refrigerator, but nothing else. A fully stocked bar in the living room. Medicine cabinet was empty. Clock radio in the bedroom. Television set and an exercycle in the living room. Some dumbbells. He musta been in pretty good shape. The last thing he watched was on ESPN. No messages on the answering machine."

"Fingerprints?"

"All over the place. He had a reception for the team when they hit town."

"He just used the place when he was here," Tweedledum said. "Easier than commuting from Phoenix, I guess."

"And did you check out his Phoenix place?"

"Sure, you think we don't know what we're doing?"

That was precisely what Penelope thought most of the time, but they *could* surprise her every once in a while. This was not one of those occasions, however. The detectives had not found anything of great interest in Adcock's office either. The files related to the team, as did everything on his computer. His office, too, was remarkably void of personal mementoes.

By the time Penelope pulled into the parking lot of The Dynamite Lounge, she had learned only that Peter Adcock had lived an apparently normal existence up to the time of his murder—except for his interest in all women (save one) and the fact that he was a majority owner of a minor league baseball team in a brand new league, and a new enterprise was always a risk.

After greedy major league baseball players and owners locked in bitter negotiations, strikes, and cancellation of the World Series, Penelope had few illusions about the great National Pastime. Baseball was Big Business personified, even for the Arizona-New Mexico League. But minor league baseball was more popular than ever, especially at the lower levels, because it was still fun. The players she had met so far were not yet tainted by huge bonuses, performance clauses, agents, personal managers, endorsements. They still played the game for glory. Still, it was a business, and those of the Coyotes who might eventually fulfill their dreams would be corrupted. It was too bad.

Well, the motivation for murder had to be found in one of those two areas—women or work. Nothing else made any sense whatsoever. Crime of passion or a deadly business clash. Adcock's interest in women was certainly no crime, although his technique was more than abrasive. Penelope shook her head. "I'm betting on business now," Penelope said, knowing full well that she wasn't certain enough to forgo an interview with Angelique, the exotic dancer.

The Dynamite Lounge was indeed, under new ownership, and Wednesday was amateur night—facts duly noted by the two trained detectives as they read the twin banners above the door.

"Forget it," Penelope said.

"We could have team matches," Tweedledee said encouragingly, "kinda like wrestling or bowling."

"Nobody bowls anymore."

"I do."

"Figures."

"I could be your coach."

"I'd rather play with Gila Monsters."

"You're no fun."

"Nope," Penelope said cheerfully, leading the way into The Dynamite Lounge.

It was . . . well . . . different from Penelope's usual haunts, although with a little redecorating it could have been a smaller version of the Double B. There was a long bar with a mirror behind it (a portrait of Lora Lou Longstreet would have added a little character), a number of tables scrunched together for the lunch crowd, and a small stage—where someone remarkably dissimilar to the Angelique of postcard fame danced enthusiastically to a medley of Andrew Lloyd Webber show tunes, while two waitresses wearing peach-colored shorts, tennis shoes, and little else served a small group of customers.

But it was definitely a clean, well-lighted place. Papa Hemingway would have been proud. So would Grandma Wolf. All the better to see you with, my dear.

"That's not her," Tweedledee said, holding the postcard to the light for identification purposes.

"Don't look, Mycroft," Penelope said.

"Help you gents?" the bartender asked. "And ma'am?" He leaned over the bar and looked down at Big Mike. "And cat?" he added. "I'm not sure he should be in here."

"It's all right," Tweedledee said. "We're cops and he's with us. Police cat on official business."

"Maybe I should call the boss."

"Don't bother him."

"Her. . . ."

"Whatever. We just have a few questions for Angelique. She may have some information on a case we're handling."

"What kind of case?"

"Murder."

"I'm calling the boss."

"Jeez, it's just a murder case."

"Angelique *is* the boss."

"Oh."

When Angelique Lamont appeared, both Tweedledee and Tweedledum made the instantaneous, albeit independent, decision that *she* was the kind of boss *they* wanted. Nothing against Dutch. He was okay as bosses went, but Dutch was no vision in peach shorts and white boxed top with an embroidered signature on the pocket that spelled out The Dynamite Lounge.

Angelique was. The postcard was but a pale imitation of reality. She was tall and had obviously been put together by an expert team of nature's plastic surgeons. Her brunette hair was long, falling beyond her shoulders, but showed blonde roots, and Penelope wondered why a blonde would dye her hair—it was against all rules, unless she had tired of dumb blonde jokes. Angelique wore the same outfit as the waitresses, although the others had left the top portion in their dressing rooms.

Penelope took charge. One look at her colleagues told her not to expect coherent conversation from them for an hour or so after Angelique departed—if ever again. Big Mike, too, was mesmerized by the new ownership of The Dynamite Lounge, even though he had never laid eyes on the old ownership. After the introductions were made and everyone sat (Tweedledee and Tweedledum bumped heads as they rushed to assist Angelique), Big Mike eliminated her as a suspect by jumping into her lap and settling in for a long stay.

"What an adorable cat," Angelique said, shattering Nora's reputation for possessing the sexiest voice north of Nogales. "What's your name, Big Guy?" the new voice in town asked.

Usually never at a loss for words, Big Mike got his tongue twisted around and said, "Meogrgh."

"Mycroft," Penelope said, helping him out. Tweedledee

and Tweedledum were on their own. "I think you can call him Mikey, though. He seems to like you."

"He should meet my Alexandra. They'd like each other."

If Alexandra was anything like Angelique, Penelope thought, Murphy Brown might get dumped. "Have you joined the Chamber of Commerce yet?" she asked.

Angelique smiled. "Do you really think my establishment is appropriate for the Chamber of Commerce?"

"Have you stopped by the Double B?"

"I had breakfast there today. Checking out the competition."

"Did you notice the portrait behind the bar?"

"It's beautiful. Do you know the artist? I'd love to have one for The Dynamite."

"I know the artist *and* the model. She's the president of the Chamber this year."

"Well, I might have to join after all—but you didn't stop by to recruit me for the Chamber." She smiled at the two detectives.

Had they been sticks of butter, they would have melted on the spot. Barely capable of movement, if not speech, they shook their heads.

"We're investigating the murder of Peter Adcock," Penelope said. "He was one of your customers."

Angelique nodded. "Such a tragedy," she said. "He was getting to be a regular, too."

"Did you know him well?"

"Not really. I try to keep a certain distance from my customers. Otherwise. . . ."

"Adcock was developing quite a reputation around town. He would have asked you out."

"He did. I let him know that I never date a customer, nor do the young ladies who work here. He accepted that."

"Gracefully?"

"Oh, yes. The alternative was eternal banishment from The Dynamite Lounge. He didn't want that."

Tweedledee held out the postcard. At least one of the detecting duo was gradually regaining his senses.

Angelique glanced briefly at it. "Quite a good photograph, don't you think?"

"You seem to have known Adcock rather well."

"Conversation only. That's part of the service we provide. You'd be surprised at how many of our patrons just want to talk. Tory, for example," Angelique said, pointing to the stage. "She's very good at it. She's a graduate student in sociology."

On the stage, the graduate student received applause as Andrew Lloyd Webber ended. Another young woman took her place and began dancing to a haunting melody of the New Age.

Penelope raised her eyebrows.

"What can I say?" Angelique shrugged. "I like Andrew Lloyd Webber and the New Age music better than the Country Western or Mitch Miller's sing-along golden oldies where I used to work. If I never hear Garth Brooks or Mitch Miller again, I'll be quite happy. I'm thinking of starting a classical day. Probably on Sundays. Dvorak's cello concerto seems to go well with Sundays, don't you think?"

Penelope agreed. She had spent many a lazy Sunday in Africa listening to that very same concerto. She was definitely overdue for an African film fest.

"And," Angelique continued, "there's no reason why exotic dancing shouldn't be instructional as well."

"Oh, I quite agree," Penelope said, rapidly revising her concept of sleaze and glancing at the two sticks of butter. They seemed fascinated by the lettering on Angelique's blouse. At least they were breathing. "But what about Peter Adcock?"

"I'm kind of a marriage counselor in that way," Angelique said. "These big executives come here. The poor dears are exhausted from making decisions all day long, and they come here to unwind instead of going home because their wives don't understand them."

"I know exactly what you mean," Tweedledee said, recovering the power of speech suddenly.

"Me too," Tweedledum said.

Angelique smiled. "Then, why haven't I seen you in here before?"

"Jesus, lady, my wife would kill me if she caught me in here unwinding, so to speak. Official business, like this, I can probably get away with."

"Me too," Tweedledum said, rather wistfully. "Maybe."

"Peter Adcock wasn't married," Penelope pointed out.

"No," Angelique said, "but he had girlfriend problems. It can be just as confusing."

Since Adcock had apparently been rejected by every woman in Empty Creek, Penelope pounced. It was what Mycroft might have done had he not been scratched and stroked by Angelique into a catatonic state. "What girlfriend?" she asked.

"I don't know her name, but normally I wouldn't tell you

even if I did. I try to keep everything strictly confidential, like a doctor or a lawyer. But when there's a murder. . . ."

"Was she connected with the team?"

The music built to a conclusion for the New Age interpretation of Summer.

"I really don't know," Angelique said, scooping Mycroft from her lap and placing him on the chair so smoothly he didn't know he had been dislodged for a moment. When he opened his eyes, they said, 'Aw, Angelique, don't go.' "You'll have to excuse me for a moment. It's my turn." She lifted her blouse over her head in a skilled and graceful motion, picked up Mycroft, and stalked to the stage.

"Nice back," Tweedledee said.

"Yeah."

Angelique stood tranquilly on the stage, head bowed, holding the shapeless and compliant lump that had once been a proud and fierce cat, waiting for the music to begin. As the overture to *Cats* filled the room, she began to stretch and move languidly, transforming herself into a cat awakening from the long nap. Big Mike played Mr. Mistoffelees to perfection.

"Lucky damned fur ball," Tweedledee said. He was definitely jealous of Big Mike's career change.

"I could do that," Penelope said.

"Next Wednesday?"

"In your dreams." Penelope took several postcards from the table.

"What are you gonna do with those?" Tweedledee asked.

"Send them to your wives," Penelope said.

"Aw, Penelope, you wouldn't do that, would you?"

"Not if you're nice to me."

"Define nice."

Hanging around the ball park was getting to be a part of the daily routine. Penelope left Big Mike to recover from his show business debut in his usual spot on the dugout roof and stepped through the gate to stand on the Field of Dreams once more. The infielders and outfielders were warming up on the sidelines. The pitchers were running wind sprints on the outfield grass under the supervision of Erika the Hun. Penelope waved to Rats and headed off to the outfield.

"Vun more time!" Erika shouted to her charges.

Their collective groan was well practiced, but they turned obediently and raced from the left field foul line back to center field. Erika beat them all.

"Vunce more."

Erika von Sturm wasn't even breathing hard when she slowed at the foul line. She was definitely Teutonic. Her short blonde hair was cut short and worn like a helmet. Her body was muscular with defined biceps and sturdy, but not unattractive, legs. "Again!" she ordered before turning to Penelope. "Hi, Cat Lady. I'm Erika the Hun."

Erika's ready smile disarmed Penelope. After Angelique's revelation of Peter Adcock's girlfriend troubles, Penelope had flip-flopped again, changing her mind about a business motive for Adcock's death, returning to the crime of passion possibility. Since Penelope had already talked with Blake Robinson extensively, she was prepared to take a hard line with Erika as the other distinct candidate for secret girlfriendhood. She was certainly pretty enough to meet Adcock's standards.

Damn that smile. Penelope liked her immediately and she hated liking people who were suspects. "Hi, Erika the Hun."

An errant baseball rolled to a stop at Erika's feet. With a deft soccer-style motion of her right foot, she rolled the ball on the toe of her cleats, tossed it waist high, caught it and threw it back. The only awkward motion was the throw. She threw like a girl who hadn't grown up playing baseball with her brothers and in Little League.

"I vill never understand this game," Erika said. "All this running for players who do nothing but stand on a little hill and throw a ball."

"All of the power comes from a pitcher's legs."

"That's what Rats always explains. I still don't understand."

"How did you happen to become the physical fitness trainer for the Coyotes?"

"My Grandfather fought with Rommel in the desert and then he was sent to the Eastern Front. He always told me to go to the desert where it was nice and, how do you say it, toasty?"

"Arizona is certainly toasty."

"So, when I grow up and want to travel I come to this desert. Libya is not a good place for a woman who is a physical fitness trainer."

"I can well imagine."

"So, I get job in Phoenix gym where I meet Peter Adcock. He offers me job. I take it. It is fun and vill be better ven I understand this game."

"What did you think of Adcock?"

"He is, how do you say it, a big *schwein*."

"A pig."

"Exactly. A pig. That's what he is."

"Was."

"Yes, was, but I didn't kill him."

"No one's accused you, have they?"

"They think it, because I dated him once. That was before I knew what he was like. Everybody looks at me with suspicion."

"Nonsense," Penelope protested, despite the fact that Erika was, indeed, moving up on her personal list of suspects and she felt guilty about it.

"Get back here," Erika shouted.

The pitchers jumped and hit the ground running.

"What *was* Adcock like?" Penelope asked of the only woman she knew who had actually gone out with him.

"Cruel and arrogant. As a woman, I would have been better treated in Libya."

Penelope retraced her steps across the outfield grass. The evening was still warm despite the setting sun and the first brilliant hues painted above the western horizon. The players gathered around the batting cage chattered hopefully, wanting their luck to change, anticipating that elusive first victory. The crack of bat on ball was crisp and sharp. Eddie Stiles drifted back lazily and gathered the ball in at the warning track in center field. Penelope paused at the dugout, reaching out to scratch Mycroft behind the ears. He looked up at her with placid all-knowing eyes, and she wished once again to know his secrets. "Ah, Mikey, who is she?"

Mycroft stood and stretched languidly and clawed at the wood of the dugout before following and settling into Penelope's lap.

One date did not a girlfriend make. Still, Angelique had been convinced that Adcock's tale of girlfriend problems had been unfeigned. "He was obviously heartbroken," Angelique had said, "and trying to recover by looking for another woman to love."

CHAPTER
SEVEN

Everyone avoided Penelope, just as Peter Adcock had apparently dodged her. Well, not everyone ducked when they saw her coming. Big Mike still loved her, even though he was on the dugout roof, front paws curled beneath his massive chest as he stared placidly at the activities on the field. And Penelope was pretty sure Andy still loved her, although he seemed to be spending an inordinate amount of time on the outfield grass interviewing Erika the Hun.

But the city fathers and mothers in attendance who saw her quickly turned away, beginning animated conversations with anyone who happened to be passing. In the case of Mayor Tiggy Bourke, he lurched into a discussion without looking and wound up getting a lecture from Cackling Ed on the need for a squad of Coyote Cheerleaders. Served him right, Penelope thought, although she was too far away to hear the specific topic. Any conversation with Old Ed would wither the warts off a toad.

City employees, usually friendly with Penelope and Big Mike, followed the example set by the elected officials.

Tweedledee and Tweedledum, heavily laden with Coyote Dogs, peanuts, and beer, didn't stop by even to engage in what they considered witty repartee.

Dutch ushered his bride-to-be to box seats directly behind home plate without so much as a wave.

"What's going on, Mikey?"

It was pretty obvious, but he answered anyway. "Meow."

Batting practice.

"If this keeps up, we'll have to ring bells and shout, 'Unclean, Unclean' as we walk the streets." If Mycroft had heard of that particular practice during the Great Plague of 1665, he gave no indication.

"Or wear a scarlet letter."

"Meow."

"I suppose they could borrow Lola's pillory for some public penance."

Mycroft nodded off.

The best thing about being ignored, Penelope discovered, was that she caught the high foul pop up that drifted over the screen without being run over by fans clamoring for the same souvenir.

"Nice catch," a familiar voice said.

"Thanks."

The lookout was at the far end of the dugout, chatting up a bird, as our English cousins used to say in Carnaby Street days. The bird at hand was Regina Pryor, the sixteen, going-on-seventeen-year-old daughter of Empty Creek's noted historian. Nora always said of her daughter, "Reggie's younger, prettier, and has a much better figure than me," adding ruefully, "it just isn't fair." Since Nora was pretty much a heart-breaking knockout in her own right, it was no wonder that the lookout was distracted by the apprentice heartbreaker.

Rats McCoy was equally distracted as he sat in the dugout, going over his lineup card, searching desperately for a winning combination. Now in the normal course of events, the look-out—one Ralph "Buddy" Peterson, a lefthander—would have been intent upon his duties. But he wasn't.

With a win or two, Rats would have been more observant himself and would not have popped out of the dugout without checking with Buddy first. But he didn't.

With a little luck, Mrs. Martha McCoy might have stopped for a beer and a Coyote Dog, stepped into the ladies room to freshen up, or taken a more circuitous route to her seat. But she didn't.

And besides all that, Mercury—the planet of civilized discourse—was in retrograde, which made communication difficult at best. There were a few other warring planets squared off against one another, too—all of which indicated that Rats would have been much better off had he stayed home in bed with the covers pulled over his head. But he hadn't.

So, while Buddy Peterson was working up his nerve to ask Reggie for her telephone number and a date, Rats McCoy threw down his stubby pencil in disgust, bounded up the dugout steps, turned, and found himself staring right into the face of the woman he cherished dearly, even under the most abnormal of circumstances.

But now, caught, trapped, cornered, and snared with no visible means of escape, Rats took the only course of action open to him.

He swallowed his chaw and instantaneously turned a deathly shade of green.

"Hi, lover," Feathers said brightly.

"Hi," Rats sputtered.

"We're gonna get them tonight."

"Yep," Rats gurgled.

"What's wrong, darling? You look positively awful."

"Something I ate," Rats managed to choke out. As his stomach did a triple gainer from the high board, Rats vowed revenge on Buddy Peterson. If there had been a league lower than the Arizona-New Mexico League, Buddy would have been packing his glove. But there wasn't.

"Would you like a ginger ale?" Feathers asked. "That's always good for an upset stomach."

Rats staggered away, shaking his head.

"That'll teach him," Feathers said to Penelope.

And it did.

The only good thing about the entire episode from the manager's point of view was that the Coyotes lost another game, fourteen to five. (At least the scores were getting closer.) Had they won, however, Rats, being of a superstitious nature like all baseball people, would have been duty bound to swallow tobacco chaws until the team lost again. The thought of a prolonged winning streak made him sick all over again.

He also quit cold turkey, and bubblegum stock slowly began to rise on the Nasdaq.

But none of that brought Penelope any closer to exposing a murderer, nor did it explain why she and Mikey were being shunned like a pair of adulterers in Cotton Mather's Puritan congregation. So, Penelope donned her cloak of indignation during the seventh inning stretch and marched to the box seats behind home plate.

"Well?" she demanded.

"Hi, Penelope," everyone chorused. "Where have you been?" Knowing her propensity for voting in every election, the mayor grabbed her hand and pumped it heartily. "April Fool's," he said.

"It's May," Penelope pointed out.

"Worked, didn't it?" Dutch said.

"You were behind this," Penelope accused.

"Yep," Dutch said smugly. "Teach you to talk to the media."

Penelope believed in accepting both victory and defeat graciously. Muffy, her long-suffering mother who had endured the various antics of her high-spirited daughters, had taught her that. "No one likes a bad loser," Muffy said countless times, "or a bad winner." Muffy's patience had been sorely tried at the screening of Stormy's first movie when her younger daughter had appeared pretty much in the altogether for most of the ninety-nine minutes of screen time. She asked only, "Who did your hair, dear?" When Penelope gathered in her Ph.D. and announced she was off to Africa with the Peace Corps, Muffy politely accepted yet another postponement in her long wait for grandchildren. "Have a nice time, dear," she said.

Penelope smiled and nodded. "Okay, what can I say? You got me. I won't do it again."

Hah!

Stormy, who knew what her sister was really thinking, was already making plans to be as far away from her betrothed as possible on the occasion of the next April Fool's Day, for

Muffy had also taught her daughters the sweet delights of a gentle but firm revenge. . . .

Perhaps suspecting Penelope's capacity for lovingly nurturing a grudge, Dutch was equally magnanimous in his small victory, issuing an invitation for post-game drinks and snacks at the house he and Stormy shared high on the slopes of Crying Woman Mountain. Penelope accepted the invitation on behalf of Andy and Big Mike.

The night was serene as Penelope and Big Mike got out of the Jeep and stood for a few moments looking down at the lights of Empty Creek, listening for the soft cries of the Indian maiden whose spirit lived in the mountain, keening at the violation of her beloved land. Although Penelope had heard the maiden's laments on any number of occasions, her spirit was at rest tonight.

The headlights of Andy's car swept over them, switched off, and he joined them, taking Penelope's hand. It hadn't been so long ago that they had driven to the top of the mountain to park in the view area like teenagers, kissing passionately after the distant lights bestowed a spell. But they had been disturbed by the sound of Dutch racing off, siren screaming, and, of course, they had followed. As she settled into his embrace, Penelope hoped there would be no repeat of that evening.

They had reached the point where Penelope was seriously considering sneaking off home when Stormy opened the door with her sense of impeccable timing and said, "Really, what would Muffy think?"

Big Mike, selfishly thinking only of lima beans, took off for the door and scooted between Stormy's legs, leaving Penelope and Andy no choice but to follow. Perhaps he was making the point that he shouldn't be locked out of the bedroom. Cats sought revenge, too.

Damn and double damn!

When Stormy and Dutch decided to share their lives and living quarters after a brief but intense courtship—all too brief and much too intense in Muffy's opinion—they had their first major argument. It raged on and off throughout a forty-five day escrow, with first Stormy and then Dutch gaining a slight advantage, only to lose it as one or the other came up with new evidence or documentation substantiating their respective positions over—of all things—who was to decorate their new home. Stormy's taste ran to the light and airy with a healthy dose of bright and splashy modern art. Dutch had nothing against light and airy, but he held strong and definite opinions on art. In the inevitable compromise, Dutch won the place of honor—the wall above the living room fireplace— the hallway, one wall in the master bedroom, and, of course, his home office. All the rest belonged to Stormy.

Thus, most of the house was light, airy, and decorated with modern art, although many of the paintings looked like Big Mike had rendered them by rolling around on open tubes of oil paints (heavy on the magenta and cobalt blue). Dutch's portion was light, airy, and dedicated to the cinematic and modeling career of one Storm Williams. "You're always flying off to L.A.," Dutch hollered during the penultimate decoration discussion, "and I want to see my sweetie when you're not here, damn it!"

The sentiment—and the fact that he seemed on the verge of a stroke—touched Stormy deeply and she surrendered.

Since Dutch was constantly redecorating, the latest movie poster was always above the fireplace and the others moved progressively down the hallway walls to the bedroom and finally to Dutch's office. And then he started over.

With a few hormones still unsettled, Penelope entered the house and automatically glanced to the fireplace.

"Good God!" Penelope exclaimed, quickly covering Andy's eyes with her hands. "Don't look, she's wearing clothes."

Sort of.

In the poster for *The Last Bride of Satan IV*, the Last Bride wore an artfully tattered gown that did little to hide her many charms. Unfortunately for the Last Bride, she was apparently going to get a big What For at the hands of a horde of Transylvanian peasants waving crude wooden pitchforks.

"Aw, Sis."

About a mile of chain coiled around the Last Bride, fastening her to a stake, managing to accentuate her every soft curve and then some. Nor was it good enough to tie the Last Bride's hands behind the post in the traditional manner. Oh, no. The Last Bride's arms were tied to a ring bolt in the stake high above her head, further emphasizing her generous endowments, leaving the remnants of her clothing poised rather precariously. One half-hearted scream or even a semi-deep breath. . . . .

"Who did your hair?"

"I wanna see," Andy complained.

"Aw, come on, Sis."

"You *are* the heroine?"

"Of course she's the heroine," Dutch said. "My honey's always the heroine."

"Thank you, darling."

"Please," Andy begged.

"Oh, all right," Penelope said. "Just don't get any ideas," she added, although a couple of interesting concepts had just popped into her mind.

"Well, I think it's very good," Andy said. "Look how she manages to convey both fear and a quiet courage with her eyes."

"Eyes, Mikey's tail."

"And the expressiveness of your mouth, Stormy. It's determination in the face of adversity."

"I'd say being burned at the stake constitutes adversity."

"And did you notice this?" Dutch asked. "Look how she depicts a sense of purity and virginity. . . ."

"I want a drink," Penelope said.

The sisters left the men to their discussion of artistic merits in cinema posters and went into the kitchen, where Big Mike waited on the counter next to the electric can opener, just in case a hint was needed.

"You pour the wine, Sis, and I'll get my very favorite cat in the whole world his lima beans."

"How *do* you manage to show fear and courage at the same time, as well as love and despair at the loss of love?"

"You saw that?"

Penelope nodded. "The guys missed a few things. You really are very good and I'm proud of you."

"Aw, shucks. T'warn't nothin'."

"No, really. I want to know."

"Part of it is becoming the character. Cassandra and Stormy go away. And then I think of certain things, like the time you rode your bike into the car and I thought you were going to die."

"All I did was cut my knee."

"Well, I didn't know that. So I remember that for fear. Love is easy. I just think of Dutch. I do stuff like that and then something happens. I can't explain it."

"What do you think of when you're tied up and waiting to shoot the scene?"

"Mostly it's boring and uncomfortable, so I fantasize about Dutch rescuing me."

"So that's how you did it. Don't think I didn't notice what was going on beneath that bodice."

Stormy grinned. "Sometimes it's kind of nice to be rescued."

Big Mike thought so, too, as his favorite aunt finally stopped talking and dished up the lima beans, staving off an imminent out-of-body experience caused by food deprivation. After all, he hadn't eaten since Blake slipped him a Coyote Dog in the fourth inning.

"So, what are you going to do to Dutch?"

"Something suitably horrible."

"Good. He deserves it."

"Don't forget you were in on it, too, my pretty." As an actress, Penelope wasn't bad herself, managing a perfectly evil smirk.

Andy and Dutch had moved on to a discussion of how the muscles in Stormy's arms showed the exact amount of tension necessary to exhibit the extent of her predicament.

"Aren't they sweet?" Stormy said, distributing glasses of wine.

"I'm going home when they get to your toes."

"I can hardly wait for the film to come out," Andy said. "I'll review it myself."

"I can hardly wait to find out who killed Peter Adcock," Penelope said. "While you were pretending I didn't exist, Dutch, did you happen to come up with anything useful?"

"I heard about your field trip to The Dynamite Lounge."

"Any ideas about the missing girlfriend?"

"Nope. How about you?"

"Blake and Erika are the only women close to the team. They claim to have despised him. Erika dated him only once, or so she says."

"What about Mrs. McCoy?"

"Feathers?"

"It's happened before. Unfaithful wife. Enraged husband. End of affair."

"Why would Rats take Debbie's bat to do the bloody deed? That doesn't make much sense."

"Murder never does."

"You're reaching."

"I suppose. You have any other ideas then?"

"Adcock offered a tryout to Marty Gault's son."

"Now who's reaching? That's no crime."

"Slightly suspicious."

"Very slightly."

"That's the trouble with this case," Penelope said. "Everything's a bit odd, like the missing bat which isn't really missing."

"Small fingerprints."

"A victim with a missing girlfriend and an eye for the ladies."

"A sweetheart deal for the deceased's baseball team."

Penelope shook her head. "I've been through the records and I can't find anything. There's nothing that makes me jump up and shout, 'Ah, ha. Gotcha!'"

"We can't find anything there, either. The city gave the Coyotes a good deal out of civic pride. Eventually, it's going to be a good deal for the city, too. And, for once, SOD went along with the program. The deal was legitimate."

Penelope swirled the wine in her glass, watching the little maelstrom she created. "But, we could be looking in all the wrong places. What if it was just a robbery?"

"He had nine hundred bucks in his wallet."

"He could have had nine thousand. A smart thief might leave a little to throw us off."

"That doesn't explain the bat. A smart thief doesn't steal a bat to commit robbery and murder."

Penelope shrugged, grinning sheepishly. "I know. It was just a thought. I'm grasping for anything that makes sense."

"If life made sense, we wouldn't need cops."

"Why, Dutch," Penelope said, "you're becoming a philosopher in your old age."

"He's not old," Stormy said. "He's my sweetie."

"He's forty-five."

"Yeah, that's pretty old, I guess."

Dutch turned to Andy. "Don't you just hate it when they gang up on you?"

"Like lionesses, closing in for the kill."

The Warren sisters growled in unison. That woke Mycroft who immediately took the side of Penelope and Stormy. "Grr."

"Yeah," Dutch agreed, "and we're the warthogs."

"And I," Penelope announced, "am taking my little warthog home."

"It's not fair," Penelope said, as she rummaged through her closet.

Andy sat on the edge of the bed watching her. "What is not fair?"

"That Stormy has all the fun." Penelope pulled out the gown she had worn as Queen of the Spring Faire, held it up, and decided it was too ornate. "Nora, Lora, and Debbie, too, for that matter. And they're just the ones I'm sure about. Pretty sure, anyway. I suspect Samantha."

"Of what?"

"Having all the fun." Penelope held up another dress from the Faire—much simpler, although still attractive in a serving wench kind of way. In fact, it was the dress she had worn when she prowled through Empty Creek's version of Elizabethan England disguised as a serving wench looking for a murderer. Perfect, she thought. "I'll be right back," Penelope said. She went into the bathroom and closed the door.

Andy discovered how Big Mike felt having the bedroom door closed in his face. Still, it was a consolation that he wouldn't be left out of the fun—whatever it might be—but as time droned on, he wished she would hurry up. It had been a long day and he was getting sleepy, although it would be folly of the highest order to nod off now. At least Mycroft could nap through the boring parts. Andy stood up and stretched. Whatever was going on, it was worth waiting for.

"Ta, da!" Penelope said, emerging from the bathroom. "The Princess Penelope."

"You don't look like a princess." He didn't really care and

only made the comment in the interest of objective reporting. The low-cut bodice and what it contained—barely—had his full attention.

"That's because I'm imprisoned in the Tower of London and they've taken all my good clothes away."

"Why?"

"Why am I imprisoned or why did they take my good clothes away?"

"Both."

"Because that's what they do. Haven't you ever read a good historical potboiler?"

Andy didn't like to admit that he hadn't. "But what did you do?" That was his inquisitorial reporter's mind taking control.

Really, Penelope thought, men could be so obtuse at times. "Nothing, but I need to be rescued," she said.

"From whom?"

"You, silly."

"All right," Andy said, although he didn't have the foggiest notion of what his beloved was talking about. "But I would never throw you into the Tower."

"No, but your evil alter ego, the Chancellor of the Exchequer, would. He wants my estate."

"Oh."

"You'll have to play both roles."

"Naturally." Andy wondered if the strain of work and detecting was taking its toll. "But what's my motivation?"

"They're going to burn the Princess Penelope at the stake. You're the Dashing Prince and you love me and don't want me to become a crispy critter."

Penelope saw the light bulb flash on—finally. Oh, that kind of rescue.

"But aren't we missing a few props?"

"We'll just use a scarf or two." I can't believe I'm doing this, Penelope thought as she furnished the necessities. I hope Laney never finds out.

"There," she said, tossing a scarf on the bed and throwing her arm across her eyes in a single motion. "Go ahead. Have your way with me, but you'll never get my estate. Never!"

Andy had just driven away a host of dastardly villains when the telephone rang.

"Don't answer it," Penelope said, knowing it was a futile request to make of her newspaper editor. "They're regrouping."

"It might be important," Andy said.

"What's more important than rescuing me again?"

"It'll just take a second. Don't go away."

Since she was firmly tied to the bedpost—hands behind her back; Penelope stressed the importance of tradition—she could only groan and roll her eyes.

"If it's Laney, hang up."

"Hello . . . no, sorry . . . she's tied up at the moment and can't come to the phone."

The Princess Penelope rolled her eyes again and tugged at her bonds. Damn, this stuff really worked. It was going to take the Dashing Prince forever to complete the rescue.

"I'd be happy to take a message . . . what . . . oh . . . let me see if I can interrupt her. Hang on a second."

The telephone cord just stretched to the Tower stake. Andy held the telephone to Penelope's ear.

She stuck her tongue out at him before saying, a little breathlessly, "Hello."

Nothing.

"Hello?"

Andy released the button and the dial tone buzzed in Penelope's ear.

"Wrong number," Andy said, doing his Cheshire cat imitation.

"Oh, you're going to pay for this."

"Where's your sense of humor?" he asked as he returned the phone to the nightstand.

"I don't have one. Not anymore."

"Well, it could have been the King calling to commute your sentence."

"I was wrong about you. You're not the Dashing Prince at all. He must have a bad twin."

"Yep."

"That wasn't in the script."

"I'm ad libbing."

"So the Princess Penelope has to be saved all over again?"

"Yep."

"Oh, what a good idea."

Andy, as the bad twin, continued his improvisations with a goodly number of stolen kisses, a lowered bodice, and a couple of other rather inspired actions. By the time the Dashing Prince finally made his grand entrance, the Princess Penelope had almost forgotten about adding Andy to her April Fool's Day list.

Almost.

And then that damned phone rang again.

CHAPTER
EIGHT

Penelope awakened early after a restless night with a good case of both the guilts and the grumps. The morning grumps could be handled, although it was tiresome being twice hauled out of bed so early in the same week. The guilts were another matter, however. While Penelope was having a perfectly wonderful time being rescued in playful make-believe, someone else had needed deliverance for real. She couldn't even blame Andy, although she fully intended loading Laney down with her own case of remorse. After all, it was Laney who always came up with fantasies like Dance Hall Girl and the Gunfighter and then went around recommending them to everyone. In fact, after her first cup of coffee, Penelope dialed Laney's number, said, "It's all your fault," promptly hung up, and then took the phone off the hook. That would teach the Ravishing Redhead to make up silly sex games.

"Why are you walking stooped over?" Andy asked as she returned to the kitchen table.

"The albatross around my neck is heavy."

Andy wisely decided to shut up, even though he greatly admired Coleridge and wanted to know who she had called and why the telephone was screeching its announcement that it was off the hook.

Eventually, however, the telephone gave up, Penelope brightened a bit at the thought of Laney redialing her number frantically to find out what in the hell was going on, and Andy was emboldened enough to observe, "Thank God, no one was seriously hurt."

That helped, too. Penelope finally removed the metaphorical albatross and gave her two guys an affectionate pat on their respective butts. Mycroft started up a pretty good purr. Andy, who didn't know how to purr (Mycroft had given up trying to teach him), grinned foolishly and asked, "What was that for?"

"Just because you're my dashing prince and I love you."

Penelope didn't think a grin could get any more foolish but Andy surprised her by cornering that particular market.

"Well, you're my princess and I love you, too."

There were two places that Big Mike didn't go in Empty Creek. He had been banned—albeit reluctantly—from the Duck Pond, Empty Creek's finest Mexican restaurant, after an unfortunate incident involving a duck, a previous mayor's rather stout wife, and an enchilada dinner. Although everyone but Mrs. Mayor agreed Mycroft had been unduly provoked by the belligerent duck from the pond that gave the restaurant its name, he was now limited to takeout service.

He had not been banned from the Empty Creek General

Hospital, though they probably had some silly notions about sterility despite the proven therapeutic and healing qualities of a warm and cuddly cat. In this case, however, Penelope was reluctant to allow Mycroft near anything that he might construe as his veterinarian's office. His aversion to water taken externally was nowhere near his antipathy to Doctor Bob's environs. Indeed, it was a major expedition, requiring a great deal of cunning and guile on the part of Penelope and several, always unwilling, helpers to get Mikey to Doctor Bob for his annual physical and booster shots. It was a good thing for all concerned that Big Mike was one healthy cat, because his last visit was still talked about with awe and respect—long after the damage to sundry human and animal participants and the curtains had been repaired.

But, by the time Penelope dropped Big Mike off at the bookstore and drove on to Empty Creek General Hospital, Blake Robinson had already been released. Still, after a prolonged search through hospital officialdom, Penelope managed to find the ward where Blake had spent the night. The nurse on duty was even persuaded by Penelope's honorary police badge to say that Blake faced no life-threatening situation.

"The doctor did want to keep her another night, just in case, however."

"Dr. Livingstone, I presume."

"Yes, Dr. Stanley A. Livingstone. How did you know?"

"A good guess." Penelope didn't bother to say she had read the hospital directory on the way in. She did wonder what kind of parents would name their kid Stanley Livingstone and figured his middle initial stood for "and."

————

Penelope arrived at the offices of the Empty Creek Baseball Club to find one Buddy Peterson tiptoeing in stocking feet on the roof of the manufactured housing unit.

"What are you doing up there?" Penelope asked. She thought it a reasonable question considering one did not often find a left-handed pitcher in nearly a full uniform on the roof of the team's offices.

"Early batting practice," Buddy replied. "Again."

"That still doesn't explain your role."

"Oh. Yeah. Blake's got a headache and Rats says if one ball hits the roof I'm dead meat. He's still really mad about last night and says he's going to feed me to a man-eating saguaro."

Only in Empty Creek.

"I hope it was worth it."

"Oh, yeah. Reggie's beautiful."

"Regina is that, and you better be nice to her. No kissing on the first date. Her mother's got a shotgun."

"I didn't do anything."

"Yet." Penelope started into the office.

"Hey, wait. You don't really have a man-eating cactus around here, do you?"

"Several," Penelope said. "And if you don't win tonight, *I'll* feed you to one."

Inside, Penelope collided with second stage security, undergoing the scrutiny of yet another member of the beleaguered Coyote roster apparently assigned collateral duties. Quincy Smith, the shortstop, wore number fourteen on his jersey and blocked Penelope's way. "Rats says I got to search every-body."

"Don't even think about it," Penelope warned. "I'm not in the mood right now. Maybe another time."

Blake Robinson emerged from her office. She wore jeans, a Coyotes T-shirt, and about a ton of makeup over her black-ened eye. "Quincy, for heaven's sake, put your libido on hold. She's practically a cop."

"Rats'll kill me if you get hurt again. And, please, don't call me Quincy. I hate that name. I'm Little Rap."

"Be good or I'll tell Penelope your middle name."

"And, whatever it is, I'll make sure it's listed in the next box score."

The dual threat sent number fourteen back to his post by the door.

"Come on in," Blake said.

"How are you?"

"Confused more than anything. Oh, my head hurts, I've got a black eye, my pride is damaged, but I'm fine. Just try to tell that to Rats though."

"What happened?"

"I worked late," Blake said. "I hate losing, just like Rats, and I thought maybe if I studied the roster some more, I might find a move we could make."

"Three games does not a season make."

"I know. Rats keeps telling me that, too, but he can always find another job. If I don't succeed, it's off to wherever they send failed female general managers."

"Probably the last circle of Hell," Penelope said.

"Or worse," Blake said bleakly. "I'll have to go to work in corporate America."

"What can you tell me?"

"Not much. I had turned the lights out because I think better in the dark. I guess I fell asleep and when I woke up I went to turn them back on. That's when *my* lights went out."

"Was it a man or a woman?"

"I don't know. It all happened too fast."

"Did you see *anything?*"

Blake shook her head. "I think there was a ski mask. I remember thinking that it was too warm for a ski mask. It seems pretty irrational now."

"Blows to the head provoke absurd thoughts sometimes."

"When I was coming to," Blake said, "I thought I was still in the dentist's office the time when I had my wisdom teeth taken out. They gave me a shot and told me to count backwards from one hundred. I was at ninety-nine when I regained consciousness and it was all over, but I kept trying to go back to sleep."

"What did the doctor say?"

Blake smiled again. "X-rays of my head showed nothing."

Penelope laughed. It was one of those legends that made baseball such a great game. Dizzy Dean, a pitcher with the St. Louis Cardinals, had been beaned during the 1934 World Series with the Detroit Tigers. Headlines the next day trumpeted the fact that the X-rays of Dean's head showed nothing. In his case, it might have been true. He didn't get his nickname for nothing.

"So, you woke up," Penelope prompted.

"With a headache, a black eye, and locked in the trailer."

"How long were you out?"

"I'm not sure. Maybe ten minutes. It might have been

longer because I kept trying to go back to sleep so they could take my wisdom teeth out. When I finally figured *that* out, I called Rats. All I wanted was for him to come let me out. The next thing I knew there were cops and paramedics all over the place, I was strapped to a gurney, and rushed to the hospital. That siren was killing my head. And when we got there, the doctor kept tickling my feet to see if I had a concussion. I hate being tickled. My brothers used to do that."

"And the prognosis?"

"Slight concussion. He came back in the morning and tickled my feet some more just to make sure. He wanted to keep me another day for observation and wouldn't release me until I gave him my phone number. 'For further observation,' he said."

"Dr. Livingstone, I presume."

Blake beamed and then said, "Ow," discovering that beaming hurts when your eye is all puffed and swollen.

"I guess he has your number if he let you out."

"Of course. He's really cute."

"So are you."

"Even with a black eye?"

"Even with a black eye."

So the questions remained. Who skulked around baseball offices in the middle of the night wearing a ski mask and what did the intruder want?

As with Peter Adcock, a personal robbery was not an apparent motive. Nothing was taken from Blake's purse. The only thing missing was her key and that was found in the lock on the outside. Blake could offer little explanation. "There's nothing here," she said. "Personnel records, business records, that sort of thing. I don't know what he could have wanted. Whatever it was, he knew where it was kept. There's not a thing out of place that I can tell."

"Do you mind if I look around?"

"Go ahead."

Penelope spent the better portion of two hours rummaging through one file cabinet after another. For such a young organization, the Empty Creek Coyotes had amassed an amazing amount of paperwork. Much of it dealt with scouting reports on their own players and those of the other five teams in the newly-formed league. Penelope skimmed over those, but after her brief examination came to the conclusion that the Sedona Red Rocks and the Bisbee Diamondbacks were the teams to beat, *if* the Coyotes ever managed to beat anyone. But the season was young and the Coyotes did have some talent. Penelope delved into her store of baseball clichés. It's a long season. Anything can happen. They put their pants on the same way we do. One leg at a time. Take 'em one game at a time. She hoped that one or another stuck for the sake of Rats and Blake. Besides, she hated losing to Sedona, too, and as for Bisbee. . . . That was unthinkable.

The business records of the baseball club were predictable. Promotional budgets, equipment budgets, projected ticket sales, projected revenues. Penelope wasn't at all surprised to find that if all went well, the Coyotes could be a profitable little team, especially if some of their players did well enough to have their contracts purchased by major league teams.

While all of that was fascinating enough, there was a paucity of clues. The only thing Penelope found of the slightest interest was a copy of the minutes of a board of directors meeting of the year before. During that particular meeting, twelve ballots had been taken before Peter Adcock had been elected as the managing general partner over one Kendall McCoffey, Jr. of computer game fame. The ten-ten deadlock had been broken finally when someone named Raymond Davenport had changed his allegiance after the eleventh ballot.

Penelope turned her attention to the computer at the late Peter Adcock's work station. She booted it up and hit the function key that listed files.

Nothing.

She did everything she knew to find a file somewhere in the recesses of the computer's electronic memory. Still nothing.

Penelope rummaged through desk drawers looking for the backup disks that Adcock must have kept. The middle drawer had pencils, paper clips, a collection of business cards (including Lora Lou's), some news clips, a staple remover, and, way in the back, a post-it note with the initials W.D. on it. The second drawer was empty, as was the third. She turned to the other side of the desk and found the backup disks. Back at the computer, she inserted them, one after another, into Drive A. There was nothing on Personnel. She drew blanks on Travel, Prospects, Scouting, Calendar, Addresses, and something called Hosanahs, whatever that was. She even tried one labeled Bad Disk and received the message, "Not Reading Drive A. 1 Retry. 2 Cancel." Penelope cancelled and leaned back in the chair, staring at the sky blue screen.

Penelope knew the disks hadn't been erased when the offices were searched by the police, but now they were.

Well.

Penelope accepted her designer key chain and followed Big Mike to the Coyote Dog stand where Blake was at her post with a handsome young man who didn't look at all like a Coyote Dog salesman, even though he wore a baseball cap and an apron adorned with the club's logo.

"Dr. Livingstone, I presume," Penelope said for the third time that day. "Sorry, I never could pass up a good line."

"Isn't it awful? Before my mother met my father, she was a medical missionary in Africa. Livingstone and Schweitzer were her heroes."

"And your middle name is Albert."

"You got it."

"Where did the Stanley come from?"

"Mom admired explorers, too."

"He insists on keeping me under observation," Blake said, "so I put him to work."

The young Dr. Livingstone evidently took his medical duties very seriously, keeping Blake's shapely backside under observation as she leaned over and pulled a bag of Coyote Dog buns from beneath the counter.

"Concussions can be very tricky things," he explained. "It's important to monitor the patient's progress."

While not up on the latest in maladies, Penelope doubted that Blake had a concussion of the butt. Still, it never hurt to be cautious. She also noticed that Mycroft, despite his hostility to medical practitioners of all specialties, was consulting with young Livingstone on Blake's activities, although that was probably because of the buns rather than *the* buns.

"Are you a baseball fan?"

"I am now. Blake's going to let me play the National Anthem on my violin."

That was Empty Creek for you.

Motivated by visions of carnivorous cacti and loaded shotguns doing the Can Can in his mind, Buddy Peterson took a no-hitter into the second inning and then the Red Rocks exploded for nine runs.

"I sure hope you're nice to him," Penelope observed, "because Rats won't be."

"I just hope he kisses better than he pitches," Reggie said.

"Regina!" Nora cried, despite the fact that she had spent most of the inning thinking about a memorable buss delivered by a certain tweedy English gentleman.

Penelope and Big Mike hung around after the game. After the events of the previous night, Penelope was determined to make sure of Blake's safety before leaving. But as the lights of the stadium dimmed, there were damned near as many people around the office waiting for Blake as had attended the game. Stanley Livingstone was there, along with Rats and Feathers, coaches, the entire team, Tweedledee and Tweedledum, and a Little League team selling cookies and gathering autographs. It appeared that Blake would be safely tucked into bed, although she might find it difficult to sleep with such an entourage hanging around her boudoir.

Penelope scratched Big Mike's chin before turning the Jeep for home. With a deadline day looming, Andy would spend the night at his place, so there was nothing to look forward to.

Little did she know.

As they pulled into the driveway, the headlights swept over a dark house. The full moon was now on the wane, but bright enough still to light the desert with a shimmering glow. Penelope held the door open for Mycroft who hopped down and headed for the front door. Penelope slammed the Jeep door shut and followed. She opened the door and reached for the light switch.

"Well, it's about time."

When her heart finished rattling around the beamed ceiling of her living room and returned to its accustomed place, Penelope cried, "Good God, Laney! You scared the bejesus out of me."

Alexander and Kelsey greeted Big Mike effusively.

"Serves you right. What do you mean it's all my fault? I put your phone back on the hook, by the way."

"Thank you, I guess," Penelope said. "Is that why you came over? To put my phone back on the hook?"

"Slumber party," Laney announced.

Oh, oh.

It happened several times a year. The volatility of Laney's temper matched her flaming red tresses. And when the sky-rockets went off, everyone—animal, vegetable, and min-eral—headed for cover. But an easy-going, unemployed cowboy named Wally was usually too lethargic to get out of the line of fire. As a result, Laney threw his lazy carcass out of her bed and home at least three times a year.

"What did he do this time?"

"Nothing."

That was often enough to set Laney off. One memorable row had started because Wally, undecided as to which movie to rent, left the choice to Laney. After a lot of "I have to make all the decisions" from her, Wally spent the next two nights bunking beneath the stars. At least he smelled like a cowboy when he was sufficiently contrite so as to be allowed back in the house—with the movie *he* had rented (which they never did see, because if there was anything Laney liked better than a good argument, it was making up afterwards).

"He must have done something."

"There I was, redialing your number frantically, wondering if you had finally lost your mind, and he just *sat* there. Eating corn flakes."

"What an ingrate," Penelope said.

"This is it," Laney declared. "He's definitely history this time."

"What are you going to do for a research assistant?"

"Put an ad in the paper." Laney clapped her hands. "Well, that's settled. What are we going to do?"

"I'm going to bed."

"You can't do that."

"Why not? You said it was a slumber party."

"Yes, but you don't sleep at a slumber party. You have fun."

"Sleeping is fun."

"Penelope!"

"Oh, all right, what do you want to do?"

"I don't know. What do *you* want to do, Penelope?"

"I don't want to sit here doing a bad imitation of *Marty*."

"It's too late to cruise for dudes, I suppose."

"I have a dude. So do you, for that matter."

"History, history, history! I'm leaving the scene of that particular crime and moving on."

"That's it!" Penelope cried, snapping her fingers.

"What's it?"

"The crime scene. Come on. I should have done this before."

"Done what?"

"Visit the crime scene."

"You really have lost your mind. You were there. We were all there."

"Not at the time the murder occurred."

"That's your idea of fun at a slumber party? Visit a crime scene?"

"We can have fun after we find out who killed Peter Adcock and cold-cocked Blake Robinson."

"The time of death was sometime between midnight and three a.m." Penelope said, as she climbed the ladder built into the side of the baseball club's offices.

Laney clambered up right after Penelope. "Well, we're right on time. It's midnight. Shall I open the wine?" If she had to go adventuring in the middle of the night, Laney insisted they take refreshments.

"Not yet," Penelope said. "Look."

"What's to see? It's an empty parking lot."

"Yes, but it's not dark. There's still enough moon to see what's going on."

"If you're expecting trouble. Adcock probably wasn't."

"Maybe." Penelope sat on the left field wall and jumped down, landing on the soft dirt of the warning track.

Laney took her place on the wall. "Here, take the wine. If I'm going to break my neck, I'll need it for anesthesia. We probably should have brought two bottles."

Penelope reached up and took the Mycroft & Company tote bag and then stepped aside.

Laney thudded into the warning track. "Ow, damn!"

"Your neck?"

"No, my bra snapped." She stood up and dusted her jeans off. "Do you have a safety pin?"

"I came unprepared for calamity."

Laney tugged her blouse free, reached underneath, and wiggled around for a bit. "There," she said, tossing the offending undergarment on the outfield grass.

"You're just going to leave it there?"

"It'll give the left fielder something to think about."

"Couldn't hurt." Abraham Jefferson Washington—The Prez—was currently hitting at a less-than-torrid .1304347826 clip, three hits in twenty-three at bats. Without cheating, his batting average couldn't even be rounded off to .131.

Walking across the infield brought back old memories for Penelope. As a child, she had been a good-fielding, hard-hitting shortstop in Little League with a paperback novel in her back pocket, until she threw her arm out when she was twelve and hung up her spikes. Baseball had always been fun, but books were better and she never regretted her abbreviated athletic career. Boys were okay, too, she discovered—especially after confronting one particular young athlete as a member of the opposite sex for the first time, rather than as a teammate.

They entered the visiting team's dugout and sat down.

"Well, here we are," Laney said. "We're having fun now. Do you want some wine?"

"Not yet. I'm working."

"Sitting in a dugout in the middle of the night is *not* work. It's . . . It's . . . It's pretty stupid if you ask me."

"Shh."

Laney concentrated on opening the wine.

Penelope closed her eyes and transported herself back to that fateful night, imagining everything as Peter Adcock and his killer must have seen it. With the moon at its fullest then, the diamond would have been well-lit, almost light enough to play a game. Adcock might have been sitting in the same spot for a time, or standing only a few feet away, where his body had fallen. The stands were in shadows and the home team dugout was dark. But otherwise. . . .

Having set the somber mood in her mind, Penelope imagined the killer walking toward Adcock, bat in hand. Not yet alarmed, Adcock rose to greet him—he had been sitting in the dugout, waiting; Penelope was positive of that now—perhaps offering his hand, or was it the other way around?

But why?

Penelope drove the nagging question away, cleared her mind, took several slow and calming breaths, and opened her eyes, fully expecting to see the recreated mise-en-scène.

Good God! I did it!

The killer was slowly advancing on the dugout, brandishing what appeared to be a very lethal baseball bat.

"Come out of there," he squeaked, "with your hands up."

Squeaked?

It was too bad Big Mike had stayed home with Alex and Kelsey.

CHAPTER
NINE

The doorbell sent Alexander and Kelsey into attack mode. They leaped off the bed doing their flying squirrel imitation, hit the floor running, and bounded away into the living room, yipping and yapping. When the doorbell rang a second time, Alexander twirled frantically, trying to raise Laney and Penelope. He would have been better off trying to wake Peter Adcock. When the pounding on the door started, Alex and Kelsey, who took their security duties very seriously, raced back down the hallway. Alex leaped to Penelope's bed and barked furiously. Kelsey was in the guest bedroom licking Laney's face.

"Good God!" Laney finally shrieked. "Everyone just shut up!" Since no one paid the slightest attention to her, she dragged herself out of bed, slipped into a bathrobe borrowed from Penelope, and stumbled to the front door, wiping away dog kisses.

"What?" Laney demanded, throwing the door open.

The floral arrangement filled the doorway of Casa Penelope, dazzling a startled ravishing redhead with all the colors of the rainbow.

"What?" Laney repeated.

"Special delivery for you," Harvey McAllister drawled. He wore his off-duty surfer's uniform, which consisted of purple shorts and sandals.

"No one ever sends me flowers," Teresa Sandia said pointedly. She was dressed more formally in shorts, T-shirt, and sandals.

"What mere flower could compete with your beauty?" Harvey responded quickly. No one had ever accused him of falling off his surf board just yesterday. While the sun might have bleached his hair, it hadn't impacted his brains yet.

"Good answer, Dude of Mine."

"What?"

"You're becoming repetitive," Penelope said. She might have slept through the minor pandemonium of irritating doorbells, repeated pummelling of her door, and strident Yorkie barks and wet kisses, but visitors on her hearth—at whatever hour—required hospitality. It was another of those things handed down from on high by Muffy. "You better get the troops, and the flowers, out of the hot sun. I'll put the coffee on."

"There's a card," Harvey said helpfully.

"It's probably C.O.D.," Penelope said, disappearing into the kitchen.

"Yes, but we gave him the good customer discount," Teresa said.

There was a card—somewhere—lost amidst the glorious floral arrangement. But after the three of them wrestled the display through the door, Teresa burrowed through the blooms, plucked it from a daffodil, and handed it over to Laney.

With trembling fingers, glistening eyes, and heaving bosom—there was no use wasting the poignancy of the moment; it could be later incorporated into Chapter Seven of *Frontier Love*—Laney opened the card and read: "I'll never eat corn flakes again." It was signed simply, "Love, Wally." She looked up at her audience and, with a sigh worthy of Scarlett O'Hara, said, "Isn't he sweet?"

"Barf," Penelope said.

"I must fly to him."

"Don't fly very far," Harvey said. "He's in the back of our van."

Laney flew.

"Double barf," Penelope said. "Coffee anyone?"

With the loony lovers reunited, cinnamon rolls heated and distributed—frozen was the best Penelope could do on short notice—Big Mike observing from the window sill, and Yorkshire Terriers each happily ensconced in a lap, a semblance of normality settled over the kitchen.

"We were beginning to think you weren't home," Teresa said.

"Tough night," Laney said, tossing a glare in Penelope's direction. "I broke a fingernail—and a bra strap."

"I should have been with you," Wally said. "How can I ever make it up to you?"

"I'll think of something."

"What happened?"

"Don't ask."

"That's the trouble with you, Laney," Penelope said. "You get upset over the slightest thing."

"Which reminds me. What was all my fault?"

"Don't ask. The blueberry muffins will be ready in a minute."

For the second time that morning, the doorbell jangled insistently.

"Good Lord," Penelope said, "now what?"

"Why didn't you just come in?" Penelope asked when she opened the door and found Dutch standing there. "We're practically related, and would be if you'd just get around to marrying my sister."

"Official business," Dutch said.

Oh, oh. "This wouldn't have anything to do with last night, would it?"

"It would."

"Oh, take that grim look off your face. I can explain everything."

"You can do it at the station. I'm taking you and Laney in."

"Are we under arrest?"

"Sort of."

"Whatever for? It was a clear case of self-defense."

"Not according to the version I heard," Dutch said. "We can probably clear this up. If you're nice. Pretty flowers."

"Wally sent them to Laney. You should send some to Stormy as long as you're here. Harvey and Teresa would be happy to take your order, I'm sure. And I'm always nice."

"I can't afford anything like that."

"Neither can Wally. Just charge them to Stormy."

"Are those blueberry muffins I smell?"

"Are you here to arrest me, sort of, or eat me out of house and home?"

"Both."

"Well, you better come in. I can hardly wait to hear why you're picking on two poor and defenseless women."

"Ha!"

"Laney, would you pour Dutch some coffee while I get the muffins out of the microwave?"

"Sure."

"Oh, and by the way, you're under arrest. Read Laney her rights, Dutch."

"I knew it! Penelope Warren, this is absolutely the last time I invite you to a slumber party."

"Now, aren't you glad we made the delivery in person?" Teresa asked. "I told Harvey we should get out more."

"What are the charges?"

"Trespassing, for one."

"I'm a season ticket holder."

"That doesn't cover the middle of the damned night."

"Well, it should. This is very bad for public relations. Particularly if they never win a game. What else?"

"Assault on a computer nerd, defamation of character, sexual harassment, littering."

"Littering? We didn't litter."

"*Someone* left a bra in left field."

"Oh, that."

"What would you do if a wild man came at you with a baseball bat?"

"Can we have conjugal visits?"

"I'm calling my lawyer."

"It was your idea to pull his pants down around his ankles so he couldn't run."

"Well, you were the one who berated him for his choice of occupations."

"I'm not going to jail in my bathrobe."

"It's *my* bathrobe."

"Do you have any corn flakes?"

"Wally!"

"Just kidding, sweetie."

Dutch groaned. Sometimes, he wished he had stayed in Los Angeles with the normal people. "Would you please get dressed so we can get this over with."

"I thought it was all settled last night. It was just a misunderstanding. Junior seemed to grasp that."

"He changed his mind."

"But why?"

"Ask *him*."

George Eden was waiting when the caravan of police car, Jeep, and red Miata convertible arrived at the Empty Creek Police Station. Dutch had been tempted to cuff them both and add resisting arrest to the complaints against them for making him wait so long while they showered and dressed. But it seemed impolite after he had finished off the blueberry muffins.

"I hope you didn't say anything," George said, shaking hands with his clients. He was the best criminal defense attorney in Empty Creek, and his attire had improved considerably since taking up with Sheila Tyler, one of Empty Creek's toughest police officers and fashion coordinators.

"They practically confessed."

"Coercion," Laney said.

"Entrapment," Penelope said.

"That's even better. Coercion *and* entrapment."

Penelope and Laney confronted their accuser—a very sheepish accuser—in Dutch's office. In the daylight, Kendall McCoffey, Jr. appeared less menacing than the night before when Penelope had dropped him with a very neat and punishing cross-body block and Laney had leaped into the fray, grabbing the bat and tossing it toward the pitcher's mound before proceeding to thrash him severely about the head and shoulders.

By the time he had squeaked out his innocence, he was already immobilized—it's difficult to run with pants around ankles. For good measure, Penelope had tickled his rib cage. It was *really* hard to run with pants around ankles while giggling hysterically. By the time the authorities arrived—he had dialed Nine-One-One before following them from the team office where he had been sleeping—everything was sorted out, and various apologies had been issued and accepted, or so it seemed at the time.

"You know her?" McCoffey, Jr. asked, indicating the still photograph on the desk of Stormy in her role as Prudence, Queen of the Dark Universe.

"My fiancée," Dutch said.

"My sister," Penelope said.

"My friend," Laney said.

"My heroine," McCoffey, Jr. said.

"My big toe," George Eden said. "We're suing for false arrest."

"What's going on?" Penelope asked. "We said we were

sorry, and it's not very polite to go around in the middle of the night charging at people with a baseball bat."

"Assault with a deadly weapon," George pointed out.

A subdued young man looked at the floor and mumbled, "Myfadermademedoit."

"What?"

"My father made me do it," McCoffey said, obviously embarrassed by his admission.

Penelope suddenly felt great pity for the young man. It was the Oedipus Complex alive and well right here in Empty Creek, one of the oldest themes in literature, the ultimate confrontation between father and son. Oedipus Cat, Penelope always called it.

Growing up on the college campus in Ethiopia, Big Mike had once been Little Mike, a thoroughly cowed young cat, attacked by his father—a big tough tomcat wearing the scars of a hundred fierce battles. Little Mike hardly dared venture out without getting clobbered by his old man. But as he grew and matured, Mycroft met the challenge. Three times he fought his father. Three times he retreated, licking his wounds (with a little first aid from Penelope).

And then one night, Penelope had been awakened by the most horrible screeching and caterwauling. Through the window, by the light of a full moon, Penelope witnessed the showdown—she had learned painfully during round one that it was folly to interfere in a cat fight. There was a great deal of puffing and howling and hissing in prelude, but the actual fight was fierce—if brief—and Mycroft was left in sole possession of the field of honor, parading in triumph. There was a new cat in town and his name was Big Mike. But that was what cats did. It was Mother Nature's noisy and disorderly way of transferring power from one generation to the next. The King was dead. Long live the King. Like Oedipus, Big Mike had no control over the fates decreed by aloof and uncaring gods.

Looking now at a most subdued young McCoffey, Penelope decided a little catharsis was in order and she was just the person to provide it. With that settled in her mind, she very neatly turned the plea bargain into an examination of Kendall McCoffey, Jr.

Penelope elicited several admissions.

"My father controls the team now."

"I hate baseball."

"My father will kill me."

"I just wanted to see you again."

Penelope smiled. "You could have found an easier way to do it."

"I'm not running a damned dating service here," Dutch hollered.

"Will you go out with me?"

"I can't," Penelope said. "I have a boyfriend."

He looked hopefully at Laney.

"Me too," she said.

"I never get to meet any girls."

It was one of the more unique plea bargains in the annals of criminal justice, even for Empty Creek. In exchange for Junior dropping the charges—again—all Penelope and Laney had to do was fix up the new managing general partner with a young woman willing to go out with him *and* introduce him to Stormy. As it turned out, Storm Williams was, indeed, his heroine, and, more importantly, Junior had nothing to do with creating computer games for the arcades. He was writing a CD-ROM program that would allow B movie aficionados, such as himself, to make their own movies starring their favorite actresses. At least it was a creative endeavor of sorts.

But as dedicated fixer-uppers, neither Penelope nor Laney realized they were facing the matchmaking challenge of their careers.

"He may be a computer genius, but I think he's a twenty-five year old virgin."

"We're going to take care of that."

"Don't look at me!"

"I didn't mean one of us. We're finding him a nice girl."

"Or a bad girl."

"Any girl."

"And we can't go around calling him Junior. Who wants to date someone with a squeaky voice named Junior?"

Back at Mycroft & Company, Penelope took the pad labeled THINGS TO DO TODAY and made a list.

1. Who took the bat from Debbie's house?
2. Who used the bat to kill Peter Adcock?
3. Who attacked Blake Robinson?
4. Why did McCoffey, Sr. make McCoffey, Jr. press charges?
5. Find girlfriend for McCoffey, Jr.
6. Unless
7. McCoffey, Jr. is the killer.
8. Why?
9. Go shopping.

10. See number eight.

11. See all of the above.

12.

Penelope couldn't think of anything to round out her list to a nice and orderly dozen. She showed the list to Mycroft who had no reaction, except perhaps to number nine.

"Thinking of your stomach again," Penelope accused.

Big Mike yawned and meowed at the same time. "Mewp," he said in what was, no doubt, agreement.

Penelope doodled, drawing little smiley faces, bigger frowning faces, several hearts, and a saguaro cactus with a buzzard sitting on it, which pretty much exhausted her artistic talents. She drew a larger heart and put P & A inside it. Penelope and Andy. Delete the ampersand and what did you get? PA. Pa equals father. What if Junior was trying to impress Senior?

Look, Pa, I can run the team better than Adcock if I have the chance.

Pay attention to me, Father!

It was ample motivation for murder.

But why steal the murder weapon from Debbie?

"Oh, hell and damnation, Mikey. It still doesn't make any sense."

Penelope went back and wrote:

12. Call Stormy.

She dialed the number.

"Hi, it's me. Want to meet one of your fans?"

"I've got nothing against you, Missy," the owner of the Sedona Red Rocks said, "but. . . ."

"Don't call me Missy!"

The fact that Blake Robinson and Emerson Heath shared matching shiners elicited no sense of camaraderie or shared misery.

"What's your point, Emerson?" McCoffey, Jr. asked, staring at the computer screen where Storm Williams was up to her waist in quicksand and sinking rapidly. The Dark Universe was populated mainly by savage mutants and quicksand bogs.

"The point is, Squirt, baseball's got no place for women in it, not when we're trying to make this league a success. Just look at the team she's put together. For Chrissake, you'll be lucky to win a game."

"Don't call me Squirt."

"Who's gonna pay to see this bunch of losers?"

"We've been sold out the entire week," Blake said.

"Yeah, that's because people in Empty Creek are too stupid to know any better. What's gonna happen when you go on the road? Nobody's gonna lay out cash to see losers. The rest of us owners gotta protect our investments."

"We'll turn it around," Blake said.

"Hunnert bucks says you don't."

"I'll take that bet," Blake said.

"So will I," Penelope said, as she led her entourage into the office.

"For Crissakes," Emerson said, "more women!"

Having been led to expect an adoring fan, Storm Williams was not prepared for the tone of disgust in Heath's voice, as if the office had suddenly been invaded by two slimy, repulsive slugs and a cat. "Oink," the star of stage and screen said, restraining the urge to darken his other eye.

"OhmyGod," Junior squeaked, leaping out of his chair, "it's you. I've got to save you."

"From what? This little piggy?" Stormy had apparently ignored Heath's bulk.

"That's it!" Blake cried. "We'll have a Babe look-alike contest."

"No, the quicksand." He swiveled the screen around.

Big Mike jumped to the desk top and had a look to see if he could be of assistance. Damsels in distress were a specialty of his.

"Oh, that," Stormy said taking a quick glance at her predicament on the screen. "Use the amulet."

Junior's fingers flew over the keyboard and the CD-ROM Stormy pulled her amulet from the muck, pointed, and pressed a hidden release. A tiny dart flew out and imbedded itself in a tree. CD Stormy used the attached wire to reel herself to relative safety.

Junior hit the pause key. They could deal with the six-footed piranha dragon lurking in the underbrush later. It was the first piranha dragon Big Mike had seen, but he didn't think it was any big deal. Six-footed dragons put their pants on like everyone else—one big paw at a time.

The reality-based Stormy said, "Hi."

"Hi," Junior managed to croak.

"You better listen to what I said," Heath grunted, heaving himself from the chair. "Otherwise the league's gonna have to take action." He stormed out.

"What about our bets?" Penelope called after him.

"You're on, Missy. You're all on."

"Misogynist jerk," Blake shouted.

"What was that all about?" Penelope asked.

"He wants Junior to fire me," Blake said. "Women have no place in baseball, according to him."

Penelope turned to Junior. "You're not going to listen to *him*, are you?"

Having saved his heroine from a mucky fate, Junior seemed overwhelmed by the magnitude of his action, although the rescue had involved no more exertion than a few simple computer commands. The office air conditioning unit was laboring a bit, but that didn't explain the beads of sweat on McCoffey's brow, the pallor of his cheeks, and his resemblance to a marble statue executed in the style of an ancient Greek Olympian about to upchuck his stuffed grape leaves.

"Is he all right?" Stormy asked.

Penelope placed her wrist on his forehead. "Clammy," she pronounced. "*Are* you all right?" she asked.

Junior indicated vital signs by nodding his head. "It's h . . . her."

"A severe case of PSS," Penelope decided.

"Is it contagious?" Blake asked.

"Not for you, I shouldn't think. Post-Stormy Syndrome."

"It's r . . . really h . . . her."

"Just think of her as plain old Cassie Warren," Penelope said. "Perhaps that will help."

"I've *never* been plain," Stormy told her sister. "Yes, it's really me," she said, stepping up to Junior and grabbing his hand, shaking it firmly. "And I'm very pleased to meet you."

Junior stared at the honored member. "I'll never wash it."

"You will if you expect to shake my hand ever again."

Having regained the power of speech and limited movement, Junior said, "I've seen all your movies. You're terrific."

"Why, thank you, sir." She curtsied slightly, managing to

convey the impression that she was a gowned and bejeweled lady-in-waiting despite being clad in an ensemble from Rodeo Drive and other Beverly Hills environs.

Big Mike, having decided that the six-footed piranha dragon was a big wuss, had no sooner taken up residence in the chair vacated by Heath—it had not escaped Penelope's notice that the rival owner had failed the lap test—than Stormy scooped him up and sat down with him in her lap. Any lesser personage than Stormy would have suffered greatly, but favorite aunts had their prerogatives.

"Tell me about yourself, Kendall," Stormy said, "and the wonderful work you're doing."

That was Penelope's clue to nod at Blake and steal out of the office. They could have banged on the wheezing air conditioner and Junior would have failed to notice. As a matter of fact, Harvey McAllister could have surfed through the office, riding the crest of the Big One, unobserved by Junior. The new managing general partner had definitely been struck by the Ga-Ga-in-Love bird.

"Well?" Penelope asked when they were back in the Jeep and heading for Mycroft & Company.

"Well, you should know. You were eavesdropping."

"Yes, but I want your impression."

"He's clean."

"Did Mikey sit in his lap?"

"Why would he leave my lap? You know he likes me best. After you, of course."

The lap test might not be infallible in Junior's case, Penelope thought. Given the choice of male or female companionship, Mikey took the lady every time, unless he happened to be momentarily upset with her.

Mikey, who could also be a little fickle, was still in Stormy's lap. Actually, his back paws were in her lap. His front paws rested on the dashboard and he peered intently through the windshield, perhaps thinking of a nice cup of non-fat yogurt. Penelope often stopped at the Ice Cream Shoppe but, distracted by the various Oedipal theories whirling around in her mind, she passed it right by on this occasion. That was the trouble with Penelope. While she had many feline attributes herself and would have made a very acceptable cat in many respects—she was an excellent sleeper, as everyone knew, and managed a very credible purr on occasion—she did not have the proper reverence for food, a mighty failing from Big Mike's perspective. Still, if he was disappointed, it didn't show, and he maintained his watchful position just in case a piranha dragon was hiding behind the next saguaro.

"Thank God," Stormy said, "we had a normal father."

"Except for making us go to Catholic school."

"Well, there was that."

"But he wasn't a Little League father like Junior's old man."

"No, we played the game and took our lumps and he was always there to pick us up if we fell down."

"Muffy, too."

"Good old Muffy and Biff."

"Poor Junior."

"Can you imagine receiving a message every morning on your answering machine giving you the marching orders for the day?"

"That's one of the reasons I don't have an answering machine," Penelope said.

"You've never followed an order in your life, Sis, except for the Marine Corps."

"Well, I'm looking forward to meeting Kendall McCoffey, Sr. He might be just the type to kill someone to make room for his son."

CHAPTER
TEN

Penelope's conjecture was in the fourth paragraph of Andy's story on Peter Adcock's murder. She read it for a second time at Mycroft & Company.

A reliable source close to the investigation commented that, "A baseball team is an extended family, a closely-knit community, and a microcosm of society. It's reasonable to expect to find the good and bad of society mirrored in that community. Since most murderers are family members, friends, or otherwise associated with their victims, it is also reasonable to look within the community for the killer, quite possibly because of a love tryst."

Penelope thought it sociological babble, but it was also true and might make someone nervous. And if the killer did not come from within the greater Coyote family, well . . . a person or persons unknown might relax just enough to make a mistake. Killers always made mistakes. If they didn't, very few would ever be caught and brought to justice. Of course, there was always the possibility that Peter Adcock had been murdered by a complete and total stranger. And if that were the case, the chances for a satisfactory conclusion were practically nonexistent, unless said stranger suddenly decided to confess.

Because there was little likelihood of that, Penelope decided to do some work. Since Adcock's death, she had fallen behind in everything. There were book reviews to glance over, novels to order, bills to be paid, telephone calls to be returned, mysteries to read so she could make intelligent recommendations to customers, and a cat to be moved before she could do anything.

Penelope had just scooted Big Mike from the center of the desk to one side, eliciting his usual complaint, when Kathy used the office intercom to let Penelope know she had a telephone call.

"Tweedledee on line one," she hollered.

"Thanks," Penelope shouted back before picking up the phone.

"I wish she wouldn't call me that," Tweedledee complained.

"It's better than Old Butthead."

"I suppose."

"Have you recovered from The Dynamite Lounge?"

"You gotta stop doing things like that, Penelope," he said. "You might get hurt."

She hadn't been surprised at Dutch's call and had listened patiently to another lecture about the folly of conducting investigations through the media, promised she would never do it again (Right!), and left him mollified. But she was touched by Tweedledee's concern. She made a mental note to send over a dozen jelly doughnuts.

"I'm just your usual reliable source. No one will know it's me."

"Yeah," Tweedledee said, his voice oozing disgust. "Who's gonna think cops talk about microcosms of society?"

"Did you have to look it up?"

"Of course not."

"There you are, then."

"Just because I didn't have to look it up, doesn't mean anybody will think I said it. They'll know it was the Cat Lady."

Eager to change the subject, Penelope said, "By the way, Tweedledee's a very nice nickname and comes from great literature. You're lucky to have it."

"I am?" He didn't sound convinced.

"Yes, you are," Penelope said. "Now, what do you know about Kendall McCoffey, Sr?"

"Other than he's on his way to see you right now?"

Kendall McCoffey, Sr. entered Mycroft & Company imperiously, glancing over the books and furnishings quickly, as though estimating their value should he decide on a hostile takeover. About sixty, he had aged well, like Paul Newman, Sean Connery, and Robert Redford had managed to do. His hair and mustache were gray and contrasted nicely with his evenly-tanned face. He was ruggedly handsome—and knew it.

"May I help you?" Kathy asked.

"Kendall McCoffey. I'm here to see Penelope Warren." He ignored the woman who had followed him into the store.

"Did you have an appointment?"

McCoffey looked affronted at the question from a mere shop clerk. "Just tell her I'm here."

"May I tell her what it's regarding?"

"You may not."

Kathy shrugged. "Ms. Warren's very busy. I'll see if she can spare a moment." She turned her back on McCoffey and disappeared into the back room. "He's a pompous windbag," she whispered to Penelope.

"I heard." She smiled. "You did great, just like we rehearsed, but try for a little more imperiousness this time."

"Ms. Warren will be with you . . . directly."

"Perfect."

Penelope glanced at her watch and went back to the novel she was reading. When she finished the chapter, she looked at her watch again and decided there was time for at least one more chapter before Kendall McCoffey, Sr. reached the point of spontaneous combustion.

Two chapters later, Penelope marked her place with the thin silver Arabian stallion bookmark Andy had given her as a stocking filler the previous Christmas, pushed her chair back, stood up, took a deep breath, pushed through the dividing curtain, and strode purposefully toward Kendall McCoffey, Sr.

"I'm Penelope Warren."

"Thank you for seeing me without an appointment."

Penelope fielded his sarcasm neatly and threw it right back at him. "It's my pleasure."

When McCoffey made no move to introduce his young

companion, Penelope did it for him. "And you are Mrs. McCoffey. "It *is* a pleasure."

"I'm Rose," she said, in a frail voice.

As a trophy wife, Rose McCoffey was decorative enough. Some three decades younger than her husband, she was tall and slender with the delicate appearance of her name. Her face was pretty, although her high cheekbones gave her the gaunt look of a model. After shaking Penelope's hand, she brushed her brown hair back nervously.

"Kathy, would you bring Mrs. McCoffey a chair, please?"

"Certainly."

"Please, don't bother. I'll just look around."

"Fine." Penelope motioned McCoffey to the chairs in front of the fireplace where Big Mike looked out with his inscrutable expression, front paws tucked beneath his chest.

"You don't have a private office?"

"This is as private as it gets in Empty Creek."

McCoffey scowled but sat down. "You've made accusations."

"Speculation, perhaps, not accusations."

"Speculation, then, but far off the mark. Although I have no wish to speak ill of the dead, Peter Adcock's sense of ethics in business was questionable at best. I believe there have been financial misdealings and official malfeasance," McCoffey stated.

For someone who didn't wish to trash the dearly-departed, McCoffey had done a pretty fair job of it. "Serious charges," she said.

"And that nonsense in the newspaper. Love tryst, indeed. That's ridiculous."

Penelope smiled. "Yes, I wondered who the reliable source might be."

"I know all about you. You meddle."

"Investigate."

"You should leave it to the police."

"Tell me about your plans for the Coyotes."

Rose browsed through the store, looking ready to wilt and cry. Penelope and Kathy both saw her slip the ceramic figurine of Mycroft Holmes, the elder and smarter brother of Sherlock and Big Mike's namesake, into her purse. Penelope shook her head slightly as Kathy looked to her for instructions.

McCoffey watched her, too, frowning, but said nothing about his wife's shopping habits. "You were saying. . . ."

"We were talking about your plans for the team."

"That's up to my son. He's in charge. I'm a silent partner."

"He's not very interested in baseball."

"He doesn't have to be. He knows what he has to do."

"And what is that?"

"Run the day-to-day operations, ensure a winning record, and show a profit at the end of the season. I'll do the rest. My attorney is looking into Adcock's dealings with city officials."

"That doesn't sound very silent, and they won't find anything."

"We'll see."

"You bought Adcock's share of the team."

"That was my right under the option terms of our corporate bylaws. Had I died, Adcock would have been entitled to purchase my financial interest in the team. That is not a crime."

"No, it isn't."

"I know what you're thinking."

"Do you?"

"It's not a motive for murder, and I won't have you going around saying it is."

"I haven't," Penelope said. Yet—she added to herself. "Are you in town long?"

"That depends."

"On what?"

"Many things."

"Your son?"

"Partly."

"I like him."

"Is that why you attacked him?"

"Disarmed him. He *was* waving a baseball bat in a very threatening manner."

"If he had taken karate as I wanted, he would have been a black belt by now and that would not have happened."

"Don't be so hard on him. We took him by surprise."

"He should have thrown his computer at you. That's the only thing he knows."

Penelope, having softened her earlier stand on Junior's chosen profession after discovering his lack of interest in noisily repelling alien invasions, felt compelled to defend him. However, if Kendall McCoffey, Sr. declared the sky blue or the earth round, Penelope was prepared to join the Red Sky Association or the Flat Earth Society. "He's well-prepared for the millennium and the new century. Those without technological skills will be left behind. They are already lagging far behind."

Kathy turned her attention away from Rose and looked at Penelope with disbelief. *This* was coming from the woman who refused to own an answering machine?

"Do you play racquetball?" McCoffey asked. His question was uttered as a challenge. I have more hair on my chest than you do.

"No."

"Or tennis?" Mine is bigger than yours.

Since she didn't have one (or hair on her chest), Penelope shook her head. "Why do you ask?"

"We might have played. It's too bad. There is more to life than staring at a computer screen. Exercise and competition sharpen the mind as well as the body. Junior, despite opportunities, never participated in sports as a child. No Little League baseball or Pop Warner football, not even soccer. I was the only father with no one to cheer for."

"I shoot," Penelope said, joining the Mine-Is-Bigger-Than-Yours-Contest with a vengeance. It was an exaggeration, but McCoffey, Sr. didn't know that she hadn't fired a round in competition since leaving the Marine Corps.

"Skeet or trap?"

"Highpower rifle." It sounded ominous even to Penelope, who knew that the sport consisted only of punching holes in targets at ranges of two hundred, three hundred, and six hundred yards.

"I prefer shotguns," McCoffey said, "or handguns."

"Well, now," Penelope said after watching Mr. and Mrs. McCoffey cross the street, "what do you make of that?"

"We'll have to replenish our supply of statuettes if she comes back very often."

"I wonder why she married him. She's a very unhappy woman."

"He's a very unhappy man."

"And intense. He wanted to run me all over a court to prove his superiority."

"He didn't invite you to shoot."

"Highpower rifle isn't his game. He wouldn't have the advantage."

"What about shotguns or pistols?"

"I've never really fired a shotgun and I can't hit a damned thing with a pistol. I'd score higher throwing it at the target."

"What's his son like?"

"You're about to find out," Penelope said, nodding toward the door. "This seems to be our day for McCoffey *Père et Fils.*"

Junior entered the store jauntily, not at all like a computer nerd, except for the paleness of his legs. He might have just left the tennis court after whomping his old man in straight sets. Although his Coyotes baseball cap was on backward the rest of his ensemble was rather dashing with white shorts, white cotton pullover with a Coyote on the breast pocket, white tennis shoes (fashionably sans socks), and wraparound sun glasses with rose colored lenses. He stopped abruptly when he saw Kathy.

"Hi," Penelope said.

"Hi," young McCoffey stammered, his cheeks doing a chameleon imitation as they rushed to match his glasses.

"This is Kathy. You don't have to worry about impressing her though. She's spoken for."

Although disappointed, Junior relaxed visibly.

Penelope straightened the baseball cap. "I've never understood the propensity of the younger generation to wear baseball caps backward. It defeats the purpose of the brim— unless, of course, you're in the Foreign Legion and wish to protect your neck from the desert sun, but they have those little white things that hang down for that. I wonder what they're called. Oh, well. Little white things will have to do for the moment." Her fashion lecture completed, Penelope asked, "Do you play tennis?"

"Hate it. Why?"

"Well, your attire for one thing, and for a second, your father seems rather fond of games involving racquets."

"You talked to him?" Junior's cheeks rushed to the opposite extreme and paled considerably.

"He just left, along with your stepmother."

That bit of news drained the jaunty away and replaced it with deflated. "I didn't know he was coming so soon. Damn."

"Perhaps he won't stay long."

"Ten minutes is more than I can stand."

Despite what appeared to be an excellent all-around deal for the Empty Creek Coyotes, Penelope decided to take another look at the city records. McCoffey Sr. might be an arrogant blowhard, but that didn't necessarily mean he was stupid. If there had been official malfeasance and financial misdealings, they were obscured, artfully hidden in the voluminous papers.

"One hundred and thirty-seven dollars!" Dutch screamed.

"And fifteen cents," Penelope replied calmly. "I should have brought this in earlier, but with everything going on, I quite simply forgot."

"Why didn't you just use our copies? Haven't you ever heard of sharing?"

"By the time Tweedledee and Tweedledum get through

everything, I'd be nearing retirement age. Besides, they'd be all yucky."

"Yucky?"

"You know. Jelly doughnuts."

"I don't care if they spill motor oil on them. I've got a budget to think about."

"Surely, $137 isn't . . ."

"*And* fifteen cents."

" . . . too much to allocate in the pursuit of justice."

"It's just like that helicopter. . . ."

"Don't bring that up again. That was years ago. Besides, no one told you to go out and commandeer the first helicopter that came along."

"Someone had to get you out of trouble."

"The situation was perfectly under control."

"Hah!"

"Hah, yourself. Now, are you going to authorize this expenditure or not?"

Dutch sighed heavily. "Oh, give me the damned receipt. I just hope you and Stormy have taken the Red Cross CPR course." He was convinced one or the other of the Warren girls would be the death of him. But since he was very much in love with one and the other came along as the future sister-in-law, it was a package deal. "You better take a refresher course in first aid, too, just in case there have been new developments."

"Thank you," Penelope said, as he signed the receipt.

Dutch groaned. "All this for nothing."

"In the light of what the new majority owner said. . . ."

"He just wanted a better deal than Adcock actually got.

He's greedy. The next thing you know, he'll probably charge us a license fee just for the privilege of buying a ticket."

"Nothing on the backup disks you made from Adcock's computer?"

"Like you said the other day. Nothing stands out."

"Then why did someone go to all the trouble of attacking Blake in order to erase the computer records in the office, especially when you had backups and there were hard copies of everything?"

"Insurance."

"Possibly. Any reference to a file called Hosanahs?"

"Nope. Did you look it up?"

Penelope nodded. "He must have misspelled hosanna— it's an appeal to God for deliverance or a shout of praise or adoration."

"Well, he probably needs some deliverance about now."

Another game, another loss.

Everyone dealt with the losing streak in their own way.

Lacking sackcloth and ashes, Rats McCoy sat in front of his locker and used a pair of scissors to methodically cut his home uniform into one-inch squares. He would have started on his road uniform if Feathers, tired of waiting, had not marched into the clubhouse and dragged him away before further damage could be done.

On the way home, she even relaxed her prohibition on his formerly rather colorful use of the English language. "Go ahead, say it."

"Really?"

Feathers nodded.

"God-damn-it-all-to-hell-anyway."

"There. Feel better?"

"No," Rats said. He reverted to the word substitution that had provided his nickname. "Rats. Double and triple rats."

At home, Feathers consoled her husband, very methodically reducing him to a whimpering, although very happy, shell of a big tough baseball manager.

Afterwards, Rats lay back on the bed, exhausted, hoping the team started a winning streak. *This* was a superstition he could handle.

Since more than half of the team was under the legal drinking age, they held a players-only meeting in the patio of McDonald's, where they all agreed more intensity and focus were needed.

"Even you, Buddy, concentrate," Earl "Big Rap" Rapp, the team captain said. Big Rap had been a part-time first baseman at Arizona State for four years. Big Rap knew his talents were not quite good enough to make it all the way to the Big Leagues, but baseball was one hell of a good summer job and he wanted to be a winner if this happened to be his last season.

Buddy Peterson was concentrating, although it was on Regina Pryor who waited inside for the meeting to be over.

Reggie had decided to show Buddy the view from Crying Woman Mountain, where she planned to employ a few motivational techniques of her own. Losing affected sixteen-going-on-seventeen-year-old young ladies, too, and she wanted Buddy to be the one who broke the losing streak.

Her mother, having met Anthony Lyme-Regis at Sky Harbor International Airport in Phoenix, was now in his suite at the Lazy Traveler Motel. As a single mother, Nora always set a proper example for her daughter. Tony, as a proper

Englishman, agreed, which explained why he was apologizing profusely for having checked into the Lilac Suite with its gaudy display of erotica for consenting adults and the water bed that had induced a slight case of seasickness in both of them.

Stan Livingstone checked on Blake Robinson's concussion, and she found it very difficult to brood in any meaningful way while being tickled unmercifully in the name of medical science.

"Are you sure they taught this in medical school?" she gasped.

"Absolutely."

Kendall McCoffey, Jr. helped a certain Queen swim three raging rivers, climb a sheer cliff face, and subdue a horde of assorted enemies along the way. It was a good way to keep thoughts of patricide away.

Kendall McCoffey, Sr. smashed a ceramic figurine against the wall of his suite at the Lazy Traveler Motel while his younger wife watched. "I'm not cleaning that up," she said, taking a second replica of the elder Holmes from her purse.

Laney thanked Wally for the wonderful flowers—several times.

Lora Lou and David's reunion consisted of an experiment with living art and a box of fingerpaints and lasted long into the night.

Debbie and Sam Connors had a solitary nightcap after the Double B closed for the night and, with one thing leading to another, very nearly broke the pool table.

And while Big Mike slept on the couch between them, Penelope and Andy watched a videotape that had been anonymously delivered to her doorstep.

CHAPTER
ELEVEN

The Empty Creek Coyotes were going on the road.

For a baseball team that had yet to record a win, the Coyotes received a pretty decent send-off. The youth of Empty Creek were well-represented by a contingent of baseball-inclined boys and girls worshipping their new heroes and still gathering autographs on their souvenir programs. Eddie Stiles, befitting his lofty status as a former major league player, drew the largest crowd, but none of the other players were left out. Penelope was pleased to see that Eddie signed anything offered to him. He even smiled and chatted briefly with each youngster.

Feathers McCoy led the significant other detachment which consisted of herself, the two coaches' wives, Dr. Stanley Livingstone, and Reggie Pryor, who was holding Buddy Peterson's hand very tightly indeed. Perhaps he did kiss better than he pitched, Penelope thought.

The sports department of the *Empty Creek News Journal* hovered around Rats McCoy, getting his final thoughts on the ten-day road trip to Sedona and Wickenburg. Penelope knew that Andy didn't have the budget to send his sports editor on every road trip and had pressed Blake Robinson into service for faxing box scores and important details of each game.

As the official poster lady of the Coyotes, Debbie Locke felt duty-bound to send them off to Red Rock country with all the best wishes for a successful trip. Her significant other was present in his black and white, along with his partner, ostensibly for crowd control if necessary.

The president of the Chamber of Commerce chatted with a tongue-tied Kendall McCoffey, Jr.—the only member of the McCoffey family present—but Penelope didn't find that odd. McCoffey Sr. was probably off somewhere browbeating poor Rose on one tennis court or another.

Tweedledee and Tweedledum were there to observe any suspicious personages who happened along.

Three members of the city council wished their new constituents well, shaking hands all around.

Big Mike took in the scene from the railing on the front porch of the club offices.

As the crowd around Eddie Stiles dwindled, Penelope joined the autograph line. He looked up in surprise after handing a program back to a grinning boy of eleven.

Penelope smiled. "Can I have your autograph, too?"

"Sure," Stiles said, opening the program with a practiced hand to the page where his photograph and write-up were.

But as he scribbled in the program, Penelope thought his demeanor had changed. A frown crossed his face rather than the easy smile and chatter he provided for the kids.

"Thank you," Penelope said, as he returned the program. "Good luck on the trip."

"Thanks. I'll need it," Stiles said. He had been hitless in his last eighteen at bats.

"You'll come out of it," Penelope said.

"I gotta go."

Stiles hesitated, and Penelope thought he was going to say something, but then he just waved and mumbled what she thought was, "See ya."

"Now that's odd," Penelope said to no one in particular as she watched him board the school bus that had been rented from the Empty Creek Unified School District for the season.

"What's odd?" Debbie asked.

"Eddie Stiles. He mumbled and took off as though I had some contagious disease."

"That *is* odd," Debbie said. "The same thing just happened to me. Shane and Jackson Baxter just ran away from me."

"And who are Shane and Jackson Baxter?"

"Neighbor kids. I asked if I could look at their autographs and they took off. Usually they're so friendly."

"Too much excitement probably," Penelope offered, "or they're in that girls-are-icky stage of life. They're probably about the right age."

"Eleven and nine," Debbie said.

"You see. But that doesn't explain Eddie's reaction, unless he thinks I'm icky, too. Oh, well. Andy likes me, I think."

"Don't worry about it," Debbie said, glancing to where Andy now stood in rapt conversation with Erika von Sturm. "I'm sure he's just doing a follow-up interview about weight-lifting milk maids in Bavaria."

"She *is* rather attractive."

"Too muscular. She could pull the team bus if it broke down."

Blake Robinson broke away from the Mad Tickler to announce the bus was leaving in two minutes with or without Buddy Peterson, provoking a chorus of catcalls from his amused—and mostly jealous—teammates. That broke up the tête-à-tête between Andy and Erika and a few others as well. Another five minutes found the bus loaded and pulling out of the parking lot, followed by last shouts of encouragement from their well-wishers.

Watching the bus disappear around a corner on its way to Interstate 17, Penelope felt a strange sense of loss. She had grown accustomed to having a baseball team around, even if it had been more trouble than it was worth in its first week of carrying Empty Creek's banner on the diamond.

Reluctant to depart, the others in the parking lot seemed to be experiencing similar emotions. Penelope approached Junior and asked, "Why aren't you going with them?"

"I have to spend the afternoon with my father." It was obvious the father-son bonding session was not a highlight of the day. "I also have to get everything ready for the next homestand. I'm in charge of Rattlesnake Chili Night and Athletic Sock Night."

"Socks? One size fits all?"

"Yeah. Where did Peter come up with these ideas anyway?"

"Blake did say he was a genius at promotions."

"But I'm the one who has to carry them out now. I don't know what I'm going to do when I get to Sexy Lingerie Night."

"Talk to Laney. She has quite a collection of mail order catalogs. She's too shy to shop in person."

"She didn't seem shy when she was taking my pants down."

"Her adrenaline was on a roll."

"Do you think she'd help? Really?"

"She'd be delighted. Call her."

Having sent Junior back to the office happy—except for the impending visit from Senior—Penelope decided that a talk with Rose McCoffey during the course of the day might be instructive. Then she turned her attention to Tweedledee and Tweedledum. They were flipping coins and matching them. "Best two out of three," Tweedledee said as Penelope joined them.

"What are you doing?"

"Trying to decide where to have lunch."

"Well, before you do that, why don't you decide who left a video tape on my doorstep last night."

"We did."

"You? Why? And you could have left a note."

"We did."

"It must have blown away."

"We thought you might see something we didn't."

"Fifteen minutes of Peter Adcock introducing the team at a city council meeting didn't leave much to see and that's not counting all the rest of that meeting I watched. Where did you get it?"

"Adcock asked for a copy of the tape. A souvenir, I guess. But by the time Alfie got around to duplicating it, Adcock was already dead. Alfie called us and asked what he should do with it."

Alfred Hicks, who videotaped each interminable moment of city council and planning commission hearings, was notoriously slow at responding to requests. Penelope believed that five years of recording the city's political history had seriously damaged both Alfie's brain and his reaction time.

"And you thought of me."

"Well, it was worth a try," Tweedledee said. "Besides, we watched it first."

"You're stuck too?"

"We need a break of some sort."

"That's what Rats says about the Coyotes."

"*They* need lots of breaks."

With the detectives shuffling disconsolately to their car, the crowd had dwindled down to Big Mike stretching restlessly on the railing, Andy stuffing his notebook into a back pocket, and Lora Lou Longstreet standing with arms flung wide, eyes closed, and face raised to the sky.

"What are you doing, Lora Lou?"

"Practicing my new pose. David calls it Wind Goddess."

"You rehearse poses?"

Lora Lou lowered her arms and opened her eyes. "Of course. Being a model is much more than just taking your clothes off. You have to help the artist find expression, vision, interpretation."

"I wondered what you called it."

Lora Lou grinned. "It's better than saying you sit around naked all the time."

"I suppose it is."

"Any progress?"

Penelope provided the brief version—bringing the Chamber president up-to-date, noting McCoffey Sr.'s charges, the futile search through business records—terminating the report with a question. "Have you ever heard of something called Hosanahs?"

Lora Lou shook her head. "Not since *Jesus Christ, Superstar*. What's it mean?"

"What's any of it mean? Haven't the foggiest."

"Well, the horse world awaits. I'll see you guys later."

Penelope turned to Andy. "Come on. I'll buy you lunch and you can tell me all about your infatuation with Erika the Hun."

When Penelope said the magic word, Big Mike headed for the Jeep at a brisk gallop. Andy, having heard a much different magic word, followed at a much slower pace, thinking fast.

Penelope tossed her program into the console and waited.

She wasn't really worried about Erika as a rival. Andy and Erika had little in common and Penelope couldn't see him taking up with a physical fitness instructor. Andy subscribed to Winston Churchill's (or was it George Bernard Shaw's?) theory of exercise—whenever he felt the urge for physical exertion, he would lie down until it went away. In addition, Andy was much too faithful and devoted—traits she admired very much—but she wasn't above making him squirm a little—or even a lot. The Squirm Factor was occasionally good for a relationship.

"Where are we going?" Andy asked.

"In the opposite direction from Erika."

"I can see that, but why? I'm just writing a feature story on her. Besides, I think she's in mourning."

"What?" Penelope exclaimed, hitting the brakes and screeching to a halt. She turned the engine off and twisted in her seat to face Andy. "Would you explain that, please."

"I think she's more affected by Adcock's death than she lets on. She told me how grateful she was to have the chance to work for the team. His death must have come as a big shock, especially since they had gone out several times."

"That's not what she told me. I thought she dated him only once."

"It was off the record. I probably shouldn't have brought it up unless. . . . You don't suspect *her?*"

"There's a missing girlfriend somewhere."

"What about McCoffey's charges? It doesn't have to be related to sex."

"Have you found any evidence in the records to suggest that Adcock was a white collar criminal?"

"No, but we're still looking." Andy had all two of his ace reporters on the case.

"We haven't either. What else did she tell you off the record?"

"That you're a very lucky woman to have me for a boy-friend."

"Hah!"

"And vice versa, of course," Andy added hastily.

Penelope started the Jeep and made a U-turn.

"Now where are we going?"

"I'm going to give you an unexpected—and undeserved, I might add—treat."

The Dynamite Lounge appeared to be benefitting from its advertising campaign. It was crowded with music appreciators of many persuasions—truck drivers, hands from the many Arabian horse ranches that filled the desert environs, several men from the city maintenance department, and four geezers from the retirement community, led by none other than Cackling Ed, at a front row table. Penelope had to admit that it was his kind of place and lessened his danger of receiving a terminal crick in the neck.

Since all the tables were occupied, Penelope took Andy's hand and led him to the bar. "It's all right," she said. "You can look."

"My goodness, I should interview Erika more often."

"Don't get any ideas. Remember, you're not in the Clinton White House."

"What nice music they have here," he said.

There was little risk of Andy endangering *his* neck because the huge mirror that ran the length of the wall behind the bar provided an excellent reflection of the young lady who danced to a tune from *Phantom of the Opera*. His unimpeded view, however, was momentarily restricted as Angelique walked up to take their orders.

"Hi, Penelope, I appreciate your bringing new business."

Angelique had changed her attire. She still wore the peach-colored shirt but instead of matching shorts, she wore a floor length black skirt and black evening gloves that snaked above her elbows. Penelope took mental notes. The visual impact of Angelique was pretty spectacular. And when she removed the top . . . well, somebody better be prepared to call 9–1–1 for Ed and his friends.

"This is Harris Anderson the Third, but call him Andy. He's the editor of our esteemed local newspaper."

"Welcome to The Dynamite Lounge, Andy. It's nice to meet you."

"Oh, no, believe me. The pleasure is mine."

"Well, thank you, Andy, and is this pleasure or business?"

"Both," Penelope replied, "but the business can wait until you're not so busy. What do you recommend?"

The food didn't rival that of the Double B but, of course, most of the patrons were not there for the delicate hint of garlic in the cheeseburgers. Still, it was more than palatable, the music *was* good, and Angelique pampered them with excellent service and a second glass of wine on the house.

A while later, the lunch hour rush had eased. Angelique squirted soda into a glass filled with ice and joined Penelope, Andy, and Mycroft. Angelique leaned over the bar and scratched Mikey behind the ears. "Got time for a dance, big guy?"

Mycroft wilted.

So did Andy. Confronted by the scarcely concealed charms of Angelique, the dancer in the mirror, and Penelope, Andy did the only gentlemanly—and prudent—act possible. He closed his eyes, put fingers to his temples, massaged gently, and announced, "I think I'm getting a headache."

"Would you like two aspirin?" Angelique asked with concern.

"Yes, please."

By the time Angelique returned with the tablets and a glass of water, the music had ended, the stage was momentarily empty, and Andy felt it was safe to take another look at his surroundings. He gulped the aspirin down and said, "Thank you."

"Perhaps you should go home and lie down," Penelope said.

"I'll be fine."

Although smiling inside, Penelope nodded solemnly before turning to Angelique. "Think back to your conversations with

Peter Adcock. Was there any indication that his mysterious girlfriend problems might have been with someone from Germany?"

"Not really." Angelique sipped her soda, a thoughtful expression on her face. "I'm trying to recall, but he was always very careful in referring to her."

"Damn."

"We always spoke in very general terms. I might say, 'A woman likes to be appreciated in little ways. An unexpected card, a single long-stemmed rose, an impetuous gesture.'"

"And what did he say?"

"A lot of it referred to the future. It was as though they had no real past history. 'When we're together, I'll adore her every moment of every day and every night.'"

"He said that specifically? 'I'll adore her. . . . '"

"Yes. I'm sure of it."

"Did he ever mention 'Hosanahs?'"

"Like from *Jesus Christ Superstar?*"

"Exactly. It's Hebrew for 'Save us' and it's used as an exclamation of adoration. He misspelled it, but I don't know what else it could mean."

Angelique shook her head.

"Do you think he met her just recently?"

Angelique furrowed her brow. "I have no clear sense of that, but I did get the impression that she might have been married."

"What gave you that idea?"

"Oh, nothing specific, really. It was just a feeling I had. You know how that is?"

"Yes, I do, and I have a feeling right now that I could use a couple of those aspirin."

Penelope dropped Andy off at his car. "I hope your headache goes away," she said, leaning over for a kiss.

"Oh, I'm a lot better. How's yours?"

"That was just preventative medicine. If something doesn't make sense soon, though, I'm going to need more than aspirin."

"How about I bring Dr. Andy's Special Stress Reliever this evening?"

"And what might that be?"

"I'm not sure yet. I'll have to spend the afternoon inventing it."

Penelope laughed. "I can hardly wait. See you tonight." She waved as she pulled out of the parking lot and headed for the Lazy Traveler Motel. It was time to have a word with Rose McCoffey, the new married woman in town.

Penelope and Big Mike were familiar with the labyrinthine layout of the Lazy Traveler Motel complex and snaked their way from the parking lot, past multiple entrances to the coffee shop, to the house phones by the Olympic-sized swimming pool. Penelope was about to pick up the phone and ask for the McCoffey's room when she saw her quarry poolside with the summer lifeguard applying sunscreen to her back.

"Well, well, well, Mikey. Would you look at that. It seems a shame to interrupt." Penelope was prepared to retreat into the background and observe for a time, but Mycroft blew their cover immediately.

It wasn't his fault. After all, he was accustomed to a little pool time in the company of one attractive young lady or another. As a result, he ambled over to the reclining lounge chair, announced his presence with a healthy meow or two, and waited for his due.

"I know you," Rose McCoffey said, angling an arm down to scratch Mycroft, but she couldn't quite reach him. "Be a dear, Tommy, and fasten my strap."

There was nothing to be done but follow Big Mike. "Hello, Rose," she said.

"It's Penelope, isn't it?" Strap firmly secured now, Rose sat up. "Would you like a drink?"

"No thanks."

"Would you get another gin and tonic for me, please, Tommy?"

"I'll put the order in right away."

"Thank you."

Penelope watched the lifeguard walk away. He was a hunk, and Penelope couldn't help but wonder what other services he provided in addition to applying sunscreen and fetching libations.

"Oh, I'm not sleeping with him," Rose said, "although it might be nice, but I've found that older lovers are better. What they've lost in endurance, they make up for in experience. Don't you think?"

Penelope wasn't about to share her experiences with older lovers. There had been only one and their time together had been very special. "I wouldn't know."

"We're getting off on the wrong foot. Please, I didn't mean anything by it. It was just an observation."

"Why are you acting like some floozy?"

"It gets Kendall's attention."

"Is that why you shoplift—to get his attention?"

"I'll pay for them. I always do."

"The money isn't important. You haven't answered my question."

The lifeguard returned with a tray. "Here you are, Mrs. McCoffey. Gin and tonic with two chunks of lime, just the way you like it."

"Thanks, Tommy, you're a sweetie." She signed the check with a room number and added a generous tip.

"Thank *you*. I'll be right over there if you need anything else."

Rose sipped her drink and again watched the lifeguard walk away. "Nice buns," she said.

"You're doing it again. You have *my* attention."

"Sorry," Rose said. "Sometimes I forget." She smiled at Penelope over the rim of the lipstick-smudged glass. "I'm Daddy's little girl and when I'm naughty, he pays attention to me. When I'm good, all he does is work. But if I'm bad, he makes me stand in the corner until I apologize."

Penelope watched Big Mike scoot under the chaise longue into the cool of the shadow cast by Rose's slender body. He peered out as though to say, Come on down. Penelope was tempted. She thought she had found two candidates for counseling, and not the kind of therapy offered at The Dynamite Lounge either.

"Did Peter Adcock ever make advances to you?"

"Do I wear a skirt?"

Except for one specific woman, Peter Adcock's record in that area was near perfect.

"Did you respond?"

"Of course not," Rose said indignantly. "He was a child and not mature enough to be taken seriously. And he was far too old to get Kendall's attention. My husband only responds to the threat of young and virile men."

"Like baseball players?"

"Exactly like baseball players," Rose said. "I'm looking forward to getting closer to the team."

"Thank you," Penelope said. "We'll have a chance to talk again soon. Come on, Mikey."

"Don't you want to know what happens when I'm really bad?" Rose called after her.

"I don't think so."

Rose laughed. She was still laughing when Penelope and Big Mike rounded the corner of the coffee shop.

CHAPTER TWELVE

With her own rather extensive record of exotic activities, Penelope never faulted consenting adults for anything that took place in the privacy of their homes so long as no one was hurt, they didn't frighten small children or animals, and were kind to their parents and neighbors.

But while Rose McCoffey was a strange piece of work, Penelope could not help but feel a degree of pity mixed with her anger. Imagine having to use petty theft and flirtations to attract your husband's attention and affections. It said little for the man. But anyone who put up with having to use such ploys was a willing partner to the humiliation. Rose McCoffey should receive the Stupid Woman of the Year Award for enduring even two minutes of such treatment.

Still, the questions remained. Had Rose teased Peter Adcock, using his interest in her to gain the attention of her husband? Had a flirtation turned into a deadly jealous rage? From what little Penelope had seen of Rose McCoffey, the answer was uncertain.

Kendall McCoffey's own personality had to be inserted into the equation as well. Was he a willing partner to the peculiar game they played? Did he react only to a potential youthful lover or to her shoplifting? Would he be driven to murder by the hint of an affair between his wife and his business partner? He was certainly competitive enough, but. . . .

To be fair, Rose was not the person who had lied about dating Adcock only once, nor was she the only wife in town. What about Feathers? She was certainly attractive enough to entice Adcock and she admitted his interest in her. If Rats discovered a secret affair between Feathers and Adcock, would he kill? A baseball bat might be *his* weapon of choice, but why go to the bother of stealing Debbie's bat when he had a clubhouse full of bats?

From what Penelope had learned of him, Adcock went after the beautiful and unattainable. And, as far as that went, the other women he had approached were just as good as married to their significant others. But Penelope knew Lora Lou, Samantha, Debbie, and Nora all too well—*and* their significant others. The possibility of a murderer among them was too grotesque to contemplate.

Which left Erika von Sturm caught in an apparent lie. Why? Why didn't she just admit she had dated Peter Adcock twice, three times, four. It didn't work out. Period. End of story. So why did Erika lie?

And that was just the search for the missing girlfriend, which didn't take into account why Adcock had Lora Lou's business card in his hand at the time of death, an attack on Blake Robinson, a computer hard disk void of information, Hosanahs (whatever that was), charges of underhanded financial dealings, possibly corrupt politicos, the mysterious disappearing and reappearing murder weapon, and tiny little fingerprints on same.

Instead of narrowing the investigation, Penelope felt she was back at the beginning, a marker on the giant Monopoly Board of Empty Creek unable to pass Go and stuck without her Get Out of Jail Free card.

Penelope rolled the metaphorical dice and came up snake eyes. It would get her out of jail, but not past Go. Having been driving aimlessly for fifteen minutes, she decided to add purpose to life and existence. With that determination firmly made, however, she had no idea of how to accomplish it. She desperately wanted to talk with Junior about his father and stepmother, if a woman only five years his senior could actually be called that, but he was spending the afternoon with his father at the club's offices and she had no desire to talk with Senior again—yet.

"Well, Mikey, there's no reason we should be the only frustrated people in town. Let's spread it around some."

The Robbery-Homicide Bureau was empty. So Penelope lingered only long enough to call Junior. The extensions must have gotten confused because he answered by saying, "Ticket Office."

"Three one-way tickets to adventure, please."

"I beg your pardon?"

"Three tickets to Adventure," Penelope repeated. "It's the title of a Gerald Durrell book in which he's on an expedition to a place called Adventure and he gets to go to the ferry boat office and ask for three tickets to Adventure, although I believe the British title was *Three Singles to Adventure*."

"I have three tickets on the first base side," Junior offered hopefully.

"Good God, Junior, this is Penelope. Where is your sense of humor? You should have replied, 'Yes, ma'am, first- or second-class?' That's what the clerk said to Durrell. But 'sir,' not 'ma'am.'"

"I don't get it."

"Oh, never mind. I'd like to buy you a drink after work. That's easy enough to understand, isn't it?"

"Oh, yes, ma'am. Where?"

Penelope briefly considered taking Junior on a true adventure, but decided he wasn't quite ready for The Dynamite Lounge. "The Double B, and come alone. Is that okay?"

"Absolutely. They'll be waiting for you at Will Call."

Obviously, Senior was in the same office. The kid wasn't such a dunce after all, and she couldn't really fault him for not having read Gerald Durrell. Not many people did anymore, probably, but they should.

"See you later, then." Penelope replaced the telephone and sat at Tweedledee's desk, remembering a disastrous adventure of her own having to do with an excess of Kumquat Liqueur, a specialty of the Greek island of Corfu where she had gone on a pilgrimage because of *My Family and Other Animals* and *Birds, Beasts and Relatives*. They were accounts of Gerry Durrell's childhood and his zany family—including his elder brother Lawrence—on Corfu before World War II. Penelope often thought it was too bad the Durrell family hadn't come to live in Empty Creek. They would have fit right in with all the other daft eccentrics. Her sojourn on the placid Greek isle had been idyllic before she made the acquaintance of Demon Kumquat Liqueur, a lethal beverage when taken in quantities, which Penelope now believed to be two sniffs—no more—of the open bottle. She hadn't looked a kumquat in the eye since.

"Come on, Mikey. Let's go see Dutch."

Big Mike opened one eye and looked up quizzically. He had taken up residence on Tweedledum's desk, having arranged the various papers to his liking. When he closed his eye again, Penelope took that to mean, Pick me up on your way out. She shrugged. Perhaps Mikey was practicing detection via osmosis. It couldn't hurt, and he certainly couldn't get into any trouble as long as Tweedledee and Tweedledum were out looking for Peter Adcock's murderer. Penelope even hoped they were having more luck than she and Mikey were.

Dutch's office, while not as much of a shrine to his beloved as their living room, was still filled with evidence of Stormy's film career. When Penelope entered, he was staring at the poster from *Space Vampires,* an early movie in which Stormy had played an astronaut who was always getting her space suit shredded by giant flying harpies with a striking resemblance to Newt Gingrich in winged drag.

"I assume your fascination with Astronaut Prunella Masterson means you're stumped, too."

"I am never stumped," Dutch said, swinging his feet across the desk to provide a view of the inestimable Storm Williams as Wild Liz in *Queen of the Pirates.* "I am, now and then, baffled, sometimes confounded, often puzzled, even on very rare occasions stymied, but I am never stumped."

"So how are we going to find Adcock's killer?"

"Beats the hell out of me."

"I know," Penelope said, "I've been driving around. . . ." She slapped her forehead with disgust.

"What's wrong?"

"*I* should get the Stupid Woman of the Year Award."

"All right," Dutch said, "I'll nominate you."

"How did Peter Adcock get to Coyote Stadium that night?"

"He walked. No one saw him. We've canvassed the entire neighborhood from his apartment complex to the stadium."

"Where was his car?"

"In the apartment parking lot under a tarp."

"Where is it now?"

"The impound lot out back."

"Did you go over it?"

"No one's nominating me for Stupid Police Chief of the Year. Of course, we went over it. Nothing."

"Thoroughly?"

"Searched it. Dusted for prints. Mostly his. None that might belong to a woman or a child. The rest were smudged. It was a quart low on oil."

"Take it apart."

"Why?"

"Something's missing. Tweedledee and Tweedledum didn't find anything at Adcock's apartment in town, nothing at his place in Phoenix, nothing at the team office. If McCoffey is right and there was something underhanded in Adcock's business dealings, there's got to be a trail somewhere. Even criminals write things down. And. . . ."

"I'm waiting."

"Cars are important to men."

"Not to me."

"You drive that dumb old truck because you like it. Adcock was arrogant enough to see his car as an extension of his personality. He probably loved his car. You said it was under a tarp. What is it, anyway?"

"Jaguar XKE. A classic."

"You see, the ultimate phallic symbol, if I remember my cars correctly. What do we have to lose?"

Thus, when the fur hit the fan, Penelope and Dutch were in the impound lot watching Terry Travis, the in-house police mechanic, drag the protective covering off a British Racing Green Jaguar XKE. "I don't know, boss," T.T. said. "What if I can't get it back together again?"

"Then, you're going to have a big pile of classic car parts cluttering up the place."

"How long will it take, T.T.?" Penelope asked.

"I don't rightly know. Generally, I'm trying to put 'em together again, not strip 'em down."

During Penelope's absence, Big Mike had migrated from the top of the desk to Tweedledum's chair to the floor beneath the desk. There, in the shadows, he kneaded the threadbare carpet to his satisfaction, turned around three or four times, and settled down for a good nap. He was snoozing quite soundly, minding his own business, when the two detectives entered their office cubicle and plopped down in their respective chairs. "Man, it's hot out there," Tweedledee said.

"Crime can come to me for the rest of the day," Tweedledum said, leaning back in his chair and stretching his feet out.

Mycroft had awakened at their entrance, twitched an ear, and feeling pretty benevolent toward the world just then, swished his tail back and forth to announce his presence.

"Snake!" Tweedledum screamed as he leaped out of his chair and stomped right on the tail that had touched his ankle.

Big Mike squalled loudly at the sneak attack and responded in kind, slashing his claws across Tweedledum's leg, and then headed for the high ground of the window sill just in case there *was* a snake down there somewhere.

"He got me," Tweedledum hollered, dancing around on one leg and holding the fleshy part of his calf on the other. "I'm bit. Oh, God, I'm bit."

By this time, Tweedledee was on top of his desk, drawing his service weapon, a 9mm Beretta.

"Get the snakebite kit!" Tweedledum screamed as he hopped out of range of a second strike.

Mycroft arched his back and hissed angrily, adding to the general pandemonium as police officers rushed down the hall to the Robbery-Homicide Bureau.

"Put that thing away!" the Watch Commander ordered from a safe position.

"Get a rake," someone else cried.

"It's a big one," Tweedledum shouted. "Look at my pants."

"How am I gonna get out of here?" Tweedledee asked plaintively. He was now on his hands and knees on the desk, peering warily underneath, his pistol at the ready.

"It's Mycroft," Sheila Tyler said disgustedly. "What did you do to him?"

Big Mike explained, emitting another horrendous, blood-chilling screech.

"Poor kitty," Sheila said. "You brutes."

Immediately upon reentering the police station proper, Penelope heard the ominous words "Poor kitty," recognizing Sheila's voice. She had been working the desk when Penelope and Mycroft had arrived.

"Now what?" Dutch asked.

"I think Tweedledee and Tweedledum are back."

Still highly offended at the affront to his dignity, Big Mike was not ready to forgive and forget, let bygones be bygones, or turn the other tail. There was nothing in the Good Book that said he had to demonstrate Christian charity to a bubblehead who didn't know the difference between a nice cuddly cat and a poisonous serpent. Indeed, had there been a fruit from the Tree of Knowledge handy, Big Mike might have chucked it at Tweedledum. Lacking that ammunition, Mycroft screeched, hissed, and bared quite formidable fangs.

"Just clear the office," Penelope said, taking charge. "Give him a chance to calm down."

"You sure there's no rattlesnake down there?" Tweedledee asked, holstering his pistol.

"How is a snake going to infiltrate the Empty Creek Police Department in broad daylight? Now get down from there."

Crisis over, police officers went back to their duties, chuckling, and already planning ways to ensure that the Great Snake Episode lived for all time. By the time the damage to Tweedledum's leg had been repaired and bandaged, the first rubber rattlesnake had already been placed in his locker.

Big Mike, left victorious on the field of battle once again, took a bath.

Junior was at a Double B table, playing with a laptop when Penelope and a clean and calm Mikey arrived. Big Mike went directly to his usual stool at the bar and waited for Pete the Bartender to bring him a shot of nonalcoholic beer. Teaching cops proper etiquette was thirsty work.

"Do you carry a computer everywhere?" Penelope asked as she pulled out a chair and sat down.

"It drives my father crazy."

"Is it a way to get his attention?"

"Good Lord, no. The less I see of him, the better."

"Where have you been, Penelope?" Debbie asked. "It's not like you to stay away so long."

"The Dynamite Lounge."

"You, too? That joint is cutting into our business."

"It's a fad, although a very nice place. The music is excellent."

"What's The Dynamite Lounge?" Junior asked.

"You're too young. Did you introduce yourself to Debbie?"

"Of course. She's the Coyote Poster Person."

"He did not," Debbie said. "He stammered and blushed. I thought he was going to crawl under the table. He typed his order on the computer screen."

"He's shy. Junior, this is Debbie."

Junior managed to meet Debbie's eyes briefly before turning to the keyboard and typing rapidly.

Debbie looked over his shoulder. "He says it's nice to meet me. Well, it's nice to meet you, too."

Again, Junior's fingers flew over the keyboard.

"Yes, I am the most beautiful woman you've ever met," Debbie said. "I'll tell my boyfriend you said so."

"Do you think you could type my order in there?" Penelope asked.

"Oh, never mind," Debbie said. "I know what you want." She put her tray down, swiveled the laptop around, and typed for a moment. "I'll be right back," Debbie said, retrieving her tray.

"What did she write?" Penelope asked.

"'Relax. You're cute and adorable.'"

"Well, you are rather cute, although I'm not sure adorable is the correct term. I'll think about it."

"How come everyone I meet is already involved with someone?"

"Bad timing. Debbie's right. Relax. You'll meet someone."

"I'm a failure. Just like my father says."

"Well, I guess I know how you spent your afternoon."

"I wish I could go there," Junior said wistfully.

"Where?"

"To Adventure. I wouldn't care if it *was* second class. Where is it, anyway?"

"British Guyana, I think. I don't know what it's called today. It's hard to keep up with all the new countries."

"Well, it sounds like more fun than Rattlesnake Chili Night."

After the episode at the police station, Penelope didn't care to discuss snakes again in the foreseeable future. "What about Sexy Lingerie Night?"

"That might be okay."

"You see, there is life after computers. Tell me about Rose."

"'Rose is a rose is a rose is a rose.'"

There was hope for Junior, Penelope—who dearly loved

a good game of literary quotations—thought. He even had Gertrude Stein correct. Penelope thought for a moment and then recited:

"'Gather therefore the Rose, whilst yet is prime,
For soon comes age, that will her pride deflower:
Gather the Rose of love, whilst yet is time.' Who's that?" Penelope asked.

"I don't know," Junior replied.

"Spenser. *The Faerie Queene*. Your turn."

"'What's in a name? That which we call a rose
By any other name would smell as sweet.'"

"Too easy. Try this one." Penelope closed her eyes, wanting to remember the exact words.

"'Gather ye rosebuds while ye may,
Old Time is still a-flying,
And this same flower that smiles today
Tomorrow will be dying.'"

"Herrick," Junior said. "'To the Virgins to Make Much of Time.'"

"Very good," Penelope exclaimed, clapping her hands. "I'm impressed."

Junior smiled boyishly, pleased at the compliment. "I like poetry," he said.

"We'll just have to find someone for you who likes to sit around by candlelight listening to poetry."

"Yes, please. When?"

"I'm working on it. But you haven't told me about Rose."

"I've said it all. Rose is Rose."

"And what exactly does that mean?"

"She's just there. A decoration for my father's arm. He's very possessive."

"And domineering?"

Junior nodded.

"If you truly don't like baseball, why don't you quit, follow your dream? Go to Adventure."

"I can't. I'm afraid."

The absence of an evening at Coyote Stadium was going to take some adjustment. Penelope had fallen into the baseball habit easily. Having grown used to a diet of Coyote Dogs, peanuts, popcorn, and beer, there were other adjustments necessary as well, and probably none too soon, Penelope thought as she looked into the mirror, estimating the soft swell of her belly as two pounds heavy. "Nothing but salads while they're on the road," she announced to Mikey. "And you're cutting back on the snacks, too."

Big Mike recognized the tone of voice and reacted in his usual manner—he ignored her. Two could play that game—whatever it was.

But Chardonnay and the bunny rabbits didn't need to go on a diet as well. Penelope loaded up on peppermint candies, lettuce, and carrots and headed off to pass out the largesse, wondering what headache cure Andy would have invented by the time he arrived.

On the way back up the incline, she remembered the program left in the Jeep. Taking a look at it might give her another headache, what with all the confusing aspects of the case, but Andy might as well have something to cure.

Penelope took the program from the console and leafed through it to take a look at her first baseball autograph. She had quite a collection of autographed first editions by authors who had passed through Mycroft & Company on publicity tours, but the thought of collecting autographs from baseball players had been a spur of the moment thing.

She found Eddie Stiles' photograph. Beneath it, he had written:

Someone is trying to get me. I need help.

Penelope looked at her watch. It was too late to catch Eddie before he left for the ballpark, but she went into the house and quickly called information for the number of the motel in Sedona where the Coyotes were staying. When the desk answered, Penelope left a message for Eddie, telling him to call when he got in, whatever the hour.

Dr. Andy's headache remedy was, unfortunately, put on hold while waiting for Eddie Stiles to call. Although disappointed, Andy gallantly suggested a game or two of Scrabble after dinner to while away the time.

She had just played Q-U-I-X-O-T-I-C on a triple word score for 128 points and a total score of 471 when the telephone finally rang. Penelope jumped for it. "Eddie?"

"Is that you, Miss Warren?"

"Call me Penelope," she said automatically. "What's wrong? Why didn't you talk to me this morning?"

"Someone might have been listening. I couldn't."

"Is anyone listening now?"

"My roommate went out for hamburgers."

"Then, tell me."

"Someone put a bottle of vodka in my locker. I found it after the game when I was getting my stuff together for the trip."

"Why?"

"It's obvious. My contract states that I can't drink or use

drugs. I have to take a drug test every week and they can test me at random anytime they want."

"Why plant a bottle then? As long as you don't drink, you're fine. There's nothing to say you can't have an unopened bottle of vodka, or anything else for that matter."

"It looks bad. Someone could get the wrong idea."

"That's true, but it's probably just a bad practical joke."

"I could handle that," Eddie said, "but . . . I was tempted. I wanted a drink so bad. . . ."

"All right," Penelope said. "Don't worry. I'll drive up in the morning and see what we can do about it." Hoping to hear a little good news that would cheer him up, Penelope asked, "How did you do tonight?"

"We lost."

Bad question, Penelope thought, but tried one more time. "How about you?"

"Oh for four," Eddie replied. "Oh for the season. Oh for my life."

CHAPTER
THIRTEEN

Penelope did not share the common Empty Creek prejudice against Sedona and the mystical qualities centered around its hallowed ground in Indian legends, the powerful lure of vortexes and their inexplicable energy, the spirituality of encountering the vision of sculpted red rocks, shaped through the millennia by the erosion of winds and rains.

At mid-century, scarcely five hundred people lived in Sedona and along Oak Creek Canyon. Now, approaching another century, another millennium, the population had burgeoned with those who chose to retire in the calm and peaceful region, New Age seekers of harmony, snowbirds who wanted refuge from the winters of their native states, artists who found their inspiration in the magnificent monuments of nature, and those who wanted nothing more than a retreat where they could shelter against the woes and violence of urban America.

Shortly after turning off the interstate, the first majestic red butte loomed, and Penelope slowly pulled the Jeep to a halt. Followed by Mycroft, who also sensed the solemnity of the moment, she walked into the desert, not far, and entered another realm. Tranquility settled over her even as she reluctantly resisted a siren's call to worship. Sitting cross-legged on the ground with Mycroft beside her, she stared at the distant red mountain and felt its enchantment, the promise to heal old wounds and protection from new heartaches. Perhaps it was what Rats McCoy sought that morning in the stadium and wanted to share with his protégé—to be at one with the experience of the moment.

The temptation to make a pilgrimage through shimmering heat waves to the foot of that sandstone butte was difficult to defy. It seemed a violation of some ancient and divine rite. It beckoned, but reality intruded when a huge recreational vehicle lumbered past on the highway behind. The spell was broken.

Penelope expected difficulty checking Big Mike into the motel and was prepared to argue vehemently for his rights, but apparently cats, those most spiritual of creatures, were welcome in Sedona. The desk clerk—a young woman barely out of high school, laden with beads and turquoise Indian jewelry and looking like a refugee from the sixties and Haight Ashbury—only smiled languidly and inquired after his health. Penelope refrained from giving her a peace sign after signing the register.

Penelope unloaded the Jeep while Big Mike explored their room. Seasoned traveler that he was, little bothered him, but he did like to find the new toys and hidey holes, stick his nose under the bed, and check behind the shower curtain to make sure they had not checked into the Bates Motel by mistake. By the time Penelope had him comfortably equipped with necessities—dishes filled with water and liver crunchies and a litter box on the small patio—and turned to her own unpacking, Big Mike was stretched out in her suitcase. If this was an elaborate ploy to get rid of him, he was having none of it.

Penelope sighed and unpacked around him. At least it was easier than packing with him in the suitcase as she had done that morning. Then, she picked up the telephone and asked for Eddie's room. "I'm going to the pool before lunch," she said. "Why don't you stop by?"

Penelope changed into her swimsuit, grabbed a towel and a paperback, and went through the patio door, leaving it open a crack for Big Mike in case he wanted to join her. It wasn't necessary, however, as he hopped out of the now-empty suitcase and trundled right after her.

Chaise longue adjusted, sun screen applied to legs and shoulders, wide-brimmed hat shading her face, Penelope opened her book—she had felt nostalgic earlier and chose several John D. MacDonald old favorites for the trip, perhaps as a result of having played Q-U-I-X-O-T-I-C the night before. Whatever the reason, Travis McGee, that wonderful knight-errant created by MacDonald, seemed just the character to spend a few hours with. She opened *The Deep Blue Good-By* and read: "It was to have been a quiet evening at home."

She closed the well-worn paperback and reflected on the prophetic nature of the sentence. She *had* planned a quiet evening at home with Andy, and here she was in Sedona waiting for a troubled, recovering addict and alcoholic baseball player to join her.

Why? she asked herself.

Because that's what you do on occasion, she answered. You save crippled birds, and shoo mice out into the garage rather than trap them, and avoid stepping on ants, and feed bunnies in the gathering dusk, and cry in sad movies, and play the matchmaker, and can't stand to see someone in despair.

That's why.

Oh.

A shadow loomed over her and she opened her eyes to find Eddie Stiles dressed in shorts and a Coyote T-shirt. "Hi, Miss Warren."

"I told you to call me Penelope. I meant it."

"Sorry."

Penelope softened her abrupt order with a smile.

Eddie pulled a chair over and sat down, squinting in the bright sunlight. "Thanks for coming."

"Why?" Penelope asked. It seemed as good a question as any to start with.

"I don't know."

"Think back. All the way to when you reported to the Coyotes for spring training. Further than that if necessary. Did anyone give you any indication whatsoever that they didn't like you, that they wanted you to fail?"

"The team's been great to me. Rats and the coaches. Everyone, really."

"Peter Adcock?"

"He's the one who signed me. Said I was going to be the big box office draw for the Coyotes. That was before I fell apart at the plate. He'd probably regret signing me now."

"How about Kendall McCoffey, Sr?"

"I only met him a couple of times during the spring. Adcock ran things. McCoffey was just there, you know."

"And his wife? Rose?"

"She's a cannibal." Too late, he looked around hastily to see if anyone was listening.

"Don't worry. We're alone and I'm not going to say anything. Why did you call her that?"

"I've seen the look before. When you're a star, you learn to recognize it. She looks at you like she's going to eat you alive and spit you out in little pieces. I hadn't seen it for a long time, but I remembered it."

"I would have thought groupies to be more adoring."

"Most are. But every once in a while. . . ."

"Did she make any advances to you?"

"I didn't give her a chance."

"Would she hold that against you?"

Eddie shrugged. "Why?"

"Have you seen her since McCoffey took over the team?"

"No."

"Maybe it is just a cruel practical joke, then."

"There is one guy. He rode me pretty hard during a couple of exhibition games. Kept calling me a junkie. He stopped during our home stand, but picked it up again last night."

"You know him?"

"Yeah. He owns the Red Rocks."

Penelope left Big Mike napping on the bed and went to the coffee shop. The manager and the general manager were in a booth near the back and when Blake saw Penelope, she waved and motioned her to join them.

"What are you doing here?" Blake asked.

"It's the game," Rats said. "Gets to you after awhile, even

when you're losing. There's always tomorrow. Which is today, or tonight. We're gonna get them tonight for sure."

Penelope slid into the booth beside Rats.

"Something's happened," Blake said.

Penelope nodded. "I'm afraid so." She related the story of the vodka bottle in Eddie's locker.

"God damn it," Rats said angrily. "Who's messing with my kids?"

Neither Penelope nor Blake cared to take that moment to remind him of his language.

"And why didn't he come to me?"

"He was confused and he didn't want to look like he was a cry baby," Penelope said. "He thought he could handle it and then impulsively cried out for help when he signed my program."

"Where is he? I better go talk with him."

Penelope smiled. "Waiting right outside." She waved and a moment later, Eddie sat down next to Blake.

"Eddie, you should have come to me."

"Sorry, skipper, but I didn't want to blame it on one of the guys."

"I don't see this as a practical joke. I mean, setting your pants on fire or putting itching powder in your underwear, that's a practical joke. This is mean and everyone on the team likes you. They're pulling for you."

"Even when I struck out with the bases loaded last night?"

"That happens. We've all struck out with the bases loaded. It's not like you're dogging it. You're hustling all the way. They know that and they look up to you."

"Well," Penelope said, "if no one on the team put the vodka bottle in his locker, who did?"

"I don't know," Rats said, "but we're closing the clubhouse to everyone. No outsiders. That's it."

"If it was an inside job, you'll scare them off," Penelope pointed out, "and if it wasn't, we'll never catch them."

"You have a plan?"

"I do." Penelope grinned wickedly.

"You have a devious mind," Rats said after listening to her proposal. "I like that in a woman."

It actually wasn't all that devious. Accompanied by Blake Robinson, Penelope went shopping and bought a small video recorder. All it took was a little shopping around, a check drawn on the Empty Creek Coyotes bank account, and a few minutes alone in the visiting team's clubhouse to find a good place to conceal it. Of course, watching several hours of Eddie's locker, even with fast forward, would be slightly less fun than watching paint dry, but better than an Empty Creek City Council meeting.

With that done, Penelope, Blake, and Big Mike went in search of Erika von Sturm. There was the matter of just how many dates she'd had with Peter Adcock.

Had they bothered to remember Erika's chosen profession, they might have gone directly to the small gym the motel provided for its more health conscious guests. But they didn't, so they trekked from Erika's room to the pool to the gift shop and back to the coffee shop before the light bulb finally flashed. And there she was, a towel draped around her neck and perspiration dripping down her face, hunched over the handlebars of a stationary bicycle, pedaling furiously.

"I just left Zurich," Erika announced.

Well, it was bound to happen, Penelope thought. The stress and tension of the continuing situation was enough to set someone's marbles to rattling aimlessly. "We can get you help," Penelope said.

"Unnecessary," she puffed. "Bicycling is an individual sport."

"No, really," Blake said, "our medical plan is very good."

"Vaht are you talking about?"

Penelope shot Blake her very best we'd-better-humor-her look.

Blake nodded and asked, "How long have you been in Zurich?"

"Not long. I am zipping straight through. I must be in Brindisi by the end of June."

"Why are you going to Brindisi?"

"Because then I can cross over to Naples and go to Rome from there. When I get to Milano, I will turn left and ride along the Riviera. It will be nice that time of year. And then on to Spain."

Penelope searched surreptitiously for a first aid kit, although she doubted it would contain anything for the onset of mental illness. At least they could take Erika's temperature. "But you'll miss the running of the bulls in Pamplona," she said.

"That is not in my plan."

"Plan?" Penelope repeated, thinking it was high time someone had a plan, even if it were slightly askew.

"Yes," Erika said. "I started in Hamburg and planned my route very carefully. It is not goot to hop on a bicycle and just start riding. Who knows where you will end up."

"Have you been spending a lot of time in the sun?" Penelope asked. "That's not good for you."

"I always ride in the shade. Like now."

"Goot," Penelope said. "I mean, good."

Erika raised up and rode no hands, slowing her pace, but still pedaling and watching the odometer creep toward the fifty mile road marker. She ended her journey precisely when the odometer showed 50.0. "There. I'm glad to be away from Zurich. The Swiss countryside is very beautiful."

"Yes," Blake said, "I'm sure it is." She turned to Penelope and said, "Perhaps I should call Stanley."

"Are you not feeling vell?" Erika asked. "Do you have a temperature? I have aspirin in my room. You must lie down and we will nurse you back to health."

"I'm not sick," Blake said. "You are."

"Me?" Erika thumped her chest. "I am, how you say it, healthy as a camel."

"Ox," Penelope said. "Healthy as an ox."

"Yes, that too."

"But what was all that about Zurich and Rome and Brindisi?" Blake asked. "Wherever that is."

"It is at the heel of Italy. On the Adriatic. A very nice little town."

"Oh."

"Just to exercise is boring," Erika continued. "So, when I ride, I travel. Much better than watching television, don't you think?"

"Indeed, it is," Penelope agreed cutting off her search for the First Aid kit, thinking it might be nice to ride a bicycle across Africa, the handlebars equipped with a basket for Big Mike. But the thought of trying to race a hungry lioness over the veldt might be a losing proposition. Besides, it might be a real bitch trying to get a bicycle to the top of Mt. Kilimanjaro and Mycroft, although he had never seen snow, probably wouldn't like it. Oh, well, some ideas were better than others. That was the way with ideas. And plans. They had a perversity all their own, always taking off on some tangent that had nothing to do with the matter at hand. "How many times did you actually go out with Peter Adcock?" Penelope asked.

"I told you. Vunce only."

"I've heard otherwise."

"Who told you this otherwise? They are lying."

In response to the flash of panic in Erika's eyes, Penelope arched an eyebrow. "It's better to tell the truth. I can't help if you don't."

Erika looked at Blake who nodded. "Three," she said finally.

"Are you sure this time?"

"Four."

"Four, not five or six?"

"Six only. I swear it."

"Why did you lie the first time?"

"I am in a strange country. I am afraid of what the police will think. I am afraid of what the Cat Lady will think."

"Did you sleep with him?"

"What kind of question is that?"

"Simple," Penelope said, "and direct. Did you sleep with him?"

Erika's face disappeared into the towel. When it reemerged, tears welled in its eyes. "Yes. It was awful."

"I'm sorry," Penelope said. "Not everyone is a good lover."

"That's not it," Erika cried. "He was abusive. He hit me."

As a courtesy, officials of the visiting team were accorded seats adjacent to the official box of the Red Rocks. This meant that Penelope, Blake, and Big Mike were seated all too close to the loud-mouthed owner, Emerson Heath, who smirked at Penelope and asked, "Come to pay up, honey?"

"Actually, no," Penelope responded. "I just wanted to make sure you weren't spending my hundred dollars."

When Eddie Stiles stepped into the cage for batting practice, Heath shouted, "Hey, Junkie! Want a fix?"

Penelope might have taken a more direct route to the concession stand, but it wouldn't have been quite as much fun. She slipped under the railing dividing the boxes and when Heath made no move to stand and allow her to pass, she stomped on his foot pretty hard.

"God damn, honey, watch where you're going."

"I am so sorry," Penelope said, managing to step on his other foot as she squeezed by.

Apparently, Heath had learned one lesson when Penelope returned laden with beer, Red Dogs, and peanuts, because he immediately stood. But he was still all over Eddie who was now in the outfield shagging flies. Penelope gave him lesson two by deftly managing to empty both containers of beer on Heath.

Heath howled. "Hot damn, that's cold," he cried, hopping around.

"If I had spilled coffee on you, would you have said, 'Cold damn, that's hot?'" Penelope asked.

"Ow, ow, ow!"

"Just curious," Penelope said.

"Clumsy broad. Now I'm gonna have to go home and change."

"Bring us some beer on your way back," Penelope said. "You made me spill ours."

The Coyotes found new and interesting ways to play the game of baseball. The Red Rock pitcher struck out the side in the top half of the first inning. Determined to reciprocate, Peeper threw his first pitch into the grandstand. He would have been well advised to put his second pitch there as well. But he didn't. He grooved a fast ball and the lead off man for the Red Rocks salivated, seeing the ball disappear beyond the center field fence. In his eagerness, however, he popped it up to shortstop.

"I got it, I got it, I got it!"

Wrong.

There was still time to get the cursing lead off man at first base. Blake groaned as Little Rap Smith threw the ball into right field. Scooter Hernandez threw a perfect strike back to Little Rap who wheeled and threw it past a sliding runner at third base. Three errors in the space of ten or twelve seconds. At least Heath wasn't there to see it.

Still thinking about the conversation with Erika, Penelope missed it too. Erika feared telling anyone of Adcock's abusive nature because she believed the police would think it ample motive for murder, which, Penelope admitted, it was. But her tearful, although belated, admission was convincing. If Erika killed him, she was in the wrong profession and should open an acting school. Even the Last Bride of Satan could learn from Erika. And if Erika was, indeed, telling the truth at last, there was still a mystery girlfriend out there somewhere, perhaps nursing the physical and psychological bruises inflicted by Peter Adcock.

When the roar of the small but enthusiastic crowd brought her back to reality, Penelope automatically looked up for the instant replay. But it wasn't like watching college football—which Penelope adored—on television where she could read until the background noise indicated excitement and network technicians worked their magic, showing the play over and over from every conceivable angle. That was the trouble with real life. No instant replay.

The blinking red light on the telephone indicated a message or messages had been received when Penelope and Big Mike returned from the game. She dialed the motel operator and found Dutch had called.

A sleepy Stormy answered the phone. "It's about time, Sis. You can talk to him. He's been a bear all night."

"You called it, Penelope," Dutch said when he came on the line.

Her heart quickened. Finally, a break. "What did you find?"

"We're keeping this our little secret. You, me, Larry, Willie, and T.T. Not even Stormy knows and she's in the other room. Okay?"

"Yes."

"It was in the spare tire. Ten thousand dollars in cash, enough cocaine to qualify as a dealer, and a computer disk labeled Hosanahs."

CHAPTER FOURTEEN

With questions multiplying faster than rabbits on a steady diet of aphrodisiacal carrots, Penelope and Big Mike deserted the Coyotes, leaving the team with its losing streak intact, and a manager who was beginning to believe that perhaps the rest of the league did put their pants on in some mystical fashion other than the traditional and revered one-leg-at-a-time.

The video tape had revealed nothing more than a three hour view of Eddie's undisturbed locker. Blake had promised to recycle the tape in the hidden camera during the rest of their stay in Sedona, but with the revelations of the night before, a single vodka bottle in a recovering alcoholic-drug addict's locker somehow seemed less important—unless it was connected to the contents of Peter Adcock's spare tire. But how? Why? "The bottle has to be a bad practical joke," Penelope told Big Mike. "But that leaves a few really big questions, like what was Peter Adcock doing with ten thousand bucks in cash and a stash of cocaine?"

Penelope might as well have asked the wind rushing past the open Jeep for all the attention Mycroft was giving to the case. Big Mike had shaken the dust of Red Rock Country from his paws with a quiet but fierce determination. From his point of view, the whole excursion had been pretty much a second-rate adventure, not at all what Penelope had promised. Except for leaving his autograph on the vinyl-covered chair in the motel room, the time had been wasted. Things had picked up a little on the way out of town when, stopped at a traffic light, a foo foo, pink-ribboned mutt in the next car over had the temerity to bark. Big Mike had raised his fur and answered with a very satisfying hiss. Now, he was on the floor, engrossed in chasing down a pesky itch. But as soon as he had licked and scratched one under control, another popped up. Penelope failed to get his attention, even after threatening him with a medicinal bath. That elicited little more than a disdainful look which said, I'll take care of my own bathing, thank you very much.

With Mycroft continuing his sulk, Penelope made the return trip to Empty Creek in little more than two hours. Pangs of guilt battered her about the head and shoulders as she passed right by Mycroft & Company. Thank God for Kathy taking charge and keeping things moving through the swirls and eddies of the book business.

Coyote Stadium looked rather forlorn with its team on the road. She wanted to check in with Junior, but that would have to wait. First, there was the matter of the computer disk incongruously hidden away with cash and cocaine. On the telephone the night before, Dutch had been uncharacteristically reticent to share anything about the contents of the disk.

"Well, what did you find?" Penelope had asked impatiently, forcing the issue.

"Pornography," Dutch finally replied, with more than a trace of disgust in his voice.

"Let me be the judge of that." As a good English major, devoted to literature and the artistic right to freedom of expression, Penelope was reluctant to put a police chief, even a usually mellow future brother-in-law, in charge of deciding literary merit or lack thereof. "I'll put it on my pornograph and play it," she added.

There had been a long silence on the telephone.

"Come on, Dutch, that's a funny line. Every household should have a pornograph."

"Ha, ha."

But Dutch had been too embarrassed to read what Penelope finally determined to be nothing more than some rather lurid and risqué love letters to an unidentified person.

Now, alone in Dutch's office—he had gone for coffee and Big Mike had stopped off at the jail for a snack with his buddies—Penelope discovered that Peter Adcock was not a bad writer at all, although he drew heavily upon the classics of erotic literature. He was overly fond of adjectives and had apparently made good use of the thesaurus function of his computer, rarely repeating a descriptive word.

There were three undated letters, addressed to "My Dearest," "My Beloved," and "My Cherished Darling." The first had apparently been written after a secret love tryst in which Adcock proclaimed both gratitude for their evening together and his undying love. He went on for several pages, reviewing their amorous activities and fantasizing about what they would do the next time they were together. Penelope felt like a voyeur, peeping into a couple's boudoir, observing their most intimate moments together, but she continued reading.

Penelope revised her opinion of Peter Adcock. The persona he had presented to one woman after another—Lora Lou, Nora, Debbie, Blake—in Empty Creek had been one of complete arrogance; a male seeking female conquests. To Erika, he had been an abusive lover. But in the beginning, Erika had lied about the extent of her involvement with Adcock. Was she to be trusted now? Could the judgment of any of the women be accurate? Penelope wished Adcock *had* made a pass at her. At least she'd have that experience to rely on rather than second hand opinion, even from women she knew and believed in.

The Peter Adcock revealed in the letters was someone quite different than Penelope had been led to see—tender, loving, compassionate, caring, and solicitous of the woman he was writing to. He took pleasure in composing the letters to her, describing each new fantasy in detail. Obviously, he had been comfortable in such blunt sexual frankness and her apparent reciprocity. Penelope was titillated, but again felt like an unwanted spectator, prying into another's personal life which she had no right to do—except Peter Adcock was dead, callously murdered, and whatever he had been in life, deserved justice.

Strangely, Penelope would have preferred to deal with the woman's responses. She was alive to defend herself, to rip the letters from Penelope's hands, to protest indignantly. But Peter Adcock had taken great care to disguise her identity. There was no mention of her name, the color of her hair, her height, her complexion. In reading the love letters, Penelope could vividly imagine the physical attributes of the woman's body, but not her face.

When Dutch returned with their coffee, Penelope looked up and asked, "When were they written?"

"Don't know."

"You know what I mean. The disk would tell the last time each file had been accessed."

"You didn't ask that."

"Why are you being so perverse?"

"I'm thinking of early retirement. I'm getting too old for this."

"What would you do?"

Dutch sighed. "Spend more time with Stormy. Hang out on movie sets."

"Are you ready to be Mr. Storm Williams?"

"Why not?"

"You wouldn't like it. You need your own identity."

"The last time he *accessed* the files. . . ." Dutch looked at his notes. "Letter1.PA, March 15th . . ."

"How appropriate," Penelope interjected. "Beware the Ides of March."

". . . at 12:14 a.m."

"The witching hour."

"Do you want to hear this or not?"

"Sorry."

"Letter2.PA, March 29th at 12:37 a.m. and Letter3.PA on April 12th at 12:05 a.m."

"Two weeks apart, always shortly after midnight. Piece of cake, Dutch. All we have to do is find out where he was on March 14th, March 28th, and April 11th and with whom."

"What happened to April 25th and May 10th?"

Penelope referred to the third letter—"My Cherished Darling." It was more romantic than the computer heading of "Letter1.PA" and Peter Adcock seemed to have been deeply in love. Penelope would give him credit for that. "There's no indication that they'll be separated for long," Penelope said. "It ends with, 'Soon, my sweetheart, we will be together forever.'"

"Soon, he was dead."

The words hung in the artificially chilled air of the office. Outside, the business of protecting the public went on quietly. Telephones rang and were quickly answered. Conversations were hushed, business-like. Penelope stared through the window behind Dutch's desk where Crying Woman Mountain loomed, its dark slopes silent and forbidding today, reticent as always to share its secrets.

Dutch lifted his coffee cup to his lips but put it back on the desk without sipping. "What about the cocaine and the cash?" he asked. "That's probably more important than some dirty love letters."

"Dope deal gone bad?"

"Looks that way."

Penelope's experience with drugs was limited. She had smoked marijuana in Africa with an older British expatriate named Robert Sidney-Veine, even inhaled, but found the narcotic effect vastly overrated. For her, it felt much like a roto-rooter reaming out her throat. She had been delighted when the stones of her fireplace transformed themselves into the gargoyles of Notre Dame, dancing in the flickering light of the fire and jabbering away at her, but that had been a brief illusion. Nor did she find that marijuana heightened her sensations when making love with Robert, her only experience with a man a number of years her senior. After smoking marijuana on several occasions with Robert, she decided that vices were better when taken in liquid form and, in keeping with the Golden Mean of the ancient Greeks, with nothing to excess. Everything was much better after that.

"Why are you smiling?" Dutch asked.

"Oh, just thinking of an old friend. I haven't heard from him in a long time and I should write." Robert's last letter had been posted from Central Africa where he was teaching and living with a young woman who was *the* Classics Department at the university in Malawi.

"Can it wait until we figure this mess out?"

"I suppose, but we better hurry. He's not getting any younger."

"Neither am I."

"Don't start that again." Penelope clapped her hands once and continued. "So, we have a dope deal gone bad, $10,000 in cash, and some erotic love letters."

"Larry and Willie are running makes on everyone listed in Adcock's computer and anybody else they can think of, including Eddie Stiles."

"Eddie's clean."

"Eddie has a record of drug involvement."

"That's in the past."

"It's never in the past. You know that. An addict is one hit or one drink away from going right back in the sewer."

"Not Eddie."

"Who then?"

"D.W." At the time, Penelope had thought little of the note in Adcock's desk. She often used shorthand in reminding herself to make or return telephone calls. A for Andy, L for

Laney, L.L. for Lora Lou. She hadn't thought it might be a primitive code.

"What's a D.W.?"

"Initials, probably," Penelope said. "I found them on a note after Blake was attacked and I don't think they correspond to anyone in his laptop. But what if it's a nickname? You can run things like that, nicknames, known aliases, can't you?"

"Burke, Stoner," Dutch roared. "Get in here!"

Blake dutifully called each morning to report that there had been no sign of the Clubhouse Phantom. There had been no sign of that elusive first victory either as the Coyotes continued in their collective slump, finding new ways to lose each night. They shook the red dust of Sedona from their cleats and headed for the series with the Wickenburg Wind where, in their first game of the new series, they managed only five hits as they were shut out—again.

"Oh, well," Blake said disconsolately, "we'll be home soon."

Penelope knew exactly how the Coyotes felt. Despite the cache discovered in the spare tire of Peter Adcock's Jag, the investigation might as well be on a jungle steamer to Adventure for all the progress that was being made. The good guys were being shut out, just like the baseball team they rooted for.

Tweedledee and Tweedledum ran the initials, every which way, even reversing them without prompting from Penelope. Nothing. There were no dope dealers who went by the nickname of D.W. or W.D.

The Empty Creek P.D. narcs weren't much help. Drugs weren't big business in the relatively clean atmosphere of

Empty Creek. For all of its civic pride, the little city was still a desert backwater. The police department's two narcs could always bust a student or two smoking a joint behind a certain convenience store near the high school, or a few refugees from the sixties, but as a big business with gangs monopolizing the trade, drugs were pretty far down on the crime scale in Empty Creek.

"Scumbags got more colorful nicknames," Tweedledee finally said.

"Yeah," Tweedledum said. "Names like Dirty Harry."

"He was a good guy," Penelope pointed out.

"You know what I mean. Colorful, like Scumbags. That's colorful."

"Rat finks. We need a snitch."

"Okay, let's call in some rat finks."

"Good idea. Where?"

"Beats me."

"Why not call the narcs in Phoenix and the Sheriff's Department?" Penelope suggested. "Maybe they've heard of D.W."

"W.D."

"W.D-40," Tweedledee chortled.

Junior was a bundle of nerves, worrying over the succession of special nights that would be the hallmark of the rapidly approaching homestand—the Rattlesnake Chili Cook-Off (the preliminaries had been held before the team went on the road), the Babe Look-Alike Contest ("Do you know how many pigs there are in Empty Creek? My God, whose stupid idea was this anyway?"), and Sexy Lingerie Night (now, mercifully shortened to Lingerie Night).

With Laney's willing assistance, the first two hundred women through the gates would receive a black negligee (courtesy of Ralph and Russell's mail order catalog—one size fits all). During the course of choosing a suitable garment from the wide array of choices, poor Junior received an education—of sorts.

"We have to find him a girlfriend," Laney later said emphatically. "The child knows absolutely nothing about anything. How about that Erika person?"

"Too muscular," Penelope said. "Besides, she's probably in Italy by now."

"Oh. Well, I hope she has a nice vacation. How about Reggie Pryor?"

"Too young."

"I suppose you're right. Angelique?"

"Too old."

"One of her dancers?"

"Too wise."

"Well, there must be someone."

"I'm working on it."

The Empty Creek Chamber of Commerce softball team gathered for its first practice. During the real game at the Fourth of July picnic, the teams would be composed of both Chamber members and players from the Coyotes. It was felt that this would be a more equitable division of talent, rather than having the amateurs take on the professionals. There was a growing school of thought among them, however, that the Chamber team might very well be able to beat the Coyotes. A discussion of this possibility lasted only until the Chamber members began to warm up. The ensuing groans as little-used muscles protested ended *that* discussion. Any thought of reconsideration was vetoed during infield practice with one bad bloody nose, several bashed shins, and one errant throw after another.

"All right, let's get two," Andy hollered optimistically as he banged out another sharp ground ball to Penelope at short-stop. She scooped it up cleanly and tossed it to David Macklin at second, who whirled smoothly and bounced his throw in the dirt. Lora Lou, filling in at first—she had no intention of submitting her freshly-manicured fingernails to the rigors of softball—scrambled out of the way.

"Sorry, hon," David called.

Lora Lou waved cheerfully. *Her* athletic reputation wasn't on the line.

What this team needs, Penelope thought, is a ringer.

She repeated the thought at home after emerging from the shower, her hair and body encased in big green fluffy towels. "Our softball team needs a ringer," Penelope said. "Like Spearchucker Jones in M*A*S*H."

"That would be cheating," Andy said. He looked up from the chopping board where he was slicing and dicing and whacking away on the radishes, cucumbers, spring onions, green peppers, and tomatoes for their salad. The vision in green distracted him, immediately turning his thoughts from salad to wondering what principle of physics or gravity kept the larger of the two towels in place as Penelope fiddled with her hair. Wisely, he decided to put the big chopping knife down.

Big Mike, looking like Sumo Cat preparing for a match, was on the counter, meditating as he watched Andy work.

Although he wasn't much for salads, he needed to keep his weight up and in wrestling trim just in case some lard-butt tomcat happened by.

"We'd get caught, anyway," Penelope said. "That's the trouble with Empty Creek. It's difficult to pull something like that off and it's too damned hard to keep secrets."

"You could play the game wearing a towel," Andy suggested. "Everyone would be waiting for it to fall off. That would break their concentration."

"Too subversive."

"How *do* you keep that thing on, anyway? I can't. It always falls off."

"Superiority of the female. And they say we don't make good engineers."

With that, Penelope left the males of the household to their own devices while she went back to the bedroom to change into something only slightly less comfortable than green, fluffy towels.

When she returned, clad in pink shorts—reminiscent of The Dynamite Lounge—and an oversized Coyote T-shirt, Andy had completed his portion of the salad and was leaning against the counter, sipping wine, absent-mindedly stroking Mycroft.

"You made too much," Penelope said. "Again."

"I like chopping," Andy said for about the one thousandth time in their relationship. "It releases my aggressions."

Penelope's task was to add the lettuce and dressing because Andy hated his own salads and he considered lettuce and dressing to be the key components. Thus, it became *her* salad. Penelope shook her head for about the ten thousandth time in their relationship. But, as Empty Creek eccentricities went, Andy's opinion on salads was fairly mild.

"I've been thinking," Andy said, stepping aside to allow her room to work. "We could sneak in one of the Gila Monsters. They had a pretty good team this year." The Gila Monster was the mascot and nickname of Empty Creek High School.

"How would we convince anyone that a high school player was a member of the Chamber of Commerce?"

"How about an associate membership," Andy said, "operating a lemonade stand or something? I always had a lemonade stand when I was a kid. Hated the lemonade, of course. It was better when my mom made it."

"Of course, you did, dear heart." Penelope went into the refrigerator for the lettuce. "No, I'm afraid the Chamber of Commerce softball team must stand on its own athletic prowess."

"We're doomed."

Penelope tossed the head of lettuce from hand to hand. "You know," she said, "Eddie Stiles could be considered a ringer."

CHAPTER
FIFTEEN

Time passed slowly, each long day dragging into what seemed—for sleephounds like Penelope and Big Mike—all too brief periods of darkness and the blessed relief of Lethean slumber.

During her waking hours, Penelope's brain became so addled in trying to put the known facts of the case together in some comprehensible fashion that she had started talking to herself at embarrassing moments—standing in line at the post office, she had suddenly exclaimed, "Flibbertigibbet!" It was not the word in her mind, but Muffy had always taught that swearing was not ladylike, and swearing in public was definitely socially unacceptable, even for the truck drivers and longshoremen who paid absolutely no heed whatsoever to Muffy's Rules of Conduct for young ladies. So, "flibbertigibbet" popped out unexpectedly. Now, the fact that this was a word Penelope didn't realize was a part of her vocabulary was not nearly as surprising as the way the line before her suddenly parted, like the Red Sea opening for Moses. People backed away, keeping a wary eye on her, wondering if this woman speaking in tongues had escaped from a lunatic asylum during a recess from finger painting. Penelope mustered her chutzpa, however, nodded graciously, said, "Thank you," and stepped up to the counter. Afterwards, she resolved to say flibbertigibbet whenever she visited the post office. It was certainly better than standing around, watching the postal clerks not work, a privilege accorded them by their union contract.

The growing frustration with the lack of progress in the case affected everyone.

Dutch sat in his office sullenly flinging darts at the small Executive Dart Board Penelope had given him for Christmas. Police officers started tiptoeing past his office, fearful that he would target them for some bizarre unwanted task, like counting locker keys.

Tweedledee and Tweedledum took to spending their lunch hours at The Dynamite Lounge, but even the passing parade of young and nubile dancers and the soothing strains of reflective New Age music failed to spark a much-needed hunch or overcome their sense of inadequacy. The search for D.W. or W.D. failed to turn up an individual who went by that nickname or any other damned thing either.

Even Big Mike took to moping around the house and the bookstore, lethargically retreating to his favorite hidey holes in each location—the kitchen cabinet at Casa Penelope and the highest shelf in the back room of Mycroft & Company— morosely considering the meaning of life. After all, as Plato had pointed out, the unexamined life was not worth living. He even turned his nose up at a generous helping of lima beans, forcing Penelope to consider a trip to the vet and all that that entailed. There *had* been an outbreak of a mild form of sleeping sickness in California and it *was* possible that a wayward mosquito had somehow migrated to Empty Creek.

The possibility of wreaking havoc on Doctor Bob, his assistants, and various critters with the misfortune to be in the vicinity when Big Mike was dragged howling and screeching into the animal hospital was forestalled, however, when Big Mike disappeared into the desert night and didn't return for three days.

And so time passed.

The Empty Creek Coyotes finally returned home, collective tails tucked neatly between their legs and with their losing streak intact, having dropped five games to the Sedona Red Rocks and another five to the Wickenburg Wind.

Desperate to win a game, any game, Rats was seriously considering an exhibition game against the Little Sisters of the Poor, except he'd heard Mother Superior had a wicked curve ball. "Probably sold her soul to the devil for it," he said, wondering where he could make application on behalf of *his* pitching staff.

So when Alyce Smith, Empty Creek's resident astrologer, psychic, and preeminent authority on all things New Age, suggested that each member of the team needed to get in touch with his inner child, Rats didn't guffaw or toss her out on her pretty little butt as another beleaguered manager might have done. To his credit, Rats set aside his pragmatic doubts, told the team to report to the clubhouse an hour earlier than normal, and said, "Omm."

Alyce met with only the players, having decided that Rats

and his coaches needed special attention as grumpy and stressed out as they were.

After the usual smirks and wisecracks typical of a group of energetic young men, they got down to the serious business of reaching inward, to give their inner children space to grow and expand, to enjoy life, and to have fun as they prepared to face the Bisbee Diamondbacks.

The Coyotes were greeted by yet another sellout crowd at Coyote Stadium.

With their inner children now serene and peaceful, the starting lineup went out and managed a very credible imitation of Superman using a bat made of kryptonite, the one element that turned the Man of Steel into mush. Had the Diamondback pitcher not slipped coming off the mound in the fourth inning to field a weakly hit ground ball, he would have thrown a perfect game against the Coyotes. As it was, he pitched a one-hitter while facing the minimum twenty-seven batters because Little Rap, who had managed the lone scratch hit, was promptly picked off first base.

A disgusted Rats McCoy didn't blame Alyce. "They were in touch with their God damn inner child, all right," he said. "Unfortunately, they picked nap time."

"Oh well," Penelope said, "they can always try massage therapy with Teresa." In fact, she thought, I could use a little massage therapy myself.

Mycroft returned from his walkabout in the desert, talkative as always, eager to tell Penelope of his adventures, dropping a lizard at her feet as a coming home present. The lizard, more than a little shocked at being kidnapped in such a rude fashion, quickly regained its senses and looked for a way out of Dodge. Grateful as she was for Big Mike's token of appreciation, Penelope aided the lizard in his or her escape by distracting Mikey with a big welcome home hug.

Debbie Locke was dressed for work when she entered Mycroft & Company carrying a baseball bat—a wooden baseball bat.

Big Mike peered out from his fireplace cave with some degree of alarm in his eyes as Debbie brandished the bat wildly. He retreated into the shadows to await developments, perhaps supposing that even a good friend like Debbie could suddenly lose her senses. Women, after all, like cats, could be most unpredictable.

"Look at this!" Debbie cried angrily.

"I think you need an aluminum bat for the softball game," Penelope said softly, although she fully intended to use her own wood softball bat. There were some traditions that should not be mucked about and Penelope had played the game when bats were wood and fields were real grass.

"It's not for the game," Debbie said. "I found it leaning against my door this morning when I was leaving for work."

Penelope took the bat and examined it with growing excitement. "The Cecil Fielder model," she said. "The murder weapon but, of course, it can't be the one used to kill Peter Adcock. The police have that. It would seem that someone took your bat and has now replaced it."

"Why?"

"Why, indeed?" Penelope turned the bat over. "It's brand new."

"Not a scratch on it, thank God. Otherwise, they'd be accusing me of stealing it back."

Penelope gripped the bat, choking up, and stepped into the batter's box. It was still difficult to think of Cecil Fielder playing for the hated New York Yankees instead of banging out those gargantuan home runs for her beloved Detroit Tigers. In the fireplace, Mycroft hunkered in the shadows. Everyone seemed to have lost their senses this morning. A full swing would demolish the Mycroft Holmes statuettes, at least those Rose McCoffey had not taken. "Now where would a person go to get a brand new Cecil Fielder bat?"

"The Coyote locker room? That's where the original came from."

"I don't think so. Let's walk down to Jeff's Sporting Goods."

Penelope would have left Big Mike in the fireplace pondering the mysteries of womanhood, but he was having none of that. His vacation had rejuvenated his spirits and he bounded out enthusiastically after determining the bat was not meant to bludgeon the handiest cat around. Penelope hung the cardboard placard in the door, and adjusted the hands on its clock face to indicate someone would be back at 11:30 a.m. "That should be time enough," Penelope said as she locked the door.

The mystery of the disappearing and reappearing Cecil Fielder bat was easily solved. Penelope wished the rest of the case would resolve itself so quickly and painlessly.

"Had to special order it," Jeff Lancaster said. "Not much call for wood bats anymore. The pros are the only ones who use them."

Ta da!

"Who ordered it?"

"Shane and Jackson Baxter. They're. . . ."

"I know who they are," Debbie interrupted. "They live next door to me." She turned to Penelope. "Remember, when the Coyotes left for the road trip. I told you two boys ran away from me. . . ."

"Shane and Jackson Baxter," Penelope pronounced. God, it was good to be able to pronounce something with a degree of certainty in this most confusing of cases. Finally!

Debbie nodded.

"Paid for it with their allowance," Jeff said. "Seemed like nice kids. Did they do something wrong?"

"I don't think so," Penelope said. "Not really, but I think we should have a talk with Master Shane and Master Jackson."

Belinda Baxter opened the door looking frazzled. She had been up for hours, making her children's breakfast, doing a load of wash, cleaning the kitchen and the living room. It was her routine to do one room each day and two on her days off. It was the only way to keep ahead of the game with two healthy boys galloping every which way during the summer vacation.

"Debbie, hi, I thought you'd be at work by now."

"Hi, Belinda, I'm taking some time off. This is Penelope Warren."

"Oh, I've read about you and your cat in the *News Journal*. It's nice to meet you," Belinda said. "It's nice to meet both of you," she added, leaning over to give Big Mike a head scratch.

Belinda Baxter was a pretty woman of perhaps thirty with

the slightly harassed look of a single mother deserted by her husband when the boys were three and one. Since then, Debbie had told Penelope, Belinda worked long and hard at a variety of jobs to support her family, while trying to be mom and dad, and carve out time to be with the boys. "She's had a tough time," Debbie had told Penelope. "I don't think I could do it."

"We need to talk with you," Penelope said, "about Shane and Jackson."

"They're out playing. My God, are they all right? Has something happened?"

Penelope shook her head quickly. "Nothing like that. They're fine."

Belinda sighed heavily. "You scared me. I thought. . . ."

"I'm sorry," Penelope said, resolving in the future to always preface such remarks with, "Everyone's fine, but. . . ."

"Come on in, then. Can I get you some coffee? I just put some on for myself."

"That would be nice, thank you."

After the usual bustling about, apologies for the state of the house, and the ceremonial pouring of coffee, Penelope and Debbie took turns explaining the importance of their mission.

After the reality of the situation intruded, Belinda protested. "But Mrs. Sanchez was here when I got home from work, watching television. She always comes in when I work late, and the boys were in bed, sound asleep. I checked on them first thing. I always do."

"What time did you get home?"

"It was after three. It was a late night for me. I stayed to help clean up. It's a new job and I wanted to make a good impression."

"Isn't it possible that Mrs. Sanchez could have fallen asleep on the couch and the boys snuck out?"

"I suppose, but. . . ."

"Nothing else makes sense," Penelope suggested gently. "You said Shane and Jackson are crazy about baseball. They borrowed Debbie's bat, went off to Coyote Stadium to pretend they were big league ballplayers, and while they were there, Peter Adcock and a killer appeared. Frightened, they dropped the bat and ran for home. Afterwards, they felt guilty about losing Debbie's bat, so they saved their allowance, ordered another, and replaced it."

"But how could they play baseball at night?"

"There was a full moon that night. Plenty of light for two boys with an imagination."

Penelope and Debbie watched the transformation. Belinda's cheeks paled and tears filled her eyes. But there was something else in those dark brown eyes as well. Something Penelope had seen often enough to recognize it—fear.

"I was afraid of something like this," Belinda cried, turning to Debbie. "They're good boys. They wouldn't steal from you."

"I know that," Debbie said. "They just borrowed the bat."

"Do we have to go to the police?"

"I'm afraid so."

Belinda burst into tears. Penelope quickly moved to sit beside her on the couch, patting her on the shoulder. "Don't worry," she said. "Nothing is going to happen to the boys, but we have to know what went on that night."

Mycroft, who couldn't stand to see a woman cry, jumped to the couch and administered a good dose of cat therapy, rubbing his head along Belinda's thigh, working up to a good, soul-satisfying purr.

"I knew something bad would happen," Belinda wailed.

"They're young, resilient. All they have to do is tell the police what they saw that night."

"It's not that. They'll find out about my new job and take my children away. They'll say I'm an unfit mother."

"No one's going to take Shane and Jackson away," Penelope said. "What *is* your new job, anyway?"

"I'm a dancer at The Dynamite Lounge," Belinda sobbed. "Only three nights a week, but the tips are good and we need the money. For a long time, I couldn't even give Shane and Jackson an allowance. This is all my fault. I haven't even been able to take them to a game yet."

"Is that all?" Penelope said. "Don't worry about it. I do phone sex on the side and I'm practically related to the police chief." It was just a little lie and for a good cause. "And I'm a member of the Chamber of Commerce."

"You do?" Belinda and Debbie chorused.

"Sure," Penelope said. "Why not? If Dutch says anything to you, I'll take Debbie's bat and beat some sense into him." She dropped her voice and said huskily, desperately searching for a good ad-lib. "Oh, that excites me so much. I'd ... I'd ... love to bite your toes." Thank God for crossed air waves on cellular phones.

Debbie looked at Penelope in amazement and shook her head.

Belinda wiped her eyes.

"Feel better now?" Penelope asked.

"A little."

"You know, I've been to The Dynamite Lounge. I've never seen your name advertised."

"Oh, I couldn't let Angelique take my picture. The boys must never find out I do this. Besides, when I dance, my name is Bambi."

"How do you feel about younger men?" Penelope asked.

Shane was eleven years old and wanted to be the tough guy, although the quivering lip gave him away—he wasn't about to make his bones on this caper. Jackson was nine and scared. He tried to hide it by squatting down to pet Big Mike. "Nice kitty," he said, although Mycroft was some years and about twenty-four pounds away from kittenhood.

Confronted with the evidence by their mother, however, they admitted, shame-faced, sneaking into Debbie's house, pinching and hiding the bat, and then sneaking off when Mrs. Sanchez fell asleep in front of the television set.

"Well, young men, the two of you are grounded for a month," Belinda declared sternly.

"Perhaps, Bambi, I mean, Belinda, that could start *after* I take them to a Coyotes game. As my guests, of course."

"Really, could we, could we, Mom?"

Knowing a good blackmail threat when she heard one, Belinda maintained the sham for a moment and then relented, nodding approval. "You're quite a woman," she whispered to Penelope. "Thank you."

"Wow, the Coyotes!"

"Now, let's go tell the police everything you saw that night."

"Are they going to arrest us?" Jackson asked. "Before we get to go to the game?"

"Not a chance," Penelope said. "All you have to do is tell the truth, just the way you did with us."

"We promise," Shane said.

CHAPTER SIXTEEN

A number of remarkable things happened on the second night after the Coyotes returned home from their disastrous road trip.

First, quite a large number of fans, all apparently suffering from a severe and collective case of Coyote fever and not at all discouraged by the inept performance the night before, arrived early and shouted encouragement to the players during batting practice, infield practice, even during pickup pepper games.

"Way to go, atta boy, that's smoking it, get two."

Kids of varying ages, including an ecstatic pair of youngsters named Shane and Jackson, clustered around the dugout gathering autographs.

Inspired by his inner child, Junior was showing a promotional flair of his own. He had set up a designated area behind home plate for Teresa Sandia to give massages for fans who needed relaxation from the tension of watching Coyote baseball and for Alyce Smith to do astrological and psychic readings for those who needed more mystical guidance. Business boomed for both Teresa and Alyce.

Half an hour before game time, the stands were filled and the Fire Marshal was called in to designate standing room only areas to accommodate the fans still clamoring for tickets outside the stadium.

The three finalists in the rattlesnake chili cookoff brought their steaming concoctions to a bench set up behind home plate where a committee consisting of Mayor Tiggy Bourke, an enthusiastic Chamber President Lora Lou Longstreet, and a reluctant Harris Anderson III waited to pronounce a winner. They dutifully sampled each of the entries, Tiggy Bourke smacking his lips loudly after tasting each, and huddled to determine the winner. Both Lora Lou and Andy agreed that number two far surpassed the others, but Tiggy "Anything-for-a-Vote" Bourke prevailed upon his committee members to announce Tri-Champions.

The beaming winners, two women and a man, had their arms raised in triumph by the mayor.

And then it was time to play some baseball—Empty Creek version.

Each player received a standing ovation as his name was announced and he jogged out to his position.

Dr. Stanley Livingstone stood at home plate and played a mournful—and amplified—version of the National Anthem on his violin. Mycroft didn't care for the high pitched whining of the instrument, nor did a dog in the stands somewhere down the right field line that howled in accompaniment, but the rest of the sold out crowd cheered and applauded politely.

The unique rendering of the Star Spangled Banner didn't help the Coyotes much because they were down eight runs after two innings. The dark cloud of the losing streak was almost palpable over the Coyote dugout.

Having left Shane and Jackson in the custody of Feathers McCoy, Penelope was behind home plate getting her massage therapy from Teresa when the first cry was heard from the seats deep down the right field line.

"Awooo."

It was during one of those lulls when even the largest of crowds fall into a sudden hush. The solitary lament rang through the stadium. Later, it was ascertained that it was Cackling Ed who initiated what was to become the war whoop of the Empty Creek Coyotes. Old Ed, however, credited Maureen and Stan Poe's dog, one Axel Betty Cocker by name, who had accompanied the national anthem, with the motivation for his inspired cry.

It didn't much resemble a sound a coyote might make, but rather more like a decrepit wolf with a severe case of indigestion. Still, it was answered by someone down the left field line.

"Awooo!"

Jesus Gomez, who was at the plate, backed out of the box, tapped dirt from his spikes with his bat, and looked up at the stands.

"Awooo!"

This curious sound came from the stands behind Penelope and Teresa.

The Diamondback catcher called time and trotted out to the mound as other Coyote fans joined in.

"Awooo! Awooo!"

Penelope shrugged off Teresa's iron fingers and stood.

"Awooo!" she howled, much to the astonishment of Big Mike, who had been comfortably napping on her lap.

All around the stadium, fans were on their feet, faces lifted to the dark skies, baying at the quarter moon.

"Awooo!"

The Coyotes jumped to the edge of the dugout, bats in hand, pounding them against the concrete floor.

A startled Diamondback manager joined the conference on the mound.

The yowling from the stands was thunderous.

"Awooo!"

The umpire went to the mound. "Play ball," he cried over the peculiar wailing that had raised Big Mike's hackles. He joined the din, screeching his version of Awooo, which was pretty hideous to human ears. But there was no stopping him. Big Mike was sick of the Coyote losing streak too.

"Awooo!"

The caterwauling grew even louder when Jesus dragged a perfect bunt between first base and the pitcher's mound. And louder still when Jesus, ignoring the don't steal sign from Rats, took off for second on the first pitch, sliding in under the tag.

"That'll cost you five bucks," Rats hollered.

Jesus grinned.

Two pitches later, Eddie Stiles one-hopped the right center field fence for a ground rule double, bringing Jesus in to score.

Eight to one.

"You can keep the five bucks, I guess," Rats said.

"Cool," Jesus replied, as he high-fived his way through his teammates.

When the inning ended, the Coyotes had narrowed the

score to eight-five. The three outs had been screaming live drives.

Well, well, well, Penelope thought as she returned to her seat with Big Mike, things are looking up.

"Awooo!"

Big Mike was minding his own business on the dugout roof when Abraham "Prez" Jefferson Washington lifted a towering foul pop up that drifted toward the Coyote dugout. The Diamondback catcher thundered over. The third baseman sprinted in. The pitcher headed toward the foul line to direct traffic, shouting, "Catcher, catcher!" The home plate umpire trailed the play to make the call.

"Lottsa room," a helpful Peeper hollered just as the catcher was about to take a pratfall into the dugout. Still, he maintained his balance, leaned over the yawning abyss of the dugout, and stretched out his glove.

Unfortunately, the Diamondback catcher had whipped off his mask as soon as the ball was hit and threw it ten yards in the opposite direction, just as all good catchers are taught to do from their first day in Little League.

It might have been better, however, had he ignored the rule just this once. All of the shouting and pounding of cleated hooves had awakened Big Mike who quickly realized a great big herd of something was bearing down on him.

The foul ball, the Diamondback catcher and his massive mitt, and Big Mike's claws arrived at the same point simultaneously. Since there wasn't enough space for all three, something had to give way.

The baseball hit the catcher's mitt at the same moment Big Mike attacked a burly forearm. Startled to wakefulness and with too little time to reconnoiter, it wasn't one of Big Mike's best shots, but it drew blood and got the immediate attention of the Diamondback catcher. The ball went into the stands to be grabbed by a delighted little girl of ten, the mitt plopped in Feathers' lap, and the catcher landed on his butt where he grabbed his forearm in horror, crying, "I've been shot!"

"Batter's out," the ump cried. "Interference."

True to baseball tradition, the Diamondback players poured from their dugout, their positions in the field, and the bullpen, rushing to the assistance of their stricken catcher. It was a credit to their courage, if not their intelligence because, had there been a demented sniper intent on evening the baseball odds in the Coyotes' favor, they would have been easy targets.

Spoiling for a good fight, the Coyote dugout and bullpen emptied to meet the challenge.

"You're outta here," the ump hollered, pointing a finger at a hissing Mycroft, and jerking his thumb over his shoulder. "Interference." Then, he hastily pulled *his* mask over his face.

"What? Who's outta here?" an immediately enraged Rats McCoy shouted, bounding out of the dugout, going face to face with the red-faced and puffing umpire.

"The cat's outta here."

"You can't throw the cat out of the game," Rats yelled. "He's not even on the roster."

"I don't care. He interfered with the right to make a fair catch and he's gone."

"Don't listen," Penelope told Shane and Jackson before

coming to the defense of Big Mike, shouting, "That's football, you dummy."

"You're outta here too."

Rats kicked dirt on the ump's nice blue slacks.

"You're gone, too, and so's your bench."

"You can't do that!"

"The hell I can't!"

All things considered, it was a pretty good rhubarb, but like all baseball fights, it ended with piles of players wrestling around on the ground, shouting dire threats, pointing fingers ("hold me back, I'm gonna kill him"), but no one was seriously hurt, except for the Diamondback catcher's pride because he now had to endure high-pitched taunts from the Coyote dugout.

"Oh, my, I've been shot!"

As he was leaving the field, Rats did a very credible Dennis Rodman imitation as he threw his baseball cap in one direction, his shirt in another, and his T-shirt in yet another. But the tour de force came when he sat on the pitcher's mound, removed his shoes, flinging them away, and then stripped off his pants, before heading for the clubhouse, wearing only his jockstrap, and mooning the home plate ump the whole way.

Take that, Dennis.

"That's my honey," Feathers said.

"Nice butt for an old guy," Penelope said, as she prepared to make her own departure, briefly considering and then rejecting a similar dramatic exit. Rather than have the Coyotes forfeit the game, as the home plate umpire threatened, Penelope issued a final razzberry at the offending man in blue, gathered up Big Mike, and left the box, leaving Shane and

Jackson once again in the charge of Feathers, just as the public address announcer summed up the toll for the fans.

"Rats McCoy has been ejected from the game. . . ."

"Booo!"

"The Coyote bench has been cleared. . . ."

"Booooo!"

"The Coyotes are now playing the game under protest. . . ."

"Yayyy!"

"And. . . ." There was a mild screech from the microphone as a hand was placed over it. Still, the announcer could be clearly heard. "You're kidding? You're *not* kidding?"

The crowd waited.

"And, holy cow, I don't believe this, but a cat and his owner have also been ejected from the game."

Penelope felt a little like Queen Elizabeth II in a royal procession as five thousand Coyote fans stood as one and issued the new battle cry of the Coyotes in their honor.

"Awooo!"

Abraham Jefferson Washington, whose pop foul had sparked the melee, later summed it up best when he said, "Man, that's one bad cat dude."

Penelope immediately placed it in the pantheon of epigraphy describing Big Mike, right next to, "That's the God damnedest cat I ever saw."

Penelope took Big Mike to the Coyote Dog stand. He was ready for a good snack after all the excitement. By the time their order was placed, Buddy Peterson had struck out the side on ten pitches.

Stanley Livingstone kissed Blake—three times, in fact. "A

kiss for every strikeout," he told Penelope. "Four for a home run."

"Man, this is great," Blake bubbled when she was allowed to come up for a breath. "We're going to win. I can just feel it." She turned up the volume on the radio. "Bottom of the seventh," the announcer blared. "Coyotes down by three. Awooo, baby!"

So much for journalistic impartiality.

Penelope left Big Mike with Blake and Stan and went to watch the game from the shadows of the tunnel. She was quickly joined by a once again fully-clothed Rats McCoy who immediately started to wig-wag signals to the remaining coach on the bench.

"Great exit," Penelope said.

"Feathers'll kill me."

"Probably," Penelope agreed cheerfully.

Big Rap followed Shrimp Federov's single to lead off the inning with a towering home run over the right field fence.

A disgruntled fan had to wait for his Coyote Dog while the young doctor received his reward. It was a pretty good deal, considering the fact that *he* didn't have to hit the home run.

Eight-seven.

Eddie Stiles singled to left.

The Prez lined out.

Little Rap flied out to center.

Scooter hit a ground ball in the hole but the shortstop backhanded it, whirled, and got Eddie at second.

Three hits, two runs.

The Coyotes were still down by one run going to the bottom of the ninth with the top of the order coming up.

Jesus walked on four pitches and trotted to first base.

The Diamondback manager came out, talked a bit, spit three times, and scratched his crotch once, but left his pitcher in after the obligatory pat on the butt.

Shrimp advanced Jesus to second with a little dribbler down the first base line. It wasn't pretty but it got the job done.

One away.

Penelope crossed her fingers when Big Rap went deep to right, but the Diamondback outfielder drifted back to the warning track and took it in. Jesus tagged and went to third.

"Damn," Penelope said, "he got under it."

Two down.

There was a lull as the Diamondback manager strolled to the mound again, conferred briefly with his catcher and pitcher, scratched and spit some more, scuffed the dirt, and then motioned to the bullpen with his right arm.

"He's bringing in Tommy Reynolds," Rats said. "He's got heat and one helluva curve ball."

"Eddie hits the fast ball *and* the curve," Penelope said, watching Reynolds make the walk in from the bullpen the way it should be done—slowly and arrogantly. Except for the hippety-hop over the chalked foul line, Reynolds was *The Man* coming in to face *The Man*.

Reaching the mound, he took the ball from the manager, received *his* pat on the butt, and went to work. After his eight warm-up pitches, Reynolds rubbed the ball, his back to the plate.

Eddie Stiles waited nonchalantly for his adversary to face him before he deliberately dug in to await the first pitch.

Reynolds knocked him down with a fast ball under his

chin. Eddie got up, brushed the dirt from his uniform, and dug his spikes even deeper into the batter's box.

"Watch this," Rats said. He scratched his nose, pulled at his ear, brushed his arms across his chest, pulled at his other ear, patted his stomach, spit twice, and made a rude gesture in the direction of the home plate umpire.

"What did you call?" Penelope asked.

"Suicide squeeze."

"You can't do that," Penelope cried, "not with two outs."

"Watch me. They'll never expect it, not in a hunnert years."

Jesus took a walking lead down the third base line, despite the fact that Reynolds was pitching from the stretch. The third baseman feinted toward the bag and Jesus retreated. Reynolds stepped off the rubber.

The eternal dance started all over again. Eddie dug in. Reynolds leaned over to get the sign from his catcher, shaking him off, once, twice. Eddie stepped out of the box. Jesus went back to the bag.

The crowd was on its feet, but hushed now, tense with the excitement of the moment. One hit, one little scratch hit, and the Coyotes would have their first big W. After that . . . who knew? Hell, they were only twelve games out of first. Anything could happen.

Eddie dug in defiantly, glaring at the pitcher.

Reynolds got his sign and went into the stretch, glancing over at Jesus walking nonchalantly down the line. The infield was playing back.

Reynolds kicked and threw.

Jesus took off.

Fast ball. Outside corner of the plate. Knee high.

"Run, Jesus, run!" Penelope screamed.

Eddie Stiles took it down to the last nanosecond before he whipped the bat around and laid the bunt down along the third base line.

The Diamondbacks were fooled, but good. Major league, big time fooled. Playing back and caught flat-footed, the Diamondbck third baseman never had a chance.

Jesus slid under the tag.

Eddie crossed the first base bag.

That's the old ball game.

"Coyotes win!"

The stadium erupted.

Penelope jumped into Rats McCoy's arms and gave him a big kiss.

"Piece a cake," Rats said.

The aftermath of the dramatic victory in the bottom of the ninth inning was equally memorable.

Having spent the better part of a nine inning baseball game howling enthusiastically with the rest of the Coyote fans, Axel Betty's voice was reduced to a pitiful croak and had to be treated for a severe case of laryngitis the next day. In grateful recognition of her contribution to their victory, however, the Coyotes voted unanimously to place Axel Betty on the honorary Fifteen Day Disabled List.

Both Penelope and Cackling Ed received baseballs autographed by the entire team for their contributions. Old Ed immediately dropped his baseball and, when Penelope automatically bent over to retrieve it for him, took the opportunity to look down her blouse. "Awooo," he said in admiration.

In making the presentation to Penelope, Rats said, "This award is for standing up to dickhead umpires."

In one of those happenstance opportunities that may come to journalistic photographers only once or twice in a lifetime—if they're extremely lucky—Greg Carroll caught the confrontation between cat and catcher on film. Outweighed by two hundred and ten pounds, Big Mike's expression showed all of the courage and determination of his larger relations in the feline world. With flattened ears and ruffled hair, Mycroft stood his ground, looking for all the world like Hamlet in his duel with Laertes. The photograph showed him at the moment of strike, right paw outstretched, claws bared, ignoring the ball and the mitt, concentrating on his soon-to-be hapless target.

Out of respect for Bad Cat Dude, the photograph was blown up, framed, and hung in a place of honor in the Coyote Clubhouse. In further recognition of Big Mike's bravery, the team refused to take the field unless Mycroft was on the dugout roof—and woe betide the umpire who objected.

The photograph should have won a Pulitzer Prize, but didn't. Penelope and Andy decided that it was an anticat bias on the judging committee. "Probably a bunch of armadillo lovers," Penelope said.

Caught up in the enthusiasm, Andy devoted the front page of the *Empty Creek News Journal* to the Coyote victory and his headline ran six columns in a type size normally devoted to the beginning of World War III or Martians landing on the City Hall lawn.

AWOOO, BABY!

CHAPTER
SEVENTEEN

The euphoria of the first win of the still young Coyote season didn't carry over to the matter of Penelope Warren, Big Mike, and the Police vs. Whoever Bumped Off Peter Adcock. The discovery of two youthful eye witnesses and the jubilation that brought lasted just long enough for Shane Baxter to say, "But we didn't see anybody. We heard a noise and we got scared and ran. I was afraid Mom would find out." His little brother agreed, nodding solemnly, eyes wide above a triple scoop cone of pistachio nut ice cream.

Still, the routine was followed and the two boys were questioned in detail. Often, eye witnesses didn't know they had seen something important until their memories were jogged. More often, unfortunately, eye witnesses screwed everything up, one person seeing a slender blond man and the next a fat bald man. Shane and Jackson fell somewhere in between.

Fortified by the ice cream cones (furnished by Officers Peggy Norton and Sheila Tyler), assurances of a ride in a black and white (red lights and siren, of course, Dutch promised), and the offer of a beer (by Tweedledee), Shane and Jackson slowly revealed what they had seen on the night in question, punctuated by an occasional diversion.

"For God's sake!" Penelope cried. "They're kids."

"So? A beer never hurt nobody. It always helps *my* memory. Besides, my mother—bless her soul—washed her hair in beer. Said it gave it body."

"We're trying to find out what happened, not get them drunk, or give them a shampoo."

"Jeez, it was just a thought."

"Do us all a favor," Penelope said. "Don't think."

"Better yet," Dutch said, "go out and get a six-pack or two."

"Dutch!"

"Hey, we're out of beer at home. Save me a stop after work."

"Make out a list, why don't you?" Tweedledee protested.

"Good idea. You need anything, Penelope?"

"Well, he could pick up my cleaning."

"Aw, boss."

At that point, Big Mike helped get the proceedings moving in the proper direction by taking a healthy lick from Jackson's ice cream cone—he had been stalking it for ten minutes. Jackson didn't appear to mind sharing germs with the "nice kitty," but his mother looked a little queasy, so Sheila went off to the refrigerator and quickly returned with a saucer of pistachio nut for Mikey—only a single scoop but he tucked in with gusto anyway.

With Mikey happy and Tweedledee (and presumably Tweedledum) reprieved from a trip to the supermarket and the cleaners, they finally got down to the important business at hand.

Yes, the boys had gone into Debbie's house to borrow her bat, planning to return it all the while.

Yes, Shane and Jackson had gleefully entered Coyote Stadium, squeezing through a narrow opening in the fence near the ticket turnstiles.

Yes, it was possible to play baseball by the light of a full desert moon (they'd find better things to do with a full moon soon enough, Penelope thought). They pretended to be big league ball players, taking turns with exaggerated windups on the pitching mound and gargantuan swings at imaginary fast balls, crashing home runs to every corner of the park, stealing bases, sliding with wild abandon. "I was Eddie Stiles," Shane said, "but I thought he'd hit better than he has."

"So did Rats," Penelope said, turning to Jackson. "And who were you?"

"I don't know," he replied shyly.

"Come on," Penelope insisted. "You must have been someone."

"Probably wants to be a detective," Tweedledee said, "like me."

Penelope thought that was a career cul de sac, but refrained from snorting derisively.

"He was Michael Jordan," Shane said, with a measured amount of disgust. "I keep trying to tell him Jordan sucked as a baseball player."

"I like Michael Jordan. He's cool."

"No hit, no field."

"Don't care."

"All right, what happened then?"

"Heard a noise."

"What kind of noise?"

"Loud," Shane said. "Really loud footsteps."

Penelope remembered her own midnight visit to the scene of the crime and attributed the loudness to the echo in an empty stadium. It *would* sound pretty spooky to kids.

"It was a monster," Jackson said.

"He still believes in monsters," his brother said, shaking his head. "I took him on two snipe hunts," he added, as though that explained everything.

Not a bad idea, Penelope thought. I'll bet I could get the Tweedle Brothers on a snipe hunt. They'd probably even go twice.

"What happened then?"

"We took off and Jackson left the bat. He was at the plate."

"Did you look back?"

"Not me," Jackson said. "I didn't want to see a monster."

Shane shook his head. "I just made sure Lame Brain was with me."

"Don't call your brother a Lame Brain."

"Well, I didn't leave the bat behind."

"Shane. . . ."

He acknowledged the warning in his mother's voice. "I'm sorry, Mom."

"That's better."

"Did you look back at all?" Dutch asked.

"Kinda," Shane admitted. "After Lame . . . Jackson was over the railing and into the tunnel, I sort of looked back. . . ."

Yes, there were two people. It wasn't a news flash. No one

had ever thought Peter Adcock committed suicide with a baseball bat.

Yes, he heard their voices, but they were speaking too low to make out what they might have been saying.

No, he couldn't tell if Peter Adcock had been with a man or a woman, because of the distance and only the hastiest of glances to ensure they were not being pursued.

"I had to go, then. Jackson was crying."

"Was not."

"Was too."

Yes, Shane and Jackson told their stories again and again. Ice cream cones were followed by cheeseburgers, french fries, and super dooper soft drinks. Even Big Mike found it difficult to keep up with those appetites, but he tried.

No, their eye witnesses did not illuminate anything about the murder of Peter Adcock, except the mystery of the missing bat and the small fingerprints, now definitely matched with Shane and Jackson Baxter.

No, the nature of Belinda's night job did not come up.

And, yes, Big Mike had his paw prints taken as well when he investigated the gooey black mess on the ink pad when everyone had their backs turned momentarily. He left a record of his passage all over the booking room of the Empty Creek hoosegow. Penelope thought the paw prints might come in handy if Big Mike was ever catnapped.

And so the promising beginning to an investigative day had ended with Penelope taking Belinda/Bambi and her boys back to their home, but even now, a day later, sitting in her office at Mycroft & Company, Penelope was still troubled by the lack of hard information. It wasn't that she thought Shane

and Jackson had lied. Quite the contrary. Time had passed
and, if anything, the boys would have had a tendency to
exaggerate what they'd seen, the events magnified in their
minds as they thought it over. But they'd told their story
simply, without embellishment. And that was what bothered
Penelope.

Surely they had seen something, a slight detail that hadn't
been revealed during the question and answer session—she
couldn't think of it as an interrogation. "We didn't ask the
right questions," she announced to the calendar hanging on
the wall above her desk, continuing her new habit of talking
to herself and inanimate objects. She wondered briefly if
hypnosis might uncover something, anything, either Shane
or Jackson might have seen but didn't remember.

Penelope took a number two pencil from her desk caddie—
decorated with the forbidding countenance of Monty Monte-
zuma, the San Diego State University mascot—and, using it
as a metronome, spoke softly to Big Mike who shared the
desk with all of the work that had accumulated during the
course of the investigation.

Big Mike's eyes followed the moving pencil, back and
forth, back and forth.

"Relax, Mikey, just relax. Allow your muscles to relax.
Feel the tension leave you now. You have a great sense of
tranquility. You feel your right front paw. It is very relaxed
and you feel that sense of relaxation traveling to your left
front paw and your back paws. Now all of your paws are
relaxed, so relaxed. You are getting sleepy, so sleepy. You're
falling asleep, but you can still hear my voice, even as you
fall asleep, and you will answer my questions."

His eyes followed the pencil as it continued its monotonous rhythmic journey, back and forth, back and forth.

"Sleepy, oh so sleepy. . . ."

Penelope dropped the pencil and nodded off.

Big Mike reached out firmly with his oh-so-relaxed right front paw and knocked the oh-so-boring pencil to the floor, yawned, stretched, yawned again, and went to look for something to eat, all without disturbing a fast-asleep Penelope.

So much for hypnosis as an investigative tool.

Penelope slept right through a flurry of activity as Kathy and Big Mike did quite a bustling business from one-thirty until three o'clock, selling nearly four hundred dollars worth of novels. Fortunately, Kathy was adept at juggling customers, telephone inquiries, the cash register, and Big Mike's assistance—sometimes simultaneously. It was enough to qualify her as a Hollywood agent.

At ten past the hour, however, a cacophony of unpleasant voices interrupted a pleasant dream in which Paul Newman allowed Penelope to ring the bell on the handlebars of his bicycle a la Butch Cassidy, while serenading her with a loud and somewhat off-key rendition of *The Yellow Rose of Texas*. Penelope didn't really care about the occasional discordant break in his voice. It *was* Paul Newman and it served Joanne Woodward right for letting him out of her sight. Even at seventy-something, those blue eyes turned Penelope's knees to mush, so it was a good thing she was firmly perched on the handlebars.

The argument had apparently started earlier, perhaps on the sidewalk, perhaps in their motel room, perhaps on their wedding night. Whenever and whatever its genesis, the quarrel entered Mycroft & Company in full bloom (appropriately enough for Paul Newman's choice of love songs) with Rose McCoffey screeching and Kendall McCoffey, Sr., clenching his fists in helpless rage.

"I don't care. It's my party and I can invite anyone I want."

"He's an unwashed lout," McCoffey fumed.

"He's a lifeguard, for God's sake. How can he be unwashed?"

"May I help you?" Kathy asked, going to stand in front of the Mycroft Holmes display.

"Are you a referee?" Rose demanded.

The game was delayed because of a rattlesnake with insomnia, perhaps brought on by the sudden disappearance of members of his (or her) extended family into bowls of chili. By rights, Mr. Snake—as he was quickly dubbed by Penelope—should not have been coiled on the grass in right field. But, as was their custom, the groundskeepers had watered the grassy portions of the baseball diamond prior to the teams emerging for batting practice. They didn't water a lot, but just enough to soften the grounds after a long day baking beneath the desert sun. The serious watering always took place after the game. And Mr. Snake, unable to sleep into a more nocturnal and natural hour for whatever reason, slithered unnoticed to a nice cool spot on the grass and took up residence just about where the right fielder would be normally positioned.

The teams straggled to the field and began tossing balls back and forth, loosening and warming their arms. But it wasn't until Rats took a fungo bat and started hitting pop ups to Jesus Gomez at second base that anyone took notice of their unwanted visitor. Rats hit a towering fly a little farther than he intended and the ball drifted into right field. Jesus hustled after it, eyes lifted into the twilight sky, concentrating on the ball. In a game, the right fielder would have called him off and made the catch himself. But this wasn't a game and Jesus was intent on the ball until. . . .

"Bzzzzzz."

The mind-chilling warning got Jesus's attention more than any right fielder ever did. He didn't know where the snake was so he did the only thing possible. In mid-stride, he stopped abruptly, leaped straight up and, arms and legs flailing at the air for purchase and momentum, reversed course like an Olympic long jumper trying to set a world's record—back-ward. He landed running and shouted, "Snake!" Arriving at the relative safety of the dugout roof next to Mycroft, Jesus burst into a furious torrent of Spanish, incomprehensible even to a native speaker of that beautiful language.

Jesus's acrobatic flight accomplished two things. First, it immediately provided a great source of amusement to his teammates and to the Bisbee Diamondbacks. Second, it gave Jesus an immediate nickname. Because of his given name, there had been halfhearted attempts to call him "Saint" or "Prophet" but Rats nipped that quickly—he had no wish to be blasphemous in the midst of a prolonged losing streak. No matter now. "And playing second base, Jesus "The Snake" Gomezzzzz!" (Decades later, after a long and distinguished career as a politician—his opponents and enemies would say the nickname was suitable—his grandchildren gathered around him at family reunions and would say, "Grandpa Snake, tell us about when you played second base for the Coyotes.")

"Go back and see if he has a ticket."

"Better get that ball. He can't throw it back."

Less than a month into the season and Rats, who had thought he had seen and experienced everything the great national pastime had to offer, shook his head in amazement. He was learning that the Empty Creek water supply affected more than the hormones of the inhabitants—it was adding to the lore of the game at a rapid pace. "Somebody get that snake out of here," he said.

His team suddenly had better things to do.

"It ain't in my contract."

"I'm calling my agent."

"You don't have an agent."

"I'm getting one now."

The groundskeepers disappeared.

Rats turned to Blake.

"Oh, no," she said, backing away hastily. "I've got to go sell some Coyote Dogs."

"I'll go with you," Penelope said. "Don't play with Mr. Snake, Mikey." It was an unnecessary suggestion. After the unfortunate incident at the police station, Big Mike had no intention of leaving Jesus alone on the dugout roof.

Rats collared the Bisbee manager at home plate. "Your snake's in right field," he said.

The Bisbee leader, one Skeeter Roberts by name, said, "I laid down the law to Eloise." He pronounced the name as "El-o-ise." "And I'm laying it down to you. We might be the Diamondbacks, but I ain't having no God damned snake in my dugout. It's bad enough we gotta put up with her foul-mouthed parrot." It appeared that El-o-ise Masters, the

Bisbee owner, had gone to the Marge Schott school of baseball management.

Now, a qualified herpetologist probably would have been unfazed by the presence of the rattler, but no one—not even the late departed promotional genius Peter Adcock—had foreseen the need for a snake expert on the roster of the Empty Creek Coyotes.

The umpires joined the discussion. "You're the home team. It's your responsibility to have the field in playing condition."

"It is in playing condition," Rats protested.

"Without snakes."

"Where's it say that in the rule book?"

"I dunno, but I'll find it if I have to. Get rid of the snake or the Coyotes forfeit."

The threat of forfeiture was enough to send Rats to the dugout to don Tank Easter's catcher's equipment. He didn't think he'd really need the mask but twisted his cap around backward and put it on anyway. Protected by shin guards, chest protector, and face mask, he clumped out of the dugout, grabbed a rake—the groundskeepers were considerate enough to leave their snake-fighting equipment behind in their unseemly haste to take a coffee break—and spotted an unsuspecting Kendall McCoffey, Jr., carrying a large cardboard box, coming down the aisle after Penelope.

"Are you playing tonight?" Junior asked. "I don't think that's legal unless we notify the league office."

"No, I'm not playing tonight."

"What are you doing with the rake?"

"What do you think? I'm going to beat it to death."

"Beat what?" Junior asked.

"You can't hurt Mr. Snake," Penelope said.

"You can't hurt Mr. Snake," Rats sneered. "Watch me."

"What snake?"

"Junior volunteered to help," Penelope said.

"What snake?"

"The rattlesnake in right field."

"Oh, no. You said Rats needed help carrying something. There was nothing about a rattlesnake."

"That's what he needs carried," Penelope said. "Of course, you have to catch it first." She looked sternly at Rats. "Without hurting it, unless you want to give it mouth to mouth resuscitation."

"I'm not going out there," Junior said. He put the box on the dugout roof. Big Mike meowed a thank you very much and immediately took up occupancy. Had there been room in the box, Jesus would have joined him.

"You want to forfeit the game?"

"No, but. . . ."

"Come on, then. You want everyone to think you're chicken?"

"I am chicken."

"Don't be silly," Penelope said. "Stormy's watching, and probably the woman of your dreams. What will they think?"

"Oh, shit."

There was a slight delay while Rats borrowed catcher's gear from the Diamondbacks for Junior. There was another delay while they coaxed Big Mike out of the box.

But, finally, they started across the infield followed by Penelope, who had decided to take command and direct snake removal operations.

The Coyotes cheered their manager and their managing

general partner. The Diamondbacks shouted encouragement from the safety of their dugout.

"Watch out, Rats, sometimes they charge when they're wounded."

"Got your insurance paid up?"

Penelope whistled a funeral dirge.

"Will you stop that!"

"The worms crawl in, the worms crawl out, and play tic tac toe on your snout."

The trio approached Mr. Snake warily, stopping twenty feet away. Andy was busily recording the dramatic moments for posterity and the next edition of the *Empty Creek News Journal*. Needless to say, he used a telephoto lens on his camera.

"Bzzzzz," Mr. Snake said, by way of howdy.

"He's just a little guy," Penelope said. "Even if he bites you, probably won't be sick for more than two or three days."

It had been a long time since Rats had attended Sunday School and he hadn't paid much attention then, always wanting to get outside and play baseball. So he wasn't particularly well-prepared in the prayers department. But he whispered all he could remember, anyhow. "Now I lay me down to sleep. . . ."

The fans encouraged the fearless snake catcher, his assistant, and his director.

"Awooo!"

"Now I lay me down to sleep," Rats repeated.

The sheer terror in Rats' voice decided it and Penelope relented, finally showing Christian charity. "You know, there is a better way to do this."

"I'm open to suggestions," Rats said.

"Me too."

"We could call Animal Control. They do this sort of thing all the time."

"You knew that," Rats accused.

"Yep." Penelope grinned.

"I'm gonna get you for this."

Baseball, Mom, apple pie, and rattlesnakes—it sure was good for taking a girl's mind off an unsolved murder.

CHAPTER
EIGHTEEN

The battle cry of the Coyotes greeted the Animal Control team, resounding through the stands as an older man and a younger woman scooped up Mr. Snake very efficiently, dropped him in a burlap bag, waved to the crowd, and went off to return a rather pissed Mr. Snake to his proper place in the ecological food chain.

"Awooo!"

The lack of batting practice—cancelled because of Mr. Snake's presence—didn't affect the Coyotes one whit. They sent thirteen batters to the plate in the bottom of the first inning, exploding for ten runs, capped off by Eddie Stiles' grand slam home run, his second hit of the inning.

"Awooo!"

As each Coyote left the dugout to take his place in the on deck circle, he paused to give Big Mike a scratch under the chin or a little pat on the butt. The players knew a good superstition when they saw one, and they viewed Big Mike's ejection from the previous game as the turning point in the

season. Mikey probably thought it was all a bit premature—
it was a long season as baseball pundits always pointed out—
but what the hell, a little chin music or a friendly pat never
hurt a cat.

By the fourth inning—the Coyotes were leading seven-
teen-zip—Rats was focused on superstitions himself. Penelope had already promised to have Big Mike in his accustomed
spot on the dugout, but Rats wondered how in the hell he
was going to get a rattlesnake to make an appearance each
night. Covering all the bases—superstition-wise—he sent a
message to Alyce Smith, who was conducting a minor seance
behind the plate at the time—contracting her to meet with
the inner children of his players before the first game in each
home stand. And, just in case, he went out between innings
to talk to the umpire with the quick thumb. "You were right,"
Rats said. "That woman sitting next to my wife is a real
troublemaker. Better keep an eye on her. Throw her out
again if you need to."

"Awooo!"

The final score was twenty-one to nothing. Peeper pitched
a three-hitter. Everyone in the starting lineup hit safely, led
by Eddie's five for five night and eight runs batted in. The
team was still in last place, but things were definitely looking
up.

With a nod to Mr. Chicago Cub, Ernie Banks, and his
famous statement when baseball was still fun at the major
league level, Rats hollered, "Let's play two!"

An apoplectic Skeeter Roberts made a rude gesture, one
more appropriate to a taxi driver at the height of rush hour
in Rome. But it was left up to El-o-ise Masters' parrot to
make the final comment on the game.

"Awk, team sucks, awk."

When everything was considered and given its proper weight in the greater scheme of the universe, it was a very satisfying evening, a pleasant diversion from more serious matters. But on the way home, Penelope found herself agreeing with Rats. They should have played two. Now, with Andy working late on his deadline, Penelope and Big Mike faced a solitary evening at home with little to do but ponder the vagaries of life as they applied to the murder of Peter Adcock.

Big Mike occasionally regressed to kittenhood, going on an energetic tear, racing from the kitchen, twice around the living room, down the hall, through their bedroom, into Penelope's home office, and back, leaping to the kitchen table, skidding across its smooth veneer to the very edge. He looked up at Penelope, not even breathing hard, despite his bulk, with the expression that said, "Cool, huh?" and took off again. It was a Big Mike version of the steeplechase. Able to leap tall computers at a single bound, easily reverse course in mid-air (he had more practice than Jesus "The Snake" Gomez), and navigate slippery surfaces without mishap, his personal best time for the course was four point two seconds. Whenever Big Mike felt the competitive urge to run, run, run, Penelope dashed for her stop watch and managed to time the second, third, and fourth circuits of the course.

Mycroft was on a record-setting pace on his fifth lap of the house when he suddenly deviated in the homestretch, much like Tom Courtenay in *The Loneliness of the Long Distance Runner*, still one of Penelope's favorite movies—she liked the way Courtenay said "cunning" in his best working class English accent. It came out as "koooning." But instead of glaring at the Guv, as Courtenay did in the film, Big Mike focused his attention on the Scrabble set, still standing as mute testimony to Andy's last defeat.

Andy had destroyed the evidence, removing Q-U-I-X-O-T-I-C from the board, but Penelope twirled the Lazy Susan of her deluxe Scrabble set and remembered the perfection of the play that had finally crushed Andy's hopes for winning. When she drew the letter tiles, the word just jumped out, even though the first arrangement on her holder read: T-X-O-U-I-I-Q. She was missing the letter C, but that was the beauty, simplicity, and luck of the play. During his last turn, Andy had played P-A-C, a type of shoe, a high moccasin, an insulated, waterproof, laced boot. But Andy forgot to play defensively, leaving the final letter one square beneath a red triple word square.

For Penelope, Scrabble was a contact sport, so she played immediately, placing the crushing word vertically up the right side of the board. But that was last week's game. It was like baseball and life. What you did last week or last night or tonight didn't carry over. There was always another game.

Penelope took the bag and began replacing the tiles in preparation for Andy's next challenge. Despite his appalling record, he always returned for another game. Penelope had once figured out that if they stayed together for the next forty years and played one game of Scrabble each week, she would win in the neighborhood of two thousand games—if he didn't improve. If he did, the lifetime record might reflect a hundred or so victories for Andy.

Big Mike interrupted the process by batting at the board with his right paw, dislodging the excellent play Andy had made that gave him a bingo—a play using all seven letters—

and a big score: H-A-M-H-O-C-K. Penelope had been proud
of him, but not enough to slack off. She immediately made
his word plural and played the rest of her tiles, following his
bingo with one of her own. B-A-C-K-E-R-S. Three bingos in
the same game wasn't bad, although not up to tournament
standards. Still, for a couple of amateurs. . . .

Once more, Big Mike batted at hamhocks, perhaps hinting
that it was time for a little snack, although he had scarfed
down a healthy portion of liver crunchies not an hour earlier
and, as far as Penelope knew, didn't care for pork in any
form. Later, of course, Penelope was quick to credit Andy
for playing the word in the first place and Mycroft for his
perspicacity. After all, had it not been for Mikey whacking
away at hamhocks, Penelope would not have been reminded
of hosanahs, although she was at a loss to explain why hamhocks reminded her of hosanahs, other than the two H's in
the words.

Whatever.

Big Mike whacked and Penelope picked out the proper
tiles and began a search for anagrams.

H-O-S-A-N-A-H-S.

She quickly rearranged the tiles.

S-A-N-H-A-S-O-H. What the hell was a sanhasoh? Absolutely nothing according to Penelope's well-worn *Webster's
Collegiate Dictionary*. That was too bad, Penelope thought. It
had a nice ring to it. The closest word was Sanhedrin, "a
great council" or "the supreme council and tribunal of the
Jews in New Testament times having religious, civil, and
criminal jurisdiction."

S-H-O-S-H-A-N-A.

Penelope looked it up. The nearest word was Shoshone of

American Indian fame, a river named after them in Wyoming, and the Shoshone dam, presumably on the same river.

Could have been typed wrong, Penelope thought.

Even if it was, what did Adcock have to do with Shoshone Indians?

Or river?

Or dam?

Damn!

Still, it had a nice ring to it. Shoshana. It might make a nice name for a daughter, if Penelope ever got around to having children and one of them happened to be of the female persuasion.

Other variations made little sense. There simply wasn't a decent word to be made from H-O-S-A-N-A-H-S, at least not using all eight letters.

H-O-S-S.

H-A-S.

H-A-N-A-H. It meant nothing. H-A-N was a Chinese dynasty from 207 B.C. to A.D. 220. Once there was a H-O-S-S in H-A-N.

S-H-A-N. A member of a group of peoples of Southeastern Asia.

Penelope went back to S-H-O-S-H-A-N-A.

There was something about the non-word she liked. Like Balaka, the name of a village in Malawi that Sidney-Veine had mentioned in one of his infrequent letters. Balaka. Shoshana and Balaka, perfect names for twin daughters. It sounded familiar to Penelope, but she couldn't explain why.

She returned to H-O-S-A-N-A-H-S, a misspelled hymn of praise for a mysterious woman. There must be a clue in that—

somewhere. Or Shoshana. Or a hoss in Han. "What do you think, Mikey?"

Having done his part for the evening—the steeplechase was a grueling event—Mikey had nodded off, but he perked up his ears at the sound of his name.

Penelope looked down at the Scrabble set, sighed, shook her head, and said, "Let's go to bed, Mikey."

Penelope brushed her teeth while Big Mike staked out his territory on the bed, like a homesteader in a Grade B Western. "There, honey, ain't it purty? There's water and grass and the sheep will have a wonderful home." Honey's eyes always filled with despair, seeing something quite different. Still, it was traditional. The pioneer woman, even the wife of a damned sodbuster and sheepherder, predated Tammy Wynette in standing by her man. "Yes, husband, it'll be just wonderful, a perfect place for little Johnny and little Jennifer," she always said, when she was really thinking, 'I knew I should have married the banker back in Ohio instead of traipsing all the way out here with this dodo and two squalling brats and a dog too dumb to find his own tail.' Big Mike might have sympathized with the sentiment, but claiming territory was serious business and needed his full attention.

Of course, as soon as Penelope plumped the pillows to her satisfaction, climbed into bed, opened her novel, and read a paragraph before promptly falling asleep, Big Mike had to do it all over again, finally winding up stretched out on Penelope's legs. Now if someone would just turn the damned light out. . . .

Penelope would never know whether it was the cramp in her finger—marking her place in the book—the weight on her legs, or the endless succession of letters dancing through her subconscious that awakened her. It didn't really matter, because at one thirty-seven a.m., she awakened with a start, shook her bookmark finger, and said, "Shan."

"Mewp," Mycroft replied. Take two aspirin and call me day after tomorrow. It was tough work leading the Coyotes to victory *and* running a steeplechase marathon. And tell those brats to knock off their whimpering.

"Shan," Penelope repeated. "Sharn. Sharon." S-H-A-R-O-N. It was simple if you added the R and then the O. The mystery woman's name was Sharon.

"Yes!" Penelope cried, pumping her fist in the air. "Sharon." There was only one slight flaw in that argument. As far as Penelope knew, she didn't know anyone by that name, at least not since the fourth grade when Sharon O'Donnell had beaten her out for class president by bribing her classmates with jelly beans. It wasn't Shoshana or Hosanahs at all. It was Sharon. But . . . there was no evidence that Peter Adcock had ever known a woman by the name of Sharon either. I suppose we could check the enrollment of *his* fourth grade class. . . .

Damn.

Sharn. There was a Sharn somewhere in all this.

Penelope had to fight Mycroft to get out of bed, but she managed it, and went off on a search of her bookcases, starting in the living room where she kept the classics of English and American literature.

The earth moved in *For Whom the Bell Tolls*, poor Jay stared wistfully across the waters at the green light in *The Great Gatsby*, and Sharn nursed a starving man in *The Grapes of Wrath*.

Rosasharn, in the Oklahoma dialect Steinbeck created.

Rose of Sharon.

Hot damn.

Hosanahs for Rose.

The Bible was next. The Song of Solomon, Chapter Two, Verse One. "I am the rose of Sharon, and the lily of the valleys."

Penelope went to the telephone and looked up the home number for Harvey McAllister and Teresa Sandia. A sleepy Teresa answered on the fourth ring. She is much more alert than I would be at this hour, a now wide-awake Penelope thought. "Teresa, it's Penelope."

"Who?"

"Penelope . . . Penelope Warren, your friend and provider of blueberry muffins." So much for alert.

"Oh, Penelope."

"What's the Spanish word for Rose?"

"She wants to know the Spanish for Rose . . . I will if you give me a chance . . . Harvey wanted to know what you wanted. I told him."

"Good, now what's the Spanish for rose?"

"Rosa."

"Oh."

"How about French?"

"Rose."

"Italian?"

"Rosa."

"German?"

"Rose."

Well, that was certainly unimaginative of the Spanish, French, Italians, and Germans. One would think that such major European languages would have come up with better words to describe such a lovely flower.

Penelope took a deep breath. "How about Hebrew? Do you know the Hebrew word for a rose?"

"She wants to know the Hebrew for rose . . . I'm going to, damn it . . . Penelope?"

"Yes?"

"Do I win something for this?"

"I'll buy all my flowers from you."

"You already do."

"That's true. I'll recommend you to all my friends."

"Penelope, we're the only flower shop in town . . . surf-boards, too, Harvey says."

"How about a double margarita at the Duck Pond?"

"No salt, blended?"

"Any way you want it."

"Okay. The Hebrew word is Shoshana."

Bingo! H-O-S-A-N-A-H-S equals S-H-O-S-H-A-N-A equals Rose.

"Did Peter Adcock ever send flowers to a woman?" Penelope asked, realizing it was a question that should have been asked long ago. Dumb, dumb, dumb.

"No," Teresa answered.

Damn.

"Well, thanks. I'm sorry I disturbed you."

"Want to go double or nothing on the margarita?"

Penelope's heart jumped. "Absolutely."

"He came in once and bought a single yellow long-stemmed rose. Does that help?"

To her credit, Penelope tried a number of other possible scenarios—just in case.

The bat boy did it. No, too small. He'd need a step ladder to reach Adcock's head and lacked a solid motive.

Nora Pryor. Ditto.

Lora Lou Longstreet. Too busy modeling for her artist.

Samantha Dale. Too busy making money for the bank's investors.

Junior. Too horny.

Erika the Hun. She could have discovered Adcock's secret romance with Rose and killed him in a jealous fit of her own. Not bad. Not good either, since there was a total lack of evidence pointing in her direction.

Eddie Stiles. Too devoted to his comeback.

Feathers McCoy. Too much in love with her husband to stray.

A supermarket clerk, a postal employee—they were always running amuck—Belinda "Bambi" Baxter, her sons, the CIA, the Columbian drug cartel—that was likely considering the cocaine, but while a substantial stash, it was hardly enough to get the attention of anyone in Medellin. D.W. or W.D., whoever that might be, was also likely, but the way things were going he would probably turn out to be Don Winslow of the U.S. Navy. Might as well say old Cackling Ed still had the strength to deliver a deadly blow with a baseball bat, or Adcock's mechanic had done it because the Jaguar wasn't brought in for its tuneup on a timely basis (whatever that was for a classic car), or his barber didn't like the way he parted his hair, or he failed to leave a big enough tip to suit one serving person or another, or Neil Simon had snuck into town just for the hell of it, or. . . .

Penelope took a deep breath and pronounced the name loudly.

"Rose McCoffey."

She had to be the mysterious girlfriend. That was now a given. But would she kill her secret lover? Had Peter Adcock abused her as he had Erika?

Have you ever made love in a dugout?

Had Rose gone to Coyote Stadium to fulfill Adcock's fantasy, been abused by him, and used the weapon at hand? Not if the letters he had written were any indication.

No, there was only one possible scenario that made sense.

It pointed the finger of justice squarely at Kendall McCoffey, Sr. Just suppose he discovered the love letters Peter Adcock wrote to Rose. Despite the fact that he and his wife were not on the best of terms, Senior was arrogant enough to be insanely jealous and quite willing to deprive Rose of the opportunity to find happiness with another man. Ergo, he arranged the meeting with Adcock, planned to kill him with a revolver or semi-automatic—he did say he preferred handguns—but used the baseball bat left behind by Shane and Jackson as a convenient weapon of opportunity. Killing Adcock also served a second purpose, allowing Senior to buy his deceased partner's share of the team and install his son as managing general partner. And it explained Rose's sad demeanor and her obsession with shoplifting as a way to anger her husband. It was a strange way to mourn a slain lover and apparent dope dealer, but each to her own.

Of course, there were a few loose ends, like the cocaine, to tie up, but all in good time.

There was also the little matter of proving it. Short of a confession (and what was the likelihood of that?), Penelope knew everything was circumstantial. There wasn't one shred of hard evidence to take to Dutch. He wasn't about to file charges against a seemingly stalwart member of the business community—even a jerk like McCoffey Sr.—without something more than a knowing smile from Penelope and her assurance, "But, Dutch, I know he did it."

Penelope was still working on the loose end department when headlights flashed across the living room window as a car turned into her driveway. She listened as a car door slammed, footsteps scrunched over the rock walkway, and the doorbell rang.

Penelope pulled her robe tight and went to greet her late night visitor.

For someone who had gone five for five and been the hero of the game only a few hours earlier, Eddie Stiles looked like his mama was in jail, his ole hound dog had run off with the neighbor's poodle, and his pickup truck had just been clobbered by the 5:15 to Yuma. It's a good thing he doesn't have a girlfriend, Penelope thought, or she'd be making tracks with the preacher man.

"Nice game," Penelope said. "Congratulations."

"Thanks."

Penelope translated that to mean, Who cares?

"It's sure nice to win a couple."

"Yeah."

Big deal.

"What's wrong, Eddie?"

"Nothing."

My life is over.

"I'll never understand men," Penelope said.

"What?"

"You come in here looking like a walking Country Western song and say nothing is wrong. Okay, have it your way. You probably just stopped by to borrow a book, something to read before you go to sleep. Let me see, what would your tastes run to? Police procedural? Spies? Locked room? A cozy, something with a Vicar and lots of tea? Hard-boiled? Yes, that's definitely it. Hard-boiled. . . ."

"It happened again," Eddie interrupted.

"That's better," Penelope said. "Another vodka bottle?"

"Worse," Eddie said. He pulled an envelope from his pocket. "I have to come up with $100,000 by Thursday, or they'll kill me."

CHAPTER
NINETEEN

Well, that certainly qualified as a loose end.

After setting Eddie up in the guest bedroom for what remained of the night, Penelope walked down to sit on the bank of Empty Creek (stomping her feet along the way to let any prowling rattlesnakes know she was coming). Big Mike, although more than ready for bed, accompanied her—someone had to protect her from the creepy crawlies if she persisted in wandering through the night.

Damn. Just when I had it all figured out, too.

Penelope stroked Mycroft in an automatic gesture of affection as she tried to make sense of the latest revelations. Instead of his usual response, the big cat sat watchfully, ears swiveling to catch and evaluate the sounds of the night.

Rose McCoffey was the mystery girlfriend, Penelope thought. Period. End of story.

McCoffey Sr. discovered the affair and killed Adcock in a crime of passion. That made sense. And there had to be a way to prove it. Killers make mistakes. They always do. We just have to find it.

But now a huge sum of money and a death threat entered the equation and jumbled everything. Someone with the initials W.D. was demanding that Eddie Stiles produce either the cocaine—which he knew nothing about—or $100,000 or else suffer most dire consequences. The note in Adcock's desk had implied a reminder to call W.D. Now that W.D. would never receive a return call, he had taken matters into his own hands and that posed somewhat of a problem since Eddie did not have the cash. And it wouldn't do to allow the death threat to be carried out, not when he had just started to hit like the Eddie Stiles of old.

And where did the cocaine fit in anyway?

Unless McCoffey Sr. and Adcock had been partners in a cocaine scheme, the murder had nothing to do with the dope and the payoff money.

Or did it?

Adcock had been involved in a dope deal with a very evil companion or companions, reneged, hid the dope, and planned to keep it, the payoff, and the subsequent profits for himself. But that was a very stupid thing to do, particularly when said evil companion or companions knew where he lived—and whatever else might be said about Peter Adcock, he was not stupid. Those involved in the drug trade were notoriously lacking in compassion or a sense of humor.

"Just suppose, Mikey, you are a dealer in black market lima beans, a very valuable commodity with a street value of millions. If someone took your lima beans, would you simply trot over one night and bash his brains out with a baseball bat? Of course not," Penelope answered for him. "You'd scratch his eyes out until he told you where the lima beans were hidden. Ergo, Peter Adcock was not killed by his dealer in contraband lima beans. I mean, cocaine. Ergo again, the murder and the cocaine are unrelated—I think."

Penelope decided to try for one more ergo. "When the dealer found out Adcock was dead, he entered the Coyote offices, hoping to discover a clue to his merchandise's whereabouts. Surprised by Blake, he knocked her out and eventually left empty-handed."

And now Eddie was set up to take the fall for a dope deal gone bad because of his background and potential earning power.

No, McCoffey Sr. killed Adcock in a jealous rage, totally unaware of Adcock's new part-time occupation as a purveyor of forbidden white powders, leaving the original owner holding an empty baggie.

That was it. It had to be. Definitely.

Probably.

Maybe.

Absolutely not.

Murder and cocaine were violent bedfellows. It was simply too coincidental to be dismissed as random. They had to be related. Therefore, McCoffey Sr. was a silent partner in more than a baseball team. He had to be involved with Adcock and the cocaine.

Didn't he?

Penelope shook her head, cleared it of too many confusing ergos, sighed, and stood up, brushing the dirt from her jeans. "Okay, Mikey, I give up. Let's go to sleep."

Penelope and Big Mike finally crept gratefully to bed. Mycroft rearranged the purty valley to his satisfaction and quickly fell asleep. "Damned cat," Penelope said with envy as she turned over. She was still wide awake, probably the only person in Empty Creek so afflicted. It just wasn't fair. There must be someone to call, someone sympathetic. But no, even Laney would probably be a little disgruntled at this hour.

Penelope squinched her eyes shut and waited for sleep to come. That didn't work, so she unsquinched them. She tried self-hypnosis again, telling her muscles to relax, trying to convince her mind that she was growing sleepy, oh, so sleepy. But it didn't seem to work without the pencil. She rolled over again and gave up, deciding it was too difficult to sleep when thoughts of cocaine, a huge sum of money, and a death threat intruded.

Hosanahs, Shoshanas, and Eddie's revelation intruded on the night.

What would Jessica Fletcher do?

Of course.

The enforcers were coming to collect from Eddie. Now, what if. . . .

Penelope smiled. Jessica would like it, and if it was good enough for Jessica. . . .

She turned the idea over in her mind, savoring every delicious nuance. Of course, there was the possibility that it would be a disaster. Dutch would rant, rave, and forbid her to do anything of the sort. But since she didn't plan to tell Dutch. . . .

Penelope smiled again. And the best part was that there *was* someone she could call now. There wouldn't be a lot of conversation, refined or otherwise, but it was contact with the outside world. She flicked the bedside lamp on and quickly dialed a number from memory.

The answering machine at the other end of the line beeped once.

"Penelope," she said and hung up. For the recipient, the single word would be as compelling as the Master's, "Come, Watson, come! The game is afoot."

Penelope was awakened by the sound of the University of Southern California fight song blaring from beneath the hood of Justin Beamish's red Cadillac convertible. So much for the discreet in Discreet Investigations, Inc.

Beamish, a dapper, diminutive man, and the principal of Discreet Investigations, Inc., knew Penelope well and had thus timed his arrival, and that of his traveling companions, for mid-morning, knowing full well from the obnoxious little voice that lived in his answering machine that Penelope had placed the call at two thirty-seven a.m.

Beamish, attired in what he considered to be the proper working duds for a private investigator of the discreet variety—cowboy hat, jeans, western shirt, and snakeskin boots—hopped out of the Cadillac, leaving it listing distinctly to the right because of the two giants who were unable to dismount as jauntily as their employer. The frame of the car creaked and groaned as they unwrapped their huge frames. At six feet eight inches and three hundred pounds each, the twin brothers were virtually indistinguishable but for the tattoos that adorned opposite arms. Ralph—or Russell—had the word MOTHER surrounded by a heart on his massive right arm. Russell—or Ralph—had the same tattoo on his left arm.

Unfortunately, Penelope could never remember which arm went with which brother, making identification impossible.

Beamish leaned into the car and tapped the horn for another rousing chorus of "Fight On."

By this time, Penelope and Big Mike had managed to rouse themselves sufficiently enough to stumble to the front door and greet their visitors, blinking in the bright morning sun. When Discreet Investigations, Inc. arrived, there was nothing for it but to awaken immediately or be awakened.

"Just," Penelope squealed. "Ralphie, Russell."

Just Beamish beamed as he disappeared into Penelope's arms. At five foot two and one hundred forty pounds (with boots), Beamish might have been the Invisible Man once Penelope set her mind to hugging.

Ralph and Russell greeted their buddy Big Mike as they awaited their own turn in the group grope. When Penelope emerged from the respective embraces of Ralph and Russell, more than a little breathless and disheveled—the twins knew how to hug a lady properly—she said, "Oh, what the hell," and went back for seconds. With hugs and kisses distributed all around, she stepped back and outbeamed Beamish.

Never one to be left out, Big Mike beamed down at her from Ralph's—or Russell's—shoulder. For Mikey, it was probably the equivalent of climbing a redwood. Now, Penelope thought, if I could just arrange to get El-o-ise's parrot on the other shoulder. . . . But that would be too mean. Not even Ralph—or Russell—would survive an encounter between cat and parrot unscathed.

"You could have called," Penelope said.

"But, dear lady, when beckoned, we boogie," Beamish

said. "Discreetly, of course. That's our new motto. Do you like it?"

"Very catchy," Penelope replied, wondering how one boogied discreetly.

"We wanted to see you," one of the twins said shyly. "Love you," he added, keeping Penelope's record for inducing blushes intact. Penelope thought it was Russell because of the T-shirt he sported with Emily Dickinson's likeness on it. Russell had a passion for thin women generally and the poetess in particular, despite having entered into a long-term relationship with a former, rather buxom, serving wench he had met while serving as one of Penelope's bodyguards during the unpleasant business at the Empty Creek Elizabethan Spring Faire some time back. In point of fact, both twins had been clobbered by Cupid's two-by-four at the Faire.

"I love you, too," Penelope said, "but who's minding the store?"

"Mother retired," Ralph said, "so we've been teaching Rebecca and Veronica."

Penelope had never met the woman who had given birth to Ralph and Russell eighteen minutes apart, but believed that she must be one remarkable lady. Sitting in as the clerk for an adult bookstore wasn't the usual matronly role. "That must be fun."

"They're expanding our line. Brought you the latest catalog. One for Laney, too."

"Yeah, how come you didn't use your gift certificate yet? Everybody else did."

"We'll have to talk about that later."

"I told my bro that you'd go for something exotic, like the love potion oils."

"Nah," Bro said, "too conventional. Penelope's more your basic bondage starter kit. Adventurous."

"Whatever I order better be processed by Becky or Ronnie, that's all I've got to say."

"Aw, Penelope, you're no fun."

"Yeah, we're taking a survey of our lady customers' preferences. Got to be business-like in our approach nowadays. Have to know the market. Anticipate trends in marital aids."

"Laney's skewed the survey so far."

"She would," Penelope said, knowing full well that Laney had probably purchased at least one of everything in the catalog with the possible exception of the home piercing kit.

"We're counting on you. Brought a copy of the market survey for you to fill out."

"Later. First, we boogie into the house for breakfast."

Ralph and Russell were on their third round of blueberry muffins when Eddie Stiles appeared nervously in the doorway of the kitchen.

"Who's he?" Ralph—or Russell—demanded.

"Eddie Stiles. He's the center fielder of the Empty Creek Coyotes."

"Where's Andy? You having an affair or something?" Their mother had instilled very strong family values.

"Of course not," Penelope said. "Eddie's the reason you're here."

"Did you use to be *the* Eddie Stiles?"

"Yes."

"You clean now?"

"Three hundred and eighty-seven days," Eddie said, not without a tinge of pride.

"Keep it that way."

"Yeah, or we break your neck."

Penelope wondered if the rehabilitation clinics utilized such direct methods. Their recidivism rate might go down drastically with Ralph and Russell on the staff as camp counselors.

"I'm staying clean," Eddie said.

"Good."

"Want a blueberry muffin?"

Penelope went through everything that had happened since Rats and Blake discovered Peter Adcock's body. No longer beaming, Just Beamish made notes on a yellow legal pad provided by Penelope, interrupting only occasionally to ask a question or two. When she had gone through the entire litany—Nora's telephone call to Laney. . . .

"She filled out our survey."

Lora Lou's business card. . . .

"So did she."

The missing bat and the questioning of Debbie. . . .

"Ditto."

"Will you please let me finish?"

"Sorry, Penelope. Just wanted you to see the wide sampling we have."

The attack on Blake and the erasure of all files on Adcock's computer, Erika von Sturm's somewhat inclusive number of dates with Adcock. . . .

"We should get them copies of the survey. . . . Sorry, Penelope."

McCoffey, Sr.'s purchase of Adcock's interest in the team,

the vodka bottle, the trip to Sedona, the stash in the Jaguar's spare tire, Hosanahs and Shoshanas. . . .

"Well, what do you think so far?"

"There's more, dear lady?" Just Beamish asked incredulously. He was getting a cramp in his writing hand.

"Oh, yes," dear lady replied.

Over more coffee, Eddie repeated his tale of finding the note waiting for him after the game.

Penelope trotted out the note Eddie had received. It demanded cash or coma in large block letters cut from *Empty Creek News Journal* headlines.

"Wild Dogs," Ralph—or Russell—said as he looked at the initials.

"Yep, Wild Dogs," his brother agreed.

"What are Wild Dogs?" Penelope asked.

"Motorcycle gang."

The twins looked at each other.

"Didn't know they were into dope."

"Weapons were their thing."

"Must have branched out."

"They always were upwardly mobile."

"Think they're bad."

"But they ain't."

"Nope. We're bad."

"The baddest." On that note, Ralph and Russell exchanged a high five, causing the windows to rattle in their panes.

The beam was restored to Beamish's face when Penelope finished explaining her plan.

"Delightfully deceitful," he said.

"Cool," the twins said.

Penelope read the first question of the marital aids survey, blushed, and hid the form away from prying eyes.

"Could I see the guest list for the party?" Penelope asked McCoffey Jr., feeling just a little guilty, knowing that she was trying to prove that his father was a murderer. Junior was too nice a guy to have a cold-blooded killer for an old man.

"Sure," Junior answered cheerfully, "but you know just about everyone on it."

Penelope glanced over it quickly. Junior was right. Rose had invited all the luminaries of the community and a few others as well, including Angelique Lamont. She must have joined the Chamber of Commerce, Penelope thought. I'll have to nominate her for office. She quickly ran down the names of the others on the list.

Some of the guests would know Beamish and the twin brothers, but that couldn't be helped. The recipient of the duplicate note signed by W.D. wouldn't recognize them, however. "How do you feel about older women?" Penelope asked.

"I love your sister, don't I?"

"You better not let Stormy know you think of her as an older woman."

"Don't worry. I'm not stupid."

"In that case, I'd like to add a name."

"Sure."

"Her name is Belinda Baxter."

"Who's she?"

"Quite possibly, the woman you've been waiting for."

"You certainly look satisfied with yourself," Andy said when he met Penelope at the Double B for a quick bite before the game.

"That's what I said," Debbie agreed. "I think she's pregnant."

Andy, who had almost settled his lanky Ichabod Crane-like frame into a chair, leaped up with alacrity, banging his knee against the table. "Ow, are you? Ow, damn!"

"I hope your liability insurance is paid up." Penelope directed this statement to Debbie as they watched Andy hop about like a scarecrow afflicted with St. Vitus Dance.

"It would be a frivolous lawsuit. The Double B is not responsible for customers who cannot seat themselves properly."

"Ow, that hurts."

"I suppose you're right."

"Well, are you?"

"Poor baby."

"Penelope!"

"No, dear heart of mine, I am not pregnant. I always look fresh and radiant, glowing with the exuberance of life." Had she been in Father John's confessional, nervously reciting her latest accumulation of venial sins—hiding her little sister's doll, beating up on the boy next door, playing doctor with the boy down the block, rolling an occasional forbidden word off her tongue for the sheer joy the sounds provided, gradually progressing to the mortal sins that endangered her soul, oh, those embarrassing lustful thoughts—Penelope might have admitted her guilt in deceiving so many of her friends. She hated keeping secrets from Andy but, although she trusted him implicitly (not bad for a newspaper guy always on the quest for a story), the fewer people who knew of her plan, the greater its chance for success. Frankly, Penelope thought, it better work or I'm giving up the detective business for needlepoint.

Armed with a leather bag filled with baseballs, Jesus "The Snake" Gomez slowly and methodically checked his position for creatures of any sort, advancing tentatively from the dugout to the pitcher's mound, throwing baseballs along the ground in a ninety degree arc, watching carefully for movement, listening intently for the buzz of poisonous snakes, the ominous hiss of a gila monster, or the click of the feared giant racing tarantula.

"Man, I'll take your average rattlesnake any day," Big Rap said. "They got antivenom for snakebite. But if a gila monster gets you, it's all over. They just hang on and chomp."

"Yeah, but gila monsters are big and fat," Little Rap said. "You can outrun one of them dudes. What I don't ever want to see is the giant racing tarantula. Fastest spider in the world. And their poison, man, ain't no cure. One of them gets you, might as well look around for a comfortable place to fall down cause it *is* all over."

"Don't they give you any warning?" Scooter Hernandez asked.

"Oh, yeah, but it's usually the last thing you hear," Little Rap answered. "Clicking sound. They warming up their teeth. You hear that clicking, man, you know somebody's getting ready for supper and you's the lamb chop."

"Hey, Snake, you looking a little green, man. You all right?"

Jesus "The Snake" Gomez weathered the dugout discussion, found the perimeters of the second base position uninhabited, and relaxed until the Coyotes took the field. As luck would have it, however, the leadoff man for the Diamondbacks hit the first pitch sharply to second base. The Snake took two steps in and was ready to scoop it up when the Diamondback dugout erupted with the buzz of the biggest damned rattlesnake ever found. The Snake's heart stopped, the ball went between his legs and, despite being clinically dead for an instant, The Snake levitated, hanging in the air for the longest time, before crashing to the ground.

Every last one of the players in the Diamondback dugout had rattles in their hands, instruments which produced a most credible imitation of a really pissed off serpent. The Diamondbacks would have razzed Gomez unmercifully, except it was too difficult to shout while collapsed in helpless laughter.

Jesus got up, brushed the dirt from his pants, and went back to his position, muttering a variety of colorful imprecations about the Diamondbacks, their mothers and fathers, their girlfriends, their unborn children, and even their favorite pets.

His invocations had no impact whatsoever as the second batter hit a perfect double play ball to shortstop. Little Rap fielded it perfectly and tossed it to second where the surehanded Jesus would have been waiting to complete the double play in the normal course of events. On this occasion, however, Jesus was desperately back-pedaling and pointing to the diamond-shaped head of a rattlesnake, mouth gaping, fangs at the ready, peering out from beneath the second base bag. The ball dribbled into short right field while the Diamondbacks circled the bases, winding up at second and third before Scooter threw a one-hop bullet to Hank "The Tank" Easter at the plate.

Rats charged the umpire, demanding an interference call. He might have gotten it, too, but the umpires were holding their sides, laughing hysterically.

Alyce Smith took that opportunity to dash out to second base, put her hands on Jesus's trembling shoulders, stare him in the eyes, and scold his inner child. She also ripped the rubber snakehead from beneath the bag to Jesus's gratitude.

By the time order was restored, Alyce had returned to the stands, climbing over the short wall, showing a rather shapely leg to the fans in the process—all without drawing the wrath of the umpires or the ushers; it *was* an infraction of the rules to enter the field of play for whatever reason, however humanitarian in nature.

With Jesus's inner child serene once more, the game continued. As luck would have it, of course, the next batter walked, loading the bases, and the Coyote infield again moved into double play depth. The Diamondback clean up hitter dug in at the plate and hit another perfect double play ball just to the left of The Snake. The play was to second, but with the damnable whir of those rattles from the Diamondback dugout loud in his ears, Jesus fielded the ball cleanly, planted his feet, and threw a strike into the enemy dugout, beaning the Diamondback manager right between the eyes.

"Better put them rattles away, boys," Skeeter said, before dropping unconscious to the dugout floor.

Two runs scored.

The fallen warrior was hauled off to Empty Creek General for X-rays.

Penelope expected Rats to pull Jesus from the game, banishing him to second base hell for the rest of the season at least, but he simply leaned back in the dugout, crossed his arms, and said, "We'll get those runs back."

Which they did, going on to win thirteen to two.

The Diamondbacks snuck out of town with their rattles tucked between their legs.

Awooo, baby!

After the game, Penelope looked up at the box where McCoffey Sr. and his wife stood, applauding their victorious team. With an off day on the morrow, it was time to boogie at the victory party.

CHAPTER
TWENTY

"'Twas the night before Christmas, when all through the house, not a creature was stirring. . . ." Except it wasn't Christmas Eve and Penelope *was* stirring—a lot—so much so that Mycroft had removed himself to the chest of drawers. It was hard but stable.

Penelope turned over for the hundredth time. These late night romps through the dark hours of the night were becoming tedious. She couldn't keep waking friends in the middle of the night just because she couldn't sleep—could she? Penelope thought briefly of placing a call to Robert Sidney-Veine in Malawi. After all, the sun was shining brightly in Central Africa now, but she discarded the idea. By the time she deciphered the intricacies of making an international call, with country codes and city codes and God knows what else, it would be midnight in Malawi and the Old Boy would be asleep. Damn, it just wasn't fair that everyone she knew close at hand was sleeping happily while the tentacles of insomnia clutched her brain, reminding her of The Plan. She tried mightily to put The Plan from her mind, but any number of diversions she tossed out to Brain Control failed to take hold for more than a few seconds, although the thought of a risqúe phone call to Andy seemed promising. But it wasn't his fault that the amateur detective hopeful of closing out a difficult and confusing case had an interminable, and sleepless, wait to see if the plan would work.

Penelope still worried about potentially pesky loose ends. Like any plan, *The Plan* would have them. It was inevitable, like packing for a two-year sojourn in Africa. Despite attempts to anticipate every need, there were important things forgotten—masa flour for making tortillas and a goodly supply of taco sauce were necessities of life not readily available on the Horn of Africa, as Penelope had discovered to her chagrin, thinking naively that good Mexican food had surely traveled to the corners of the globe. In her next entrepreneurial venture, Penelope was determined to open a Mexican restaurant in Nairobi. That thought was good for fifteen seconds before her mind slipped right back to the current matter. Where was Paul Newman when you needed him? Penelope smiled in the darkness as another ten seconds passed. A little late night dalliance with Paul would be just the thing. . . .

A leaf-blowing, weed-whacking, bug-zapping loose end thundered into Brain Control, zinging her, but good.

Penelope sat up in bed and slapped her forehead in disgust. "Oh, my God, Mikey, how could we have been so stupid?"

Mikey twitched. Barely. Speak for yourself.

"Come on, we've got to get to the library."

That presented a slight problem as it was past midnight and the library's hours were normally from ten in the morning until nine in the evening. Since thieves had never been known to break in after hours to steal books and any overdue fines hanging around would be considered chump change, there was no need for a night watchman to patrol the stacks of fiction, non-fiction, reference, or out-of-state telephone books.

Undeterred by such a minor detail, Penelope picked up the telephone and called the home number of the librarian.

After several rings, the line was answered by a sleepy feminine voice doing a very credible imitation of Penelope when she was rudely awakened.

"Herro?"

"Leigh, wake up, it's Penelope. I have a research problem."

"Liburry's closed."

"I know the library's closed. That's why I'm calling you. We have to open it."

"Open what?"

"The library," Penelope repeated patiently, sympathetically. "It's important or I wouldn't have called."

"Why?"

Penelope plunged on. "What do you know about popular music of the fifties and sixties?"

"It's popular," Leigh replied. "Or it was," she added, slowly grasping the situation. "Is this some kind of test?"

"You'll probably get a medal of valor from the American Library Association."

"I think I'll have a key made for you."

"That might come in handy later, but it doesn't help me now."

"All right, but you'd better stop for coffee. Black coffee. A large black coffee."

Big Mike was not pleased at being forced out into the cold, cruel night—it was a balmy seventy-eight degrees at one-fifteen a.m., according to the flashing thermometer and clock above Empty Creek National Bank. In point of fact, his annoyance was unwarranted as Penelope had told him he could have the bed all to himself for awhile but, of course, his desire to be in on any fun and his natural curiosity forced him to go, complaining loudly all the way to the Jeep, probably asking unsympathetic deities how he was expected to get his accustomed twenty hours of sleep at this rate.

At least, Penelope thought gratefully, he slept all the way into town, during the brief stop for coffee, and while waiting for Leigh to arrive.

When Leigh pulled up next to the Jeep, she again dispelled the popular stereotype of librarians. Even a tousled and sleep-deprived Leigh was a most suitable candidate for immortality on David Macklin's canvas. Many a young man vowed to give up reading for all time and enough tears were shed to fill the local creek bed to overflowing when Leigh married Burton Maxwell, an English instructor at the local college. And now that she had taken up training for the triathalon, Leigh's always trim figure had settled perfectly in all the right places.

"Good morning," Penelope said brightly, as she handed over the coffee. "How's Burt?"

"Sleeping," Leigh said curtly.

"I'm not surprised. You're too grumpy in the morning. I'd sleep too."

Leigh stared at the darkened building. "You know, I don't think I've ever been in a library in the middle of the night."

"You see. This is a new experience. Everyone should be open to new experiences. You should be grateful I called."

"Ha!"

"Next time, bring Burt and boff him in the stacks."

"Penelope!"

"Well, that would be a new experience, too," Penelope said somewhat defensively. "You could write an article for *Library Journal:* the advantage of making love in Reference rather than Circulation."

"Periodicals," Leigh said. "There's a very comfortable couch in Periodicals."

"There you have it, then. You've already done the preliminary research. Which is what I have to do now. Why don't you give old Burt a call? It'll give you something to do while I work."

"I'll read while I wait, thank you very much."

Penelope shook her head. "And when you could be breaking new ground in librarianship. . . ."

In the reference section, Penelope quickly found what she was looking for. "Gotcha," she whispered sadly.

At the microfilm machine, Penelope threaded the newspaper film expertly, picking a recent year at random and working backward from there. Sitting at the machine, Penelope passed through the weeks and months as she pleased. With the touch of a finger, she could make time stand still or pass before her eyes in a blur of newsprint. After forty-five minutes, she stopped the machine and stared at the screen for a long time. Again, she whispered, "Gotcha." Then, she rewound the film watching *tempus fugit.* Penelope knew the tense was wrong, but she wasn't about to start conjugating Latin verbs at this point in her life. She only wished she could fast forward as easily to Rose McCoffey's party and bring an end to the whole unhappy business. An even better alternative would be to reverse time, and go back to that fateful night to prevent murder.

Penelope sighed and called the answering machine of Discreet Investigations. She left instructions for amending The Plan.

The McCoffeys: Senior, Junior, and Rose, formed the receiving line at the entrance to the Lazy Traveler Motel pool area, greeting their guests affably, although Junior's face had the peculiar expression of a hyperventilating monster from his computer game.

Penelope did not offer her hand to Target Numero Uno, using the squirming Big Mike in her arms—he was eager to check out the hors d'oeuvres—as an excuse to avoid physical contact with a man she hoped might yet turn out to be a killer. She looked for a trace of nervousness, but McCoffey Sr.'s expression was noncommittal. If the communication he had received anonymously—a revised version of the W.D. note to Eddie—caused him any consternation, he showed no sign of it. "Welcome to Rose's little soiree," he said, passing Penelope on to Target Numero Dos as he turned to smile at Mayor Tiggy Bourke.

"Good evening, Shoshana," Penelope said, smiling at her hostess. It was the last chance to see if Rose might yet turn out to be Peter Adcock's mysterious girlfriend. Just in case, Rose, too, had received a demand from W.D.

But Rose McCoffey looked truly confused. "Excuse me? What did you say?"

"It's the Hebrew for your name. I think it's very pretty." Penelope quickly moved on without waiting for a response. The odds were beginning to favor Target Numero Tres. Damn.

"Nice cologne," she said. Big Mike wrinkled his nose at the strong scent wafting from Junior.

"Did I use too much?" Junior asked, as he watched Big Mike wiggle free and chart a stately course for the chow line. "I want to make a good impression."

"I wouldn't worry about Mikey's reaction. He doesn't have the feminine appreciation for such things."

"But she's not here yet."

"Belinda's fashionably late. She'll want to make a good impression, too. Just don't fall into the pool." Penelope left him with a reassuring smile, hoping that Belinda did like him.

"Scouts are coming in for the weekend series," Eddie Stiles said. "This is my chance. I wish I could just concentrate on baseball."

"It'll be over soon," Penelope promised, hoping she was right—about everything—as she looked around nervously for the other principals involved in The Plan. If no one showed. . . . Penelope shook her head. "You just keep hitting. Everything else will take care of itself."

"That's what Rats says."

"Believe him."

"I've finished Kathy's painting," David Macklin said. "I can slip you into my schedule right after Angelique and before Laney."

"Laney, too?"

"It's a present for Wally," Lora Lou said. "You should pose. You'd look good hanging over Andy's fireplace."

"He doesn't have a fireplace." Penelope had a vision of herself mounted in a trophy room between the twelve point buck and a mountain lion.

"Well, he should," Lora Lou said, "and you don't *have* to take your clothes off. He can always use his imagination, I suppose."

"Oh, come on," Laney said, joining the group, "don't be such a stick in the Empty Creek mud."

"Fine talk from someone who's supposed to be my best friend."

"I'm just thinking of you. You should want to support the arts. Nora's doing it. Even Samantha, but she's going to wear a mask, of course, which I'm designing. It wouldn't do for the financial community to recognize their bank president. We could even do a calendar. The Women of Empty Creek. We'll make a fortune."

"I thought we were supporting the arts."

"I'm just thinking of David. He's a fine painter. There's nothing in the rule book that says you *have* to be penniless and cut off your nose."

"Ear."

"Whatever."

Further discussion of the embryonic Empty Creek Foundation for the Arts was interrupted by a curious sound. Clump, clump, shuffle, shuffle. The three ladies and the artist turned to find Cackling Ed bearing down on them armed with a walker.

"Who invited you?"

"And what are you doing with a walker?"

"Borrowed it from Tilly Goodnight," Old Ed cackled. "Hope she doesn't have to go to the bathroom before I get home."

The purpose of the walker soon became evident as Cackling Ed utilized it as a stepladder to hoist himself to a level suitable for peering down blouses. "Nice party dress, Laney," he said.

Laney gave the walker a powerful kick.

"Whatcha do that for?"

"You're a disgusting old man."

"Aw, come on, Laney, you wuz always my favorite. How about you come to the dance with me Saturday night? You need an older gentleman to put out them fires."

"Then I'll find a gentleman."

"Oops, gotta go." Old Cackling Ed shuffled and clumped his way to greet Angelique Lamont, another potential patroness of the arts.

When Dutch and Stormy arrived, Penelope avoided them. Dutch would be one unhappy police chief when he found out what had been set up without bringing him into the information loop. As Dutch and Stormy circled the pool, Penelope sidled away from them, heading for Andy who had just left the receiving line. She waved, caught his attention, and waited for him to make his way over, keeping one eye on the receiving line, wondering when and how Discreet Investigations would make its dramatic entrance.

"You look like you just swallowed a pickled herring," Andy said.

"Is that any way to greet the love of your life? Yesterday,

I was glowing and radiant. Today, I look like a pickled herring?" She stretched up on tiptoes to kiss him anyway.

"I didn't say you *were* a pickled herring, just that you looked like you ate one. Pickled herrings are yucky. I don't know how the Dutch can stand them. Their gin is quite palatable, however. Amsterdam is rather a nice city, too. Except for the pickled herrings, of course."

"I suppose you browsed through the *Walletjes?*" It was the famous red light district where prostitutes sat in windows displaying their charms.

"Naturally," Andy said grinning. "I believe in sampling all the delights of a city. Nothing but window shopping though," he added hastily.

"Well, just remember that *I* am the delight of Empty Creek, Arizona."

"They were too Rubenesque for me. I like my women lean and mean."

"Well, thank you, I think."

"Why don't we sneak away? It seems like forever since we played Rescue the Princess."

"That would be rude," Penelope said, "but hold the thought." She looked over at the receiving line where arriving guests had slacked off. Damn near everyone was present and accounted for—except Discreet Investigations. For the thirty-seventh time since beginning to count, Penelope wondered where they were and how they would arrive. Belinda and Junior were at the bar. Belinda smiled, bobbing her head in agreement with something Junior managed to stammer. At least that was going according to plan. Damn Beamish and those twin brothers, anyway. Penelope looked back at Andy.

"And, by the way, don't you dare have me stuffed and mounted," she said.

Andy sighed. "What *are* you talking about?"

Big Mike quickly tired of the noise—feet tripping not so lightly all around him, dangerously close to his tail—and headed off to find a hidey hole. The food wasn't all that great, anyway. The sausages were too spicy for his taste, there wasn't a Coyote Dog to be had, and for a hostess who wanted acceptance by the upper reaches of Empty Creek society, Rose McCoffey had not provided proper delicacies such as lima beans.

The cocktail party chatter diminished as he entered the parking lot, intending to curl up in the familiar surroundings of Penelope's Jeep, but he was sidetracked by a Mustang convertible with the top down emanating a familiar fragrance. Big Mike paused and sniffed the air. Doubtless, he approved, for he tensed, gathered his muscles, and leaped effortlessly into the car. Even with its top down, the interior was dark, for the car was parked well away from any of the light stanchions that provided illumination for the Lazy Traveler's guests. The black leather seat was pleasantly warm. Big Mike turned around several times, plumped the leather with his claws, and curled up, doing his furry beach ball imitation. After a good sigh to savor the rewards of a day well-spent, he promptly fell sound asleep.

When she heard the deep throaty roar of motorcycles, Penelope wondered no longer how her enforcers would make their entrance. They rode their hogs right into the party—or at least two of them did. Beamish's motorized steed hardly quali-

fied as a hog. It was more of a piglet, better suited to his
own diminutive stature. But what he lacked in motorcycle
horsepower, he more than made up for with a panache of
costume. Penelope particularly liked the purple hat with
feathers, although she said, "You're supposed to be someone
who can break kneecaps, not a pimp."

Beamish accepted her criticism cheerfully. "It's all in the
props, dearest Penelope," he said, lifting a purple pant leg
to display a tire iron strapped to his leg. "I *am* Purple Dog
the Collector," he snarled.

Ralph and Russell, on the other hand, wore greasy jeans
that looked as though they would stand up on their own
and dingy T-shirts. The backs of their denim jackets were
decorated with snarling, salivating wild dogs. Their huge
frames strained the seams of the jackets.

"Where did you get their colors?" Penelope asked.

"Had a little discussion group."

"Quoted Emily Dickinson."

"Didn't they have any that fit?"

"Jeez, Penelope, we beat up the biggest Dogs we could
find."

"Never mind," Penelope said. Rose McCoffey, eyes flashing, was bearing down on them. "It's boogie time."

"You actually know these people?" Rose asked, skidding
to a halt. She was angry, but she showed no sign of guilt or
of making a connection between her note and the three party-
crashers.

"I was just explaining that it's a private party," Penelope
said, looking past her for McCoffey Sr.'s reaction. He was
talking to a private security guard hired for the occasion.
Damn, Penelope thought, a perfectly normal response to the

arrival of outlaw bikers. It was looking bad for Contestant Number Three.

"It certainly is."

"Bitchy little thing, ain't she?"

Had there been any doubt remaining in Penelope's mind about Rose's guilt in the death of Peter Adcock, her attitude— bitchy, indeed—dispelled it. Rose stamped her foot, demanded that the intruders leave her party, and threatened to call the police to have them removed if they did not exit voluntarily. Even Jessica Fletcher would have been convinced of Rose's innocence.

"I'll escort them out," Penelope said.

"We only wanted to say hello to an old friend," Beamish said, acknowledging Penelope's signal to ignore Uno and Dos and to wait for Tres.

"You'd better," Rose said. "Five minutes. Period. End of story."

The twins turned on the charm.

"Anger brings out your beauty."

"Absolutely."

"Absolutely stunning."

"A vision."

"Worthy of a gift certificate."

"Two."

"Nay, three—a thousand gift certificates would be unworthy of her splendor."

"All the oils of the east."

Rose smiled and touched her hair coyly. "Do you really think so?"

Oh, good God, what drivel, Penelope thought, but she was forced to admit it worked, although she'd better warn the twins to keep one hand on any figurines they happened to have lying about.

"Where is the other one?" Beamish asked after Rose had departed, promising each of the twins a dance later.

"In the ladies room, I think," Penelope replied before she was interrupted by the roar of another herd of motorcycles descending upon the Lazy Traveler Motel.

"You were supposed to make sure we weren't followed," Russell—or Ralph—said.

"I thought you were," his brother replied.

"I think it may be time for another discussion group," Penelope said, as several very real and very big Wild Dogs entered the crowded confines of Rose McCoffey's soiree and spotted their little gathering.

When the private security guard saw what he perceived as Wild Dog reinforcements, he handed his cap to McCoffey Senior and headed for higher ground.

Penelope saw Dutch on Stormy's cell phone and suspected he was calling for backup. Good idea, she thought, as she hurriedly prepared to participate in her very first gang fight, wishing that she had thought ahead enough to rent *The Wild Ones*. She suspected a few pointers from the youthful Marlon Brando and Lee Marvin might be rather helpful just about now. Her rifle might be handy too. And just where in the hell is Big Mike in my hour of need? He was going to be really sorry he missed the Wild Dogs. This was his kind of encounter.

Oh, well. It was too late for research, going home for suitable armament, or looking for Big Mike now. It was High Noon at the Lazy Traveler Motel Corral. Penelope girded her queasy loins for battle and thought, This isn't going at all the way it does for Jessica Fletcher.

The real Wild Dogs advanced five abreast.

"Let me handle this," Purple Dog said.

"It was my idea," Penelope said.

"I'll take the two on the right," Ralph—or Russell—said. "You take the two on the left."

"Okey dokey," Russell—or Ralph—replied.

"Good plan," Penelope said. "I'll take the big ugly guy in the middle."

"He's mine," Purple Dog said gallantly, as he lifted one purple pant leg and fumbled for his tire iron.

Dutch was coming up behind the Wild Dogs, but he was still too far away. Andy was on the far side of the pool, his back turned. Most of the other guests were wisely backing away from the impending confrontation.

"Don't start yet," Purple Dog said. He was still trying to get the tire iron loose.

Penelope took a deep breath. She wasn't sure about the protocol for starting a gang fight. Probably there were a few blustery male rituals to go through first.

As it turned out, everything took care of itself.

Just as Penelope was about to pop Big Ugly Wild Dog, he pointed across the pool. "There she is," he said. "Yoo hoo, Rose."

Yoo hoo?

Penelope risked a glance over her shoulder and nodded grimly. Target Numero Tres had just emerged from the ladies room. Angelique Lamont smiled at Andy and took a glass of champagne from a passing waiter.

"Yoo hoo, Rose, over here."

Angelique heard the second cry, saw the Wild Dogs, and dropped her glass.

Gotcha, Penelope thought, with more than a little remorse. She had liked Angelique, but. . . .

When Penelope turned back, Big Ugly Wild Dog was still waving. Penelope popped him right in the nose anyway. Yoo hoo, indeed. What kind of way was that for a biker to talk? Protocol be damned. That was as good a way as any to start a rumble.

Big Ugly Wild Dog grabbed for his nose with one hand and Penelope with the other, but she slipped his grasp easily and took off after Angelique, who was rapidly exiting the premises.

"Awooo!" Cackling Ed hollered as he bashed a Wild Dog with Tilly Goodnight's walker.

By all later accounts, Penelope would realize she had missed a pretty good fight, but she was preoccupied in forming her own little discussion group with a certain exotic dancer. And if she didn't get moving, she might have to chase Angelique all the way to Nogales. Angelique had a good head start and it would take too long to circle the pool and give chase.

Although she hadn't ridden a motorcycle since her days in Africa, Penelope hopped on Beamish's piglet, cranked it over, revved the engine a couple of times, and popped a wheelie as she headed for the parking lot, scattering a group of late arrivals as she roared down the sidewalk and jumped the curb, spotting her quarry running hard through the parking lot.

Red lights and sirens keened through the streets of Empty Creek, converging on the Lazy Traveler Motel.

Penelope picked an aisle between the parked cars and

pointed the machine at Angelique. The exotic dancer glanced over her shoulder and dashed between a pickup and a Mazda to the next aisle.

Damn it.

Penelope skidded through the turn at the end of the drive and headed back toward Angelique, who was now fumbling in her purse as she ran.

Penelope was still fifty yards away as Angelique threw her purse in the convertible and vaulted over the side into the driver's seat.

Penelope had already visualized her course of action. She was fully prepared to lay the motorcycle on its side and step off, letting it slide beneath the Mustang, thereby impeding any immediate exit by Angelique. It was an excellent plan—in theory. With enough time to take another lap or two around the parking lot, Penelope might have come up with a better plan, one with less risk to her delicate skin, but. . . .

Angelique had no sooner landed her shapely derriere in the car than she shrieked and attempted to reverse her course, succeeding merely in banging her knees against the steering wheel and falling back again, only to scream and leap up again.

With the motorcycle engine roaring in her ears, Penelope did not hear the horrible caterwauling and could only wonder if the exertion of Angelique's dash through the parking lot had brought on a seizure of some sort. As Penelope skidded to a halt and cut the engine, Angelique managed to open the car door and throw herself from the car with a very large, very angry Abyssinian alley cat from Abyssinia attached to her backside.

CHAPTER
TWENTY-ONE

The night manager of the Lazy Traveler Motel, a normally mild-mannered gentleman named Fenton Vavasour, screamed at his staff. "Do something!"

They did. Quickly evaluating the situation and deciding that riot control was not in their job description, the waiters and waitresses headed for cover, setting up a barricade behind the tables laden with hors d'oeuvres, all but one making it unscathed through the combatants.

Rose McCoffey's victory celebration was definitely out of hand.

Fenton Vavasour took a quick look around, saw the chief of police wrestling a little ugly Wild Dog to the ground, and decided to join his staff, particularly after watching the chief's statuesque fiancée join the fight by hopping on a biker back, damn near scratching his eyes out as he bucked and hollered.

The irate hostess broke a heel hammering away on a giant of a Wild Dog—Russell, as it turned out—until he was rescued by his brother, who tossed Rose into the pool to cool off.

Rather than having the desired effect, it only served to enrage Rose even more and the spluttering spitfire climbed out of the pool and went after Ralph wielding a chaise longue.

Andy, intent on rescuing Penelope—although he had lost track of her—broke several bones in his right hand on a Wild Dog's jaw, but it was well worth it for the glassy-eyed expression on the Dog's face as he crumpled into a heap.

McCoffey Junior shielded Belinda Baxter from the charge of the Wickenburg Wind—who had just arrived in town for the next series with the Coyotes, crashing the party shortly after Penelope's abrupt departure—and the countercharge of the Coyotes, receiving *his* black eye for gallantry in action.

Rats and the Wind manager traded blows until they spotted the umpire crew and united against the common enemy.

Since there weren't enough Wild Dogs, Wind players, or Coyotes to go around, the invited guests began pummeling each other just for the sheer hell of it in some cases or to exact revenge for some past slight or insult in other cases (L. Malcolm Osterburg also wound up in the pool, the result of a collaboration between his staff and the president of SOD).

By the time the local constabulary began arriving, it was impossible to tell the good guys from the bad guys—all five had been subdued anyway—so the police officers waded in, throwing the belligerents to the four points of the compass, taking care not to manhandle or womanhandle (Officers Peggy Norton and Sheila Tyler hardly ever got to toss miscreants against the traditional wall) the mayor or the other elected public servants.

Big Mike glared from the hood of the Mustang.

Angelique ignored her wound. "Poor Mikey, are you all right?" she crooned softly. "I'm sorry, baby doll. I didn't mean to squash you. Can you ever forgive me?" She reached out tentatively and stroked his fur.

Big Mike shriveled. So much for the Feline Lap Test.

"I think he's fine," Angelique said, turning to face Penelope, rubbing gingerly at her posterior.

"Are you all right?" Penelope asked.

"Just a scratch. I wonder who'll take care of Alexandra now?"

It was the most compassionate admission of guilt Penelope had ever heard. "We'll find a good home for her." She was unafraid even though she faced a murderess. How could you fear anyone—even a killer—who was more worried about the animals than herself?

Angelique nodded. "How did you know?"

"Shoshana," Penelope said. "You were the mysterious girl-friend."

"He liked to call me that. I liked it too . . . until he became abusive—again."

"Would you like to sit down?"

Angelique smiled ruefully. "I think I'd better stand for a while. Mikey's claws are pretty sharp."

"Well, I'm beat," Penelope said, kicking her shoes off. "Let's go lie down on the grass."

"It's too bad we can't call room service."

"Good idea." Penelope put two fingers between her lips and whistled at the doorman, who was looking rather bewildered as yet another black and white raced past. But he responded to Penelope's shrill summons and took their order for a bottle of wine without a second thought. He had obviously lived and worked in Empty Creek long enough to understand local mores. "And hurry," Penelope said, "but you'll have to run a tab. I left my purse back there."

There was a great deal of noise coming from the cocktail party.

"No problemo," the doorman said, hustling off to fill their order.

"It's on me," Angelique said. "My purse is in the car."

"Thanks."

The two women stretched out on their stomachs with Big Mike between them. All three stared out pensively at the lights of Empty Creek.

"I'm going to miss this place," Angelique said. "I didn't mean to kill him, you know."

"He wrote you letters. He loved you."

"Peter seduced you with words. His letters were beautiful, but he had a very mean streak. I was always bruised somewhere, but he was careful to make sure it wouldn't show."

"And then he wanted to make love in a dugout."

"How did you know that?"

"Something someone said."

"I agreed to meet him, but I just wanted him to give the cocaine back and get the Wild Dogs off my back. It was awful. I knew what he was like, but he was worse than I'd ever seen him before. He just wouldn't listen, and then he attacked me, dragging me into the dugout by my hair. I had to do something."

"And the bat was there."

"I hit him with it, but I didn't mean to kill him. And then I panicked and ran. I was so scared."

"It was self-defense. You should have just called the police."

"I know that now, but I was confused. I *really* didn't mean to kill him."

"I know." Penelope plucked a blade of grass and stuck it in her mouth. "How did you get involved with him?"

"We used to date, but he started hitting me and I stopped seeing him. I thought it was over and then we were both in Empty Creek together. He swore he had changed and I started dating him again."

"Then he needed money and got involved with the cocaine."

Angelique nodded. "I should have bailed out right then, but I still cared for him. I gave him the contact with the Wild Dogs. They used to hang out where I danced before. That was really stupid of me. He was supposed to keep my name out of it but he used me as a reference to get the dope on credit. Can you imagine that. Well, the Wild Dogs were never too bright."

"Why Eddie Stiles?"

"He had nothing to do with any of it. That was the Wild Dogs. They thought they could blackmail him, especially if he went back to the big leagues. Adcock was just a little guy to the Dogs. They got greedy."

"One bottle of chardonnay," the doorman interrupted. "Shall I pour?"

"Yes, please," Penelope said, sitting up. She took the glasses from the tray and handed one to Angelique.

"Can I get you anything else? Some hors d'oeuvres, perhaps?"

"I'm not very hungry," Angelique said.

"We'll just drink," Penelope said.

"It's a good night for it."

When they were alone again, Penelope and Angelique
clinked glasses automatically, realizing belatedly there was
nothing to toast.

"You knew all along?"

Penelope shook her head. "Not until today. When I figured
out the meaning of Shoshana, Rose McCoffey was the obvious
candidate to be Adcock's secret girlfriend. I thought she might
have killed him, but I was betting on her husband as having
discovered their affair. He could have gone after Adcock in
a jealous rage. I was convinced one of them had killed Adcock,
but things kept nagging at me. I knew Adcock had bought
a single yellow rose and it had to be for his girlfriend."

"It was the last nice thing he did for me."

Penelope nodded. "But I was still thinking Rose McCoffey," she said. "And then I couldn't sleep last night, and I
finally remembered something you said—about how you were
sick of Mitch Miller. I wasn't sure until I looked him up in
a popular music reference book, but I was right. One of his
biggest hits was 'The Yellow Rose of Texas.'"

"'The Yellow Rose of Texas,'" Angelique said quietly.
"God, I was sick of that song. I really hate it now."

"After that, I went back through the newspaper files and
found an advertisement for the club where you danced before.
You were billed as the Yellow Rose of Texas. It all started
making sense then. Before, I couldn't figure out why a natural
blonde would want to be a brunette."

"I wanted to be someone new," Angelique said. "I didn't like the old me anymore."

"The gloves fooled me for awhile, too," Penelope said. She was in a hurry to get it over with now. "I finally realized you were hiding bruised knuckles. It had to be you who broke into the office and hit Blake."

"I had a duplicate of Peter's key and I didn't expect anyone to be there. I felt awful about hitting Blake. I'm glad she's all right, but I needed to find out where he hid the cocaine. I didn't want anything to do with the old life, but it just kept coming back."

"'So we beat on, boats against the current, borne back ceaselessly into the past.'"

Angelique smiled sadly. "It's over for me too, just like *The Great Gatsby*. I wonder if anyone will come to my funeral."

"It's still self-defense," Penelope said. "We'll get you a good lawyer. George Eden is the best. He'll know what to do."

The battle of the Lazy Traveler Motel, as it came to be known in Empty Creek lore, ended with Wild Dogs—the real ones—lying face down by the pool, handcuffed and babbling alternately for their attorneys and medical attention from the paramedics, while Dutch stood over them thundering out their Miranda rights. He was a little ticked off because his perfectly good shirt—brand new—had been practically ripped off his back during the melee.

The casualty list was extensive and black eyes were *the* growth industry locally. After ensuring his lady love was unharmed, except for being drenched in beer as the result of breaking a full bottle of the stuff over a Wild Dog's head,

Dr. Livingstone went into triage, rapidly sorting out the various injuries in need of attention.

When order was finally restored, couples slowly reunited, and an unofficial roll call was taken to ensure no unattended bodies were left beneath a table or chaise longue.

Cackling Ed stood over poor Tilly Goodnight's walker. It was battered beyond recognition.

Rose cried at the destruction wrought on her cocktail party. McCoffey Senior took her in his arms. "By God, Rose," he said, "you've got fire in your soul."

Rose smiled through her tears. "Do you really think so?"

"Come on, woman, I'll buy you a drink and then. . . ."

"That would be nice. I'd like that."

His hand dropped from her shoulder to pinch her pretty backside.

"Kendall! Not here."

They had to step around Junior whose head was in Belinda's lap.

"Way to go, Son. Helluva right."

"Thanks, Dad."

Andy, his hand in an ice bucket, said, "We'd better find Penelope."

"There they are."

The posse, many of them sporting the marks of hand to hand combat, found a bemused cat watching as an amateur detective and a confessed murderess, both more than a little tipsy now, alternately laughed and cried in each other's arms.

EPILOGUE

Angelique Lamont was charged with murder in the first degree, but that was later reduced to second degree. George Eden plea-bargained that charge down to voluntary manslaughter and Angelique was sentenced to six years in state prison. With time off for good behavior, she would be released in three years.

In due course, five Wild Dogs went to the slammer for narcotics trafficking and conspiracy to commit extortion. After their conviction, Lola LaPola did yet another follow up story featuring Penelope and Big Mike.

Although no formal announcement was made, The Dynamite Lounge was again under new management. Bambi Baxter retired as a dancer and Belinda Baxter took over the establishment as manager, acquiring a significant other by the name of Kendall McCoffey, Jr. and a cat named Alexandra in the process.

Eddie Stiles went back to the major leagues in mid-season. Despite his absence, the Coyotes went on a tear and put together winning streaks of eleven, eight, and fourteen games, and won the pennant going away.

Penelope never did find out why Peter Adcock had Lora Lou's business card in his hand or who had put the vodka bottle in Eddie's locker. Some mysteries were not meant to be solved. She did suspect Edwin Heath of the latter action and made him pay off his bets.

Awooo!

A Vietnamese pot-bellied pig from Cambodia named Hamlet won the *Babe* Look-Alike contest, even though he didn't resemble the little sheep-herding porker from down under in the slightest. Wasn't that just the way things always went in Empty Creek?

Shortly before Blake Robinson became Blake Robinson-Livingstone in ceremonies at home plate before the last game of the season, the winning entry of her nickname contest was announced. In deference to the sell-out crowd in attendance, Butterfly Butt was shortened to Butterfly. In addition to her closest friend from high school, Blake's bridal party consisted of the heroine of the moment, an actress soon to be acclaimed for a theatrical triumph, a former Las Vegas showgirl, and a large cat.

Rats and Feathers McCoy moved to Empty Creek permanently and Rats kicked the bubble gum habit.

Rose and Kendall McCoffey, Sr. entered marriage counseling and shortly thereafter Rose announced that she was pregnant.

On Penelope's advice, Erika von Sturm chalked up new miles on the stationary bicycle, pedaling through the United States. By Christmas, she was in the Mississippi Delta.

Penelope inflicted an African film festival on her friends and wrote to Robert Sidney-Veine.

When things finally settled down and she was caught up on her sleep, Penelope went to the closet, removed the catalog of adult toys and its gift certificate. Sitting on the bed, she leafed through the entire catalog. There were so many interesting and varied items that it was difficult to make a choice. But with everything back to what passed for normal in Empty Creek, complacency just wouldn't do. After all, it was part of *her* job description to make life interesting for Andy and keep him off balance. The combination of items she finally selected would do just that.

"Awooo!"

At the Fourth of July picnic, the Chamber of Commerce Blue team beat the Red Team by a score of thirty-seven to twenty-nine.

When the store next door fell vacant, Lora Lou Longstreet expanded The Tack Shack, knocking out the wall to install a tasteful art gallery devoted primarily to works by David Macklin, whose first local showing consisted of a great many nude studies.

"Come on," Lora Lou exhorted her friends, "if I can do it, you can do it."

And thus art was served.

"Pretty cool, Mom," Reggie said at the opening, when she looked on Nora's painting with admiration, "but you're still grounded for the rest of the year."

The Women of Empty Creek sixteen-month calendar quickly sold out and Laney had to order a second and then a third printing to satisfy all the orders. The proceeds benefited a children's charity.

Andy kept his calendar turned to June year round ("I can't believe I'm doing this," Penelope wailed), although he occasionally peeked at January (Debbie), February (an exotically-masked Samantha), March (Bambi, not Belinda), April (Kathy), July (Nora), August (Laney), September (Blake), October (Angelique—her painting was rendered from a post-card), November (Feathers—a major triumph for the AARP crowd), December (Lora Lou), the following January (Alyce, on a sheet decorated with astrological symbols), February (Leigh, winner of the sexy librarian pageant), March (Teresa, holding a margarita—Penelope paid her debts, too), and April (Stormy, forgoing the nudity clause one last time).

Laney was enthusiastically planning The Men of Empty Creek Calendar, although those bozos were giving her a great deal of resistance.

Many months later, Andy suggested a game of Scrabble and Penelope quickly brought the set out. They drew to see who would go first. Andy revealed an O. Penelope pulled out a B. She would draw and play first. When she had taken her seven letters, Penelope looked at the tiles, quickly rearranged them, and smiled.

Ah, sweet revenge.

She began the game by playing H-A-M-H-O-C-K.

Bingo!

"I challenge," Andy said. "Hamhock is not a word."

"Of course it's a word," Penelope said. "Like hamburger. Besides, you played it. I would never have figured out it was Angelique if you hadn't played it and Mikey hadn't batted it around."

"Look it up."

Penelope went to the *Official Scrabble Dictionary*. No hamhock. *Webster's Collegiate Dictionary*. No hamhock. *The Random House Dictionary of the English Language* revealed a paucity of hamhocks. She would have gone to the *Oxford English Dictionary* had Andy not called her for delay of game.

"Well, damn it, what are those ugly things in the supermarket?" Penelope asked.

"Ham," Andy replied, with a big grin on his face, "hocks. Two words."

"Cheater." Her reply was automatic. Secretly, she was impressed. "Why didn't you challenge me when I made it plural?"

"Sandbagging. Waiting for this moment."

Penelope revised her estimate. A running score over forty years might turn out to be pretty even, after all.

But just wait until April Fool's Day. There were scores to settle.

And Big Mike was . . . well. . . . Big Mike, which is to say just about the damndest cat who ever ate a lima bean or subdued a six-footed piranha dragon.

ON THE CASE WITH THE
HEARTLAND'S #1 FEMALE P.I.
THE AMANDA HAZARD MYSTERIES
BY CONNIE FEDDERSEN

DEAD IN THE WATER   (0-8217-5244-8, $4.99)
The quaint little farm community of Vamoose, Oklahoma isn't as laid back as they'd have you believe. Not when the body of one of its hardest-working citizens is found face down in a cattle trough. Amateur sleuth Amanda Hazard has two sinister suspects and a prickly but irresistible country gumshoe named Nick Thorn to contend with as she plows ahead for the truth.

DEAD IN THE CELLAR   (0-8217-5245-6, $4.99)
A deadly tornado rips through Vamoose, Oklahoma, followed by a deadly web of intrigue when elderly Elmer Jolly is found murdered in his storm cellar. Can Amanda Hazard collar the killer before she herself becomes the center of the storm, and the killer's next victim?

DEAD IN THE MUD   (0-8217-156-X, $5.50)
It's a dirty way to die: drowned in the mud from torrential rain. Amanda Hazard is convinced the County Commissioner's death is no accident, and finds herself sinking into a seething morass of corruption and danger as she works to bring the culprits to light—before she, too, ends up 6-feet-under.

Available wherever paperbacks are sold, or order direct from the Publisher. Send cover price plus 50¢ per copy for mailing and handling to Kensington Publishing Corp., Consumer Orders, or call (toll free) 888-345-BOOK, to place your order using Mastercard or Visa. Residents of New York and Tennessee must include sales tax. DO NOT SEND CASH.

THE MYSTERIES OF MARY ROBERTS RINEHART